DRAWN FROM THE NILE

ROBERT BENNETT

Dedicated to Nancy,
My biggest cheerleader and best friend.
She has always been by my side.
My wife, who I love.

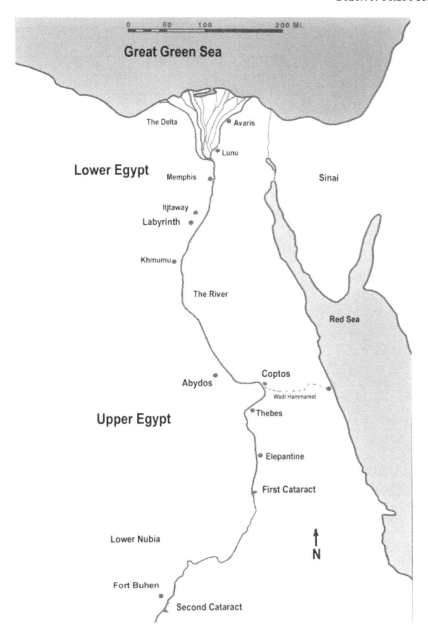

ROBERT BENNETT

Hatshepsut
Metropolitan Museum of Art

INTRODUCTION

Ancient Egypt was a unique country made up of two totally different land areas, the Black Land and the Red Land.

The Black Land is the narrow strip of fertile land along the banks of the Nile, called the River, by the ancient Egyptians. Along these narrow banks, the common people called "rekhyt" live and die without ever leaving their small portion of the river.

The Red Land is the desert were the average Egyptian did not venture far into. The people that did inhabit this region were small bands of wanderers, the "Bedouin", who were looked down on by the inhabitants along the River and were considered to be outcasts and outlaws.

Ancient Egypt could not have existed without the Nile which runs over 4,000 miles from the south to the north, starting in Lake Victoria and ending at the Mediterranean Sea.

The nation of ancient Egypt consisted of two regions called Upper Egypt and Lower Egypt. Lower Egypt is the Nile Delta region, here was the ancient city of Memphis and the pyramids. Up the River to the south is Upper Egypt, here was the ancient city of Thebes. The Valley of the Kings, Luxor, and the religious center of Karnak are in Upper Egypt.

The pharaohs wore a double crown that represented the two lands that had been united 500 years before the age of the pyramids. There were two periods in Egypt's long history when the two lands were not united as one nation.

The story of Hatshepsut, Pharaoh's Daughter, takes place after the second period of "chaos" when Egypt was divided. Lower

Egypt, the Delta area, had been conquered by foreign kings called Hyksos. Hatshepsut's ancestors from Thebes in Upper Egypt had defeated the Hyksos and reunited Egypt. These Kings did not just live the life of luxury but were fearsome warriors.

Hatshepsut's father, Tuthmose I, was the third such warrior King in the 18th Dynasty of Egypt and ruled from Thebes now the capital of Egypt. Memphis in Lower Egypt was no longer the capital, but powerful men and priests in Memphis wanted the riches and power returned to their ancient city.

CHAPTER ONE
Hatshepsut

Pronounced, hat SHEP soot

The cobra is looking at me with its hood extended and it is as tall as me because I am very young and still wearing my side lock of hair. I see no menace from its intense gaze, I am not afraid. My nanny, Sitre, comes close and the cobra turns toward her and makes a loud hissing sound.

She slowly backs away. The cobra returns its gaze toward me, it is watching me intently, as if it is trying to tell me something. But this dream is different than all the others I have had about the cobra, I see movement out of the corner of my eye, it is a lioness running very fast and taking quick glances behind her.

Sitre runs between me and the cobra, her only thought is to protect me, knowing that she will most certainly be bitten by the deadly cobra. It does not strike Sitre but moves its broad head back and forth, then it lowers to the ground and slithers off into the garden. Sitre holds me tight, she is one of just a few people who are allowed to touch me.

Pharaoh's Palace in Thebes

Hatshepsut wakes from a dream that she has had many times and wonders about the lioness in this dream. It is early in the morning and still cool with the pale morning light entering

7

the high windows in her bedroom from the first rays of the sun god Ra. The brightly colored scenes of trees, flowers, animals and birds painted on her bedroom walls seem alive with their apparent movement from the flickering oil lamp flames. On her bed at her feet lies her favorite cat, called Mau, curled up and still asleep. He is one in a long line of black cats with white feet and a white nose that have been in her family for many years. Most homes in Egypt had a cat, they hunt mice and rats to help protect valuable grain, which is used for trade and an important source of food.

She sees Sitre sitting beside her bed through the thin veil draped over her bed, offering her some protection from insects. The veil is held by a wood frame with gold reliefs of lotus flowers on the top of each post. Sitre's eyes are closed, but Hatshepsut knows she is not asleep because she is rocking slightly as she prays to her God. Sitre is always there when she awakens, when she was very young, Sitre was the last person she saw at bedtime and the first person in the morning. Now that she is older and enjoys staying up late, Sitre has stopped staying up with her at night. Today an older Sitre is sitting by her bed, she wears the makeup and dress of an Egyptian but her complexion and hair are that of her people, the Hebrew. Hatshepsut has fond memories of Sitre's bedtime stories and particularly the songs about her people. The songs tell stories, her history, and sometimes the song is a long list of her ancestors, her people have no written language.

The encounter with the cobra did happen to her when she was five years old and still living on her mother's country estate playing in the gardens by one of the pools. All she remembers now are the stories about the encounter, her dreams about it, and being told how brave she was standing still. But, as the fog of sleep clears, she wonders about this dream and the lioness. The dream has become a sign to her, a message from the gods perhaps. Sometimes after the dream something good will happen or it can also be a warning. One time after her dream, Hatshepsut's father returned from a victorious foreign campaign into Nubia earlier than expected. The defeated king was dead and hanging upside down on the bow of Pharaoh's Royal Barge the "Falcon". Then there was the time when her half-brother, the future Pharaoh, was murdered after one of her dreams. Hatshepsut was depressed for a long time after his death, she loved him and was looking forward to the time when she was his Queen. Since the murder of her half-brother two years ago, she has been living in the palace for security reasons. She is continuing her education and preparations to be the next Queen of Egypt. She must be alert after the dream, the cobra goddess Wadjet, may be trying to tell her something important.

The day has already started for the rekhyt, the common people of Egypt, much work needs to be done before the heat of the day becomes intense. Within the palace are the hushed sounds of activity and the aroma of cooking as the morning meal is being made by servants and slaves for the Royal Family. She stretches and her movement wakes Mau, he jumps down off the bed, beginning his day of hunting. Sitre realizes that the princess is awake, so she finishes her silent prayers. Her parents gave her an Egyptian name, as many Hebrew families did, hoping to make life easier for their children and to help them blend into the Egyptian society.

Hatshepsut reaches for her gold and blue handled dagger, to insure it is still on the ebony and ivory table next to her bed. The dagger is very old and was given to her by her mother. Sitre opens her eyes and a warm familiar smile comes over her face, "Good morning, My Noble Lady, I pray God watches over you today."

"I have many gods to protect me," Hatshepsut replied smiling at Sitre, it is a morning greeting that they have exchanged for years. When Hatshepsut was younger, she felt sorry for Sitre because she had only one God. Even the poorest Egyptian family have many gods they can pray to, "Sitre, I had my dream last night about Wadjet."

"That terrible serpent, it still haunts my memory, I was so afraid that I would lose you that day!"

"This dream was different because I saw Wadjet and then I saw a lioness running from something. What do you think that means?" Hatshepsut asked as she jumped out of bed and pulled back the veil.

"I am not sure, maybe a warning. If you hear or see a lion today, perhaps you should start running, very fast." Sitre replied with a smile.

Hatshepsut laughed, "Don't worry, I will." They began the morning routine they have been doing for as long as Hatshepsut could remember. She enjoys her private time with Sitre because she can be herself. When in public, she must maintain a royal attitude and be in complete control of her emotions. Sitre went to call in the servants to serve the morning meal to the young princess, she stopped short of the door and appeared to be thinking about something.

Hatshepsut saw her hesitate, "What's wrong?"

"I believe the lioness in your dream is a message from my God."

"Why would your God use my dream?"

"Perhaps God used your dream because it is the one dream you pay attention to."

"I don't believe in your God."

"Yes, but that does not make him any less real." Sitre continued, "Also, the Great Wife came by this morning and requested that you join her today, she is going to the Temple of Amun."

"How is mother, I am worried about her?"

"Pharaoh's Great Wife looks tired." Hatshepsut knew she was correct because her mother had been under a lot of stress for a long time. Besides the demands of being the Great Wife of

Pharaoh and Queen, she now is required to spend many hours daily tending to the affairs of Egypt. Her father, the Pharaoh, is ill and often in pain. After her meal, Hatshepsut chose to wear a less elegant short pleated gown. She preferred it over the long formal gowns required when she was in the Royal Court. Sitre commented, "Pharaoh's Great Wife will not approve of your choice, My Lady."

Hatshepsut looked at herself in the highly polished bronze mirror, "I am pleased," she said stubbornly. The only jewelry she has on, is a solid pink gold necklace that is always around her neck, it is unique because the centerpiece is of only half the image of Maat with just one wing. Maat is the goddess of truth, justice, and perfect order. Her half-brother Amenmose, who had been assassinated, wore the other half. After their planned wedding and when they ruled Egypt together, the two halves would have been joined and Maat then completed. His necklace was stolen by the assassins, she often touches her necklace and thinks about what could have been, a slight surge of anger always courses through her body.

Sitre performed a few final loving strokes to Hatshepsut's hair before placing on her head a small gold and lapis headband with a Uraeus in front, it is very old. The Uraeus, a likeness of a cobra, is a symbol of protection because the cobra appears ready to strike or spit its venom on anyone that could be considered a threat. It had been passed down to her from her great-great-grandmother, Queen Ahhotep, who is still remembered and honored as a ferocious warrior that revenged her husband and son who had died in battle against the vile Hyksos. The Queen is Hatshepsut's role model and she hopes to be remembered as the great Queen still is, to be remembered is required for eternal life.

A day away from dull studies in the Royal House of Books and being with her mother will be a welcomed change for Hatshepsut. She has never spent much time with her mother, on the country estate where she once lived, the Queen seldom came and then just for a few days. Duty always required her to return to the Royal Palace because Pharaoh was often away on foreign military campaigns for months at a time. When he was home, he preferred not to get evolved in palace politics or the mundane jobs of administration. He was a mighty warrior who loved adventure and enjoyed spending time with Hatshepsut and her three older half-brothers.

His youngest son and namesake, Tuthmose II, had always been weak and could do only limited physical activities. Hatshepsut always came to his defense when he was often picked on by his two older brothers. He was older than Hatshepsut but he considered her his protector and older sister. He was not groomed to be Pharaoh because he had two older brothers and many including his father did not think he would live to be an adult. But the gods had their own plans, one brother died after having severe pain in his lower abdomen and the other was assassinated. Tuthmose II was now in line to become Pharaoh, he was unprepared. Hatshepsut did not wish to marry him, but for the family's dynasty to continue, she had to become Pharaoh's Great Wife. Hopefully, one day after she had a son, she could add the title of Pharaoh's Mother.

Before Amenmose was assassinated, he and Hatshepsut had traveled with their father. Pharaoh taught both the skills a warrior needed, he shared stories of battle that occurred in distant and mysterious lands. He told of mountains that had white frozen rain on top and of a great river, in Mitanni, that ran in the opposite direction of their River. Pharaoh had tried in the beginning to include his youngest son, but the boy could not keep up with his older siblings, he grew tired of always failing and eventually refused to continue. Hatshepsut loved being with her father and would do anything to please him, what she lacked in strength she compensated with speed and skill. She became even closer to her father after Amenmose was murdered, Pharaoh knew that the future of his dynasty was on her shoulders. Hatshepsut may be Queen to her half-brother the

Pharaoh, but her father planned for the real power to be hers.

She applied a small amount of myrrh, her favorite perfume, from an ornate ostrich egg container. On her way out near her door, was a small altar of Amun-Ra, she stopped and prayed for a long life, an easy death, to be remembered, and a resting place undisturbed. It was a pleasant walk through the palace's complex maze of halls, courtyards, and bridges, there was always some new art or sculpture to enjoy. While going through one of the courtyards that had many columns resembling palm trees, some movement caught her eye, it was only a pet mongoose, but she already had her dagger in her hand. A palace guard came out of the shadows, she dismissed him as she returned the dagger to its sheath. There were many tame mongooses called "Pharaoh's Rats" in the palace and grounds to seek out any serpents that may find a way inside the palace walls.

Even after two years in the palace, she was still not use to always being under the watchful eye of guards. They tried to be inconspicuous, but she knew they were always there, a very slow and painful death awaited any guard allowing any harm to come to her.

Leaving the Palace she used the King's Bridge that went over the Royal Avenue to the Royal Court complex, a quick glance into the Throne Room revealed that the Queen was not there. Only guards with several men were waiting in the reception area to plead some cause or concern to Pharaoh, the Queen, or Vizier. Some most likely had traveled a great distance from their respective Nome's, one of the forty-two territorial divisions along the River. They wished to be heard by the House of Pharaoh, this was their last appeal.

She did find her mother in the Queen's private chamber with the Vizier of Upper Egypt, their conversation about a captain and owner of a ship that had sank, stopped as she entered the room. Hatshepsut realized that their conversation was most likely concerning a case to be heard today. Her mother dismissed Vizier Hepuseneb, he bowed and smiled at the young princess as he departed, it was a truly friendly jester from Hepuseneb. He was the Queen's cousin and had been the Vizier of Upper Egypt for many years. His role was purely administrative, involving many tedious jobs including domestic disputes, a census of livestock, and keeping records of all crops and riches that came into Egypt. Hatshepsut did not envy his duties because she was not interested in dull matters like dikes and canals.

The Queen's expression turned from concern to a polite smile, she was a master of self-control and expression, she had seen her mother melt the hearts of ambassadors from enemy nations and put fear in once trusted officials who had betrayed her. She loved her mother, but they were different, she had inherited her love of adventure and action from her father. But she hoped she had some of her mother's poise, grace, and elegance. Queen Ahmose noticed how her daughter was dressed, Hatshepsut knew that she was being inspected and had come up short, "I am pleased to see Pharaoh's Daughter," her mother formally stated.

"I am happy to have the day with you because I know that duty demands so much from my mother." Hatshepsut answered using less formal language, her mother was Pharaoh's Great Wife and preferred to be addressed by that title, but Hatshepsut needed her to be just her mother.

"It is nice that I can combine duty and have time with Pharaoh's Daughter, we should be on our way." Hatshepsut was used to brief encounters with her mother, but this was even less than normal, the Queen's personal guard followed them as they proceeded to the Royal Avenue. The Queen gave various commands and instructions to officials and scribes that were trailing along with her. A royal carrying chair awaited them with guards and fan bearers carrying large colorful fans made of ostrich feathers. The blue and white royal standard was carried in front of the possession by one of the guards, eight strong Nubian men lifted the carrying chair and proceeded down the

Royal Avenue to the Temple Complex.

Hatshepsut could see that her mother's thoughts were on some issue, so she observed their surroundings. Few people were on the paved avenue reserved for officials, priests, scribes, and the royal family. Palm trees lined the beautiful avenue with several bridges crossing over canals with lush vegetation, many statues, and arches that were designed to make the journey pleasant for the privileged travelers. When the Royal Standard was seen by others, they would give way and bow, Queen Ahmose did not seem to notice them. The other travelers did not stare at the royal procession, it was not proper, because the radiance of royalty was too bright to look at very long. There were a few who tried to catch a curious glimpse of Pharaoh's Great Wife and Daughter, Hatshepsut enjoyed making eye contact and seeing their reaction as they quickly turned away.

The soft calls of doves were interrupted by a small monkey that jumped from a nearby acacia tree with its distinctive feathery leaves and started barking. Obviously, he expected to be given a treat, Hatshepsut smiled at the noisy little beggar. The Queen commented, "They are not supposed to be fed, soon it will be in our laps." The obnoxious little monkey did accomplish one thing, the Queen's thoughts returned to Hatshepsut, "How are your studies going?"

"They are going well, I don't like accounting and law, so not having to study today in the House of Books is nice. Is the Temple being readied for father's obelisks?"

"Yes, I want to visit the temple before the mountain of sand and mud bricks are placed in the temple to raise the symbols of Ra, the statues and art must also be moved. The architect has also requested my advice on some final arrangements."

Hatshepsut wanted to keep her thinking about the temple, "Vizier Hepuseneb could not advise the architect on details?"

"The Vizier wanted me to get away from palace matters

for a day because he knows I love walking the grounds of the Temple. The architect worked on Pharaoh's tomb and has some exciting new ideas for the temple, he will be polite and listen to my suggestions. He is someone that your father wants you to meet, we both feel that he may be important to you in the future. In any case, I too get tired of accounting and legal matters." She said smiling for the first time at her beautiful young daughter, Hatshepsut returned her smile. "The architect first served your father on military campaigns when he was a young scribe, he is very talented and someone that can be trusted. You need to be thinking about those that can serve you when you are the Great Wife." When she mentioned the future, Hatshepsut noticed that her mood drifted away again, she hated to see her mother unhappy, with thoughts of Pharaoh's death. The events of the near future were out of even her mother's control, the Queen liked to be in total control.

"I appreciate your advice mother, did Tuthmose not want to come today?" Hatshepsut asked about the future Pharaoh.

"He said that he did not feel well," was the Queen's short answer then she added after a pause, "I think that all he wants to do is play games with those that pretend to be his friends, drink too much beer and wine, and be entertained by his dancers and harem girls. He is using the powder from the "Joy Plant" too much for pain and is not aware of his surroundings most of the time."

Hatshepsut replied defensively even though she knew that the drug from the flower was addictive, "He does have difficulty breathing and does not feel well most days."

The Great Wife turned her attention to the Temple, "We are almost there." They approached the Temple Complex at the King's Gate, a private side entrance to the complex used only by royalty, the main entrance was used by noblemen and rekhyt. The temple complex was empty except for priests, in anticipation of their arrival, no one was allowed to interfere with a royal visit. Hatshepsut saw the bald High Priest wearing his cloak made of leopard skin and a young man standing next to him. If he was the architect, he was much younger then she expected. He was tall and very impressive, as they drew closer, she recognized the young man, he had entertained her during her father's inspections of his tomb.

She especially remembered his unusual hair that was brown, curly, and lighter around his face. It had been four years since she last visited the site with her father across the River to the mysterious desolate western side. The tomb was finished now and inspections were no longer required in the sacred valley. Her father had chosen to be the first Pharaoh to have his royal tomb hidden in the valley and not near his mortuary temple, hopefully the hidden location of his tomb would protect it from robbers. The mortuary temple was at the end of a canal from the River, there the King's cult could make offerings for him to the gods for eternity.

The rays of Ra were now making the day warmer as the two men stood watching, anticipating their arrival, they wanted the Great Wife and Daughter to see them waiting respectfully. The architect asked the High Priest Pamose, "I haven't seen the Daughter in four years, what is she like now?"

"She is Pharaoh's Daughter," was the High Priest's short answer.

Senenmut thought, I didn't get any information about her from him. He had attended one function at the palace since his return to Thebes after working in the quarry that had taken him six months to lift the first obelisk from the quarry and float it down the River to Thebes, the second obelisk had taken just as long. The King and Great Wife were in attendance, but not the Daughter. As he waited, he thought, I will have to write my mother and inform her that I personally met the Great Wife and Pharaoh's Daughter. She will be very proud and brag to her friends and neighbors in his little home village, he smiled as he thought of the many questions he must answer at their next family gathering.

The work had been hard in the valley where Pharaoh had selected to build his secret tomb and he also did not like living in the remote village called the Place of Truth, where all the workers and craftsmen lived with their families. The isolated village was built by Pharaoh so the location of his tomb could be kept secret, workers lived and died there without leaving. They and their families were well cared for, but were guarded by the newly formed state police force called the Medjay, the elite force now used throughout Egypt.

Had the Daughter, whose name meant, Foremost of Noble Ladies, turned into a spoiled and aloof young woman. He hoped not, she had been a bright and charming young girl with a thousand questions. There was very little gossip about her after Amenmose was murdered, he knew the assassins had never been caught but no one knew any details.

It was the way of the Pharaohs, one only heard good news, the rumors from the palace lately were about the health of the Pharaoh. He was seldom seen and this saddened Senenmut who remembering how Pharaoh was, as a roaring lion and all men respected and feared him. He had been introduced to Pharaoh during a military campaign to Nubia, when he was the personal scribe for one of the generals. Pharaoh and the General had grown up together, he was frustrated that he could not remember if they were related in some way. Perhaps the General was related to the Great Wife, he wasn't sure. There were many nights that the General and Senenmut were invited to his tent, Senenmut was envied by all the other scribes, because Pharaoh called him by his name.

The General retired shortly after that campaign and he had arranged for him to be sent to Thebes. First, he studied as a priest in the temple and then with the Royal Architect Ineni.

He had found his true passion and was honored when Ineni had suggested to Pharaoh that he be in charge of the Temple project that included the addition of the two obelisks. He was glad to be back in Thebes where life was easier and much more pleasant, with good food, sports, and the company of the ladies. It was a chance of a lifetime for him if he was successful in raising the obelisks, he would have other opportunities. If not, well he didn't want to think about that!

Queen Ahmose stepped out of the carrier regal in her pleated full-length linen gown with gold trim, she wore a large crown, fine jewelry and sandals with gold threads and jewel decorations. Then Senenmut saw Hatshepsut, she is a beautiful young woman.

Memphis, the Royal Palace

Ambassador Ipi, Egypt's Ambassador of Foreign Affairs, arrived at the Memphis dock without any fanfare while Vizier Tinfurer watched from the balcony of Pharaoh's palatial quarters. As Vizier he had his own quarters, but he was sure that the aging Pharaoh would never use the quarters in Memphis again. Plans were being made to ensure the next Pharaoh was going to be from Memphis and not the weak son of a brutal soldier from Thebes. The Ambassador disembarked and hurried toward the Palace, the Vizier sent a messenger to inform Rewer, the High Priest of Ptah, of the ambassador's arrival.

Later, the three men enjoyed wine and a lavish meal served by young servant girls, they were to be entertained by nude dancers, but Vizier Tinfurer stopped the entertainment. He sent everyone out so they could talk in private.

"King Shuttarna of Mitanni is very supportive of our plan," Ambassador Ipi proudly stated.

"I'm sure he is with all the gold we promised him," a resentful Vizier commented.

"Can we trust Shuttarna?" Priest Rewer questioned.

"I think we can because I demanded that he bring one of his daughters to Egypt when he comes for the gold, he would not dare attack Egypt as long as we have her. She is very beautiful and exotic."

"Don't worry Tinfurer about the gold, when I am Pharaoh, we will send our army back to Mitanni and get ours and all of their gold too. Ipi, you can have the young princess, we do not desire her, isn't that right my sweet Tinfurer?" The High Priest said as he smiled and placed his hand on the Vizier's hand.

Ambassador Ipi watched the two, "When you see her you may change your mind," knowing that they would not want her, then he could have the young girl he lusted for.

CHAPTER TWO

Senenmut, the Architect

Pharaoh's Daughter was taller than her mother and appeared to be looking directly at him, perhaps she is trying to remember where she had seen him. He then realized that he is being arrogant, the young princess would not remember him after four years. Her appearance is very striking, if not as elegant as the Queen. Hatshepsut's short linen gown is pleated with a pale green sash over one shoulder, her small waist is accented by a wide intricately braided leather belt, holding an elegant scabbard and dagger. The dagger is not just a small ceremonial dagger, it is a real weapon that is larger and has a curved blade. He first thought her necklace was broken with one wing missing off of the goddess Maat symbol, then he saw that it is made that way, a strange design. Pharaoh's Daughter did not wear a wig, there is only a small pink gold head band in her silky black hair. Her sandals are made of soft leather with leg straps that accented her long slim legs. Occasionally, she touched the dagger, he could not take his eyes off of her.

Hatshepsut followed her mother and noticed that Senenmut was looking at her, good, I have his attention she thought. Then he saw her looking directly at him, he looked away, not wanting to offend her. Both men then bowed very low to them.

"Rise," Queen Ahmose commanded. With much effort and self-control, Senenmut focused his attention on the High Priest and Queen Ahmose. Pamose, the High Priest of Amun, introduced him to the Queen and Hatshepsut as the architect in charge of the current temple construction. Queen Ahmose acknowledged that she knew of Senenmut and looked forward to seeing his work at the temple. Senenmut slightly bowed to her, "It is an honor to serve Pharaoh and his Great Wife, the project is ahead of schedule and will be finished before the annual inundation."

"I will inform Pharaoh."

Hatshepsut, who was not one to be ignored, "It is a pleasure to see the favorite architect of the great builder Ineni again."

High Priest Pamose looked surprised, "You have met Pharaoh's Daughter before?"

Hatshepsut answered before Senenmut could reply as she smiled at him. "Senenmut is remembered for his excellent work, when Pharaoh and his Daughter inspected the King's tomb."

Senenmut's mind and heart was racing because the beautiful Daughter of Pharaoh had remembered him, "Pharaoh's Daughter honors her humble servant by remembering him." He would remember this moment for the rest of his life.

Queen Ahmose dismissed the guards as the four of them walked through the King's Gate into the temple complex. High Priest Pamose and Queen Ahmose walked in front, with Hatshepsut and Senenmut following as they made their way to the Holy of Holy place reserved for priests and royalty. There was activity in the temple, priests were busy moving everything out of the area that was to be filled with sand and mud bricks. The stone obelisks would be pulled up the man-made mountain and then lowered onto the stone bases that were already prepared and waiting for the towering obelisks. Senenmut was pointing out the large square base with a small square hole in the center that will support the tall obelisks.

Suddenly there was a lot of yelling and commotion coming from a nearby side room, followed by a loud crash. His heart sank, because he knew that a statue had fallen, a young priest was running toward them holding his injured blooded hands.

Out of the corner of his eyes he saw that Hatshepsut had quickly stepped between her mother and the approaching priest with her dagger drawn. He had not given any thought of possible danger for the Great Wife or Pharaoh's Daughter, the Royal Family always live with the possible threat on their lives, he realized. The young priest fell to his knees before the High Priest Pamose, "I beg forgiveness for letting the statue be destroyed, I tried to stop the fall," he explained as he showed his injured hands with his head bowed to the floor.

Embarrassed and angered that this had occurred in the presence of the Great Wife and Daughter, Pamose yelled, "The statue is worth more than your miserable life."

Senenmut saw Hatshepsut put her dagger back into its scabbard with one quick smooth practiced motion, he only had a quick glance of the gleaming blade of her dagger, it was not bronze but a lustrous metal he did not recognize. Hatshepsut confronted Pamose, "The priest is injured, he should be attended to."

Queen Ahmose always in control, softly spoke to Pamose, "Tend to his wounds and reward him for his brave attempt to save the statue."

"As Pharaoh's Great Wife commands," relieved that he would in no way be responsible for the damage to the priceless statue. Other priests cautiously came to the aid of their injured colleague. Senenmut was pleasantly surprised by the compassion the young princess had shown, coming to the defense of the injured priest.

"I wish to be alone," Queen Ahmose said as she walked from the spacious open forecourt into the cooler shadows of the temple. The interior of the temple was brilliant with many different colors, a blue ceiling with gold stars and a polished black granite floor. On the walls were colored reliefs of wild life, vegetation, and the gods, she was going to the sacred pool to cleanse herself before offering prayers to Amun.

High Priest Pamose boldly stated that he was going to ensure proper care of the injured priest as he gladly left Hatshepsut and Senenmut alone. Hatshepsut looked at Senenmut, his
face showed intelligence and an inquisitive nature in his large
almond shaped eyes. He reminded her of her older half-brother,
who had been murdered, with a square jaw that showed determination and resolve, the same strong characteristics that
would have made her brother a great Pharaoh. To Senenmut's
relief, she finally spoke, "Show me the obelisks."

"As Pharaoh's Daughter commands."

They walked down a paved avenue with sphinx on each
side guarding the entrance to the temple, behind the rows
of sphinx were palm and sycamore trees that provided cool,
pleasant sitting areas next to pools. Through a large monu-
mental gateway, called a pylon, they entered a courtyard and
continued toward the main gate of the tall white wall that surrounded the temple complex. Near the main gate were two
portals in the shape of large human ears. Depending on the
offering, the priest hidden behind the "listening ears" may answer their prayers favorably. Rekhyt could go no farther into
the temple complex than the courtyard.

Departing the temple complex, large white and blue pennants on tall cedar poles were fluttering and making slapping
sounds in the prevailing north wind. Several men and a few
women were waiting to enter and make an offering to Amun.
They had been a little restless and perhaps impatient because
they had to wait for the royal party to leave the Temple. But
now they were pleasantly surprised at the rare opportunity to
see Pharaoh's young daughter, a respectful silence fell over the
crowd as they bowed to Hatshepsut. Senenmut was proud to
be seen with her, as they continued toward the River, palace
guards joined them. The paved walkway of white granite led
to the canal that came from the River to the dock for Amun's
Royal Barge. Next to the canal were a large number of tents that
had been erected around the two granite obelisks that lay on

the ground. Hatshepsut stopped and from a distance looked at all the activity, there was a mixture of sounds, men talking and laughing, stone being hammered, and women singing. "Wonderful," she exclaimed, "so many people working on Pharaoh's obelisks."

Senenmut commented proudly, "Pharaoh's obelisks will be the tallest in all of Egypt, each obelisk took two large barges to carry."

She continued toward a large tent that was at the upper end of one unfinished obelisk, Senenmut and three guards followed her. The guards were visibly nervous, they did not like being among so many people with Pharaoh's Daughter. When they arrived, Senenmut raised his arm motioning for everyone to stop working. He then announced, "Welcome the Royal and Most Beautiful Daughter of Pharaoh, may she have good health, The Foremost of Noble Ladies." Everyone bowed, including Senenmut.

"Rise and continue your worthy efforts."

Most of the workers returned to their activities, but watched her as much as they dared. "Here architects are shaping the obelisk's tip," Senenmut pointed out the precise work. Moving to a large table with drawings held down by small granite carvings of different gods, she closely examined the plans. The architects stepped back to allow ample room for her and they did not wish to step on her shadow, which is a part of a person's soul.

"This writing I do not understand," she stated looking at Senenmut.

Senenmut hesitated and then explained, "This is the language that the Royal Architect Ineni taught us, the writings were created by the great architect Imhotep."

"Imhotep the builder of the first pyramids, astronomer, and physician, created this language? I did not know such a language existed!"

"It is not known by many, My Lady, only those that have been trained under Ineni. It is an easier and faster way to write, to calculate, and to keep our building secrets safe." He was impressed that the princess knew so much about the man who built the first pyramid over a thousand years ago.

She then went to the obelisk with one side completely engraved with writings and was being polished to a smooth finish by women. The top was being carved by craftsmen, who had stopped working, so there would be no dust or granite chips in the air. Senenmut had motioned for them to not start back to work after Hatshepsut had commanded everyone to continue. The other side was being written on by an artist, with the hieroglyphs in red paint that were to be carved into the stone. "What about the side that is on the ground, how will you engrave that side?"

Impressed by her question, "That side will be finished after the obelisk is erected, moving the stone would damage the engraving, if done now." Hatshepsut nodded her understanding and started walking back toward the temple, the relieved guards and Senenmut followed.

Entering the main gate, Hatshepsut dismissed the guards with a slight motion of her hand and proceeded to a shaded area under a larger sycamore tree near a pool with white lotus blossoms fully open. After sitting down, she gestured for Senenmut to join her on the granite bench. It was pleasant on the cool bench in the shade with a gentle breeze, the only sounds were calls of birds and the occasional bark of monkeys. She noticed that Senenmut was uncomfortable, "How did you arrive here in Thebes in service to Pharaoh?"

"I was born in the little dusty village of Iuny, up River and educated in the temple of the local god Montu and then joined the army of Pharaoh as a scribe for a general at the age of thirteen. But I decided that the military life was not for me."

He paused and smiled slightly, Hatshepsut nodding her understanding. "So, I sought other ways to serve Pharaoh, first I studied as a priest and then I was given the opportunity by the Royal Architect to work in stone. That is where I first met Pharaoh's Daughter," he made a slight nod to her. "I have found much satisfaction working in stone."

"I wish to learn the mysterious writing that you use."

Senenmut wondered if he dare offer to teach her, perhaps a chance for her to know him better, "Your servant would be honored to instruct My Noble Lady."

She thought for a moment, "The palace guards will be informed of your visit this evening when your work on Pharaoh's obelisk allows. I will not keep you any longer."

Senenmut rose to his feet, bowed to Hatshepsut, "I look forward to this evening." He walked toward the main gate, trying to control his emotions, his thoughts were flying through his mind about the events of the morning. He wanted to take full advantage of meeting the Daughter, what an opportunity for a mere commoner, perhaps he could serve in the Royal Palace.

Watching Senenmut, she heard her mother walk up behind her. "Did you enjoy your time with the architect?"

"Yes, he is very smart and is easy to look at. Does he remind you of anyone mother?"

"I see the resemblance of the one who should have been your husband. Senenmut is a man that your father and I feel could serve you well in the future."

Hatshepsut thoughts turned from Senenmut to her mother, "Our time today here at Amun's Temple was more than just your desire to be away from the duties of the palace wasn't it?"

"Yes, but I must return to my duties now. Pharaoh will want to hear your opinion of Senenmut at the evening meal and he has news for you."

Ra was about to descend into the west, to start his journey through the underworld as Senenmut made his way down
the Royal Avenue to the palace. The River paralleled the avenue and the final rays of Ra made the River appear as liquid
gold. Torches were already burning and the large pennants were
hanging limp in the still wind. Senenmut wished his nerves
were as calm as the wind when he walked under the King's
Bridge that connected the palace and living quarters on one side
of the avenue to the Throne and Royal Offices on the other side.
Arriving at the open gate, the Captain of the Guard approached
him, "I am Senenmut, here at the request of Pharaoh's Daughter."

The captain maintained an aloof and bored attitude,
"Yes, the architect, follow me."

Senenmut followed him through the large open doors
into the central court were several people were walking with
a sense of urgency and mission to finish their daily duties. He
had been here before, but now with darkness setting in and
the flickering torches, there was an ominous feeling. Crossing
the central court to a heavily guarded door under the covered
bridge, he realized that these ornate heavy doors led to the private residence of the royal family. The Captain of the Guard
introduced Senenmut to the guards, he was pleased to learn that
there might be other visits. Through the doors they entered a
palm tree edged courtyard, a large pool was in the center with
rare sacred blue lotus blossoms that were starting to close for
the night. The unescorted people had different color sashes on,
the different colors indicated who they represented, but he did
not see anyone in the green color that represented Pharaoh's
Daughter. Green symbolized, to flourish or to grow, Pharaoh's
Daughter was becoming the future queen.

Leading off the courtyard were several halls that had two
guards posted at each entry. Out of one hall came a troupe
of musicians and thinly clad almost nude female dancers. He

wasn't sure if the hall went to Pharaoh's quarters or Prince Tuthmose. Most likely not Pharaoh's he thought, Pharaoh was rumored to be ill. As the troupe passed by there was a flirting exchange between the dancers and the captain. One dancer looked at Senenmut trying to see if she recognized him, teasingly she smiled and spoke to him as she removed a thin scarf reveling herself.

They entered a different hallway past it's guards, into a high enclosed atrium, with a forest of columns. The flickering light from large oil lamps caused the columns and statues shadows to move slightly, as if alive. Then he noticed some movement among the columns that was not shadows, but were guards that looked almost like statues in the dim light. Going through the atrium they arrived at a door that had several inlays of lotus flowers, a large watchful eye of Horus made of ebony and ivory, and at the top of the door was a menacing gold Uraeus protecting those behind the door.

Knocking on the door, the captain came to attention. After a few moments, the door was opened by a lovely middle-aged woman dressed in a long pale green gown. She thanked the captain and then gave a warm smile to him, "Senenmut, My Lady is expecting you. I am Sitre."

The reception room was well lit, with the sweet fragrance of frankincense and myrrh, cedar furniture, and expensive oils. The ceiling was three stories high, with sky lights that let in light and a breeze during the day, they were closed now as the cold desert night air settled in. Sitre offered Senenmut a seat, as she left the reception room, he politely declined and remained standing as he examined the lavish surroundings. The art in the room was decorated in traditional Egyptian style and of the Minoan Island People, he was surprised to see a few pieces in the style of the Hebrew, that style of art was not very popular. There was a Hebrew style banner that had white, black, and red stripes and next to it was another banner that was yellow in the shape of a shield with twelve small different colored squares on it. He did not know the meaning of any of the Hebrew pieces of art pieces, the Hebrew people were mostly servants and slaves, this puzzled him.

On the walls were murals of river scenes, The Great White Wall Palace in Memphis, and of the three Great Pyramids. The pyramids caught his attention the most because he had always wanted to see them. While examining the murals, he realized someone was behind him, turning he saw that Hatshepsut had entered the room. He bowed and waited for her permission to rise. "My friend Senenmut, rise."

He was surprised to be called, her friend, to be known as a friend of royalty was a great honor. When he was able to look at Hatshepsut, he thought she was the most beautiful woman he had ever seen, all the women he had known paled in her radiance. She was pleased with the effect she was having on him, perhaps she thought, I have learned more from my mother than I realized.

Her full-length shear pleated gown had gold trim on the bottom edge. She wore white linen shoes with gold thread, gold beads were braided in her hair. A green sash was draped over one shoulder that was kept tight at her small waist by a belt made of gold cowrie shells. Attached to her belt was the same dagger he had seen earlier that day. "Pharaoh's Daughter honors me with her audience." She smiled at him, he thought the look on her face was like a cat playing with a mouse, a very patient cat.

"Follow me." Expecting to stay in the large reception area, he was able to observe her lovely shape in the sheer gown, as they went into her private quarters. Sitre watched Senenmut, he did not notice her at first, he quickly started taking in the surroundings. Hatshepsut sat on a large cushion lounge, motioned for him to be seated by her as she chased off a cat. Sitre brought wine as Hatshepsut picked up a blue lotus bloom, holding it close to her face. "How difficult is it to learn the secret writing of the architects?"

Senenmut took his glass of wine noticing the wine had the faint aroma of the lotus blossoms, he had been served wine made with the sacred blue lotus flower once and knew it had a very strong relaxing effect. He just sipped the wine to keep his wits about him, "I'm sure My Noble Lady can learn the writings in about three months. But Pharaoh's Daughter may soon lose interest, she has many duties, shall we start now?"

She leaned back on her lounge in thought, still holding the flower. "I do want to learn the language, it intrigues me. There could be many uses of the ability to communicate with trusted staff that no one else understood, but we will not start tonight."

Senenmut drank some of his wine, it tasted very good, but he immediately noticed the effect. "We find that the writing is much quicker and easier to use once it is learned. We do not use it for personal writing."

"To keep the secret language from becoming common knowledge?"

"Yes, My Lady," he was enjoying the relaxing effect the wine was having.

"I understand that you enjoy astronomy, let's go to my roof, there you can show me something."

Leaving her living quarters, they climbed the stairs to her roof with her cat leading the way. He was thinking about what Hatshepsut had just said, she knew of his interest in astronomy because she had taken the effort to find out about him. It was a beautiful evening with the temperature still pleasant but soon becoming much cooler. In the distance there were many flickering flames from the city below, he could just make out his living quarters near the temple, the clear night sky was full of stars. On the roof were a small table and lounge, an elegant carved wooden bed frame that he knew she would use soon at night during the coming hot, flood season. The item that caught his interest the most was an elegant cooper bathtub, the water in it would have been warmed by the previous day's rays of Ra. The stonework around the tub was wet in some spots and wet foot prints could be seen, Hatshepsut had recently bathed. He was embarrassed when she caught him looking at her footprints.

Quickly he looked up into the night sky and wondered what was in tonight's sky that she might find interesting. Joining them, Sitre offered a warmer tunic for Hatshepsut, which she accepted, "Thank you Sitre, that will be all for the evening."

"Your servant Sitre is very lovely," Senenmut stated, not sure what he was supposed to talk about.

"Sitre is not a servant, she is my companion and friend."

Realizing he may have made a mistake referring to Sitre as a servant, "I apologize, My Noble Lady, I did not know."

"You could not have known about Sitre, she was my wet nurse, then my nanny, and now my constant companion. When I was very young, she risked her life to save me from a cobra, her family were Hebrew slaves on my mother's country estate. When the Queen learned what Sitre had done, she gave Sitre and her family their freedom and land of their own, Sitre chose to stay with me."

"The gods blessed My Lady with a loyal friend."

"Yes." After a brief pause, "This is one of my favorite times of the day. I enjoy the early mornings, planning my day and in the evenings, I review my day."

"How was this day for Pharaoh's Daughter?"

"It was a good day." Her father indeed had important news for her at the evening meal, she was to travel to Memphis, after the flood season. "Show me something in the night sky."

By the end of the evening she had learned about his many interests including his love of horses, he had never been married, she enjoyed his company. "I have enjoyed the evening."

Knowing he was being dismissed, "It has been a pleasure to be with Pharaoh's Daughter, I will always remember the honor," as he bowed.

Hatshepsut smiled and the look on her face was again that of a mischievous cat. "You speak as if you will never be here again, this is only the first night of many that I hope we spend together." She untied the green sash that was over her shoulders and handed it to Senenmut, "This is my color, when you wear it, you will not have to be escorted to my quarters. I command you to return tomorrow night," she said with a smile.

Senenmut took the sash made of fine linen, it had the sweet fragrance of myrrh, oil, and lotus flowers. The fragrance would become one that he would always associate with Pharaoh's Daughter, "I look forward to teaching Pharaoh's Daughter the language of Imhotep.

The following months Senenmut spent many evenings with Hatshepsut, he would receive a message from her servant, a young girl named Naomi. She had requested that he bring other architects for her to meet, most were young and single. The life of an architect demanded so much of their time, first there was the commitment of learning the many skills and acquiring the experience. Their work with stone monuments, which were to last for an eternity, then often took them to remote areas. Hatshepsut loved their enthusiasm, intelligence, and logic but one architect named Nehsi became the one she asked Senenmut to bring most often. His father was the Governor of the nome named Min. He was brilliant and knew several languages, he commented that languages just came easy for him.

Senenmut was amazed at how quickly Hatshepsut

learned the secret language of the architects, it had taken her only a month. He had seen the result of royalty marrying close relatives, their weaknesses were often magnified in their children. Now he had seen the rare positive results of an individual acquiring only desirable traits, Hatshepsut was very intelligent and beautiful. One of her learning skills he had noticed was interesting, she would look away and listen to whoever was talking. It appeared that if she heard something, without being distracted, she would never forget it. They practiced writing notes to each other, on the most elegant papyrus sheets Senenmut had ever written on. He saved these notes with her distinctive hand writing in a plain cedar box that was given to him by his mother. The notes like her sash had the fragrance of Hatshepsut on them.

The two obelisks of Pharaoh's were successfully raised and Senenmut was relieved when the last one finally settled onto its base. Queen Ahmose had rushed the raising of the second obelisk because she wanted Pharaoh to see the grand event attended by many noblemen from all of Egypt. Senenmut was not even allowed time to complete the carving on one of the obelisks, it could be completed later, the Queen commented. She wanted Pharaoh to enjoy the work he had commissioned now.

Senenmut wanted to please Pharaoh and prayed often that one of the obelisks would not crack or fall while being erected. But most of all he did not want Hatshepsut to see him fail, he would never forget the proud look on her face when she, the Pharaoh, the Great Wife, and Ineni the Royal Architect, congratulated him in the palace the night after the obelisks were raised. In celebration of the obelisks successful raising, there was a grand party with Senenmut the guest of honor. There was music, dancers, wonderful food, and he sat at the head table with the Royal Family. He made certain that he did not look at the beautiful princess too much.

The Royal Family departed first, no one dared to leave before they did, Hatshepsut congratulated him and then left. As the Queen was leaving, she almost said something, but decided not to. Senenmut saw her hesitation, did she see how much he cared for Hatshepsut? Was she amused, did she feel pity for his predicament, or more likely was she going to warn him? He knew that he had to keep his emotions under control and his dreams to himself, the least that could happen, was that he made a fool of himself or he could be fed to the crocodiles. After all, she had the royal blood of many Kings in her veins.

After the evening in his honor, he did not see Hatshepsut for a very long week, then he received a message to meet her. She was kind and polite as always, but a little distant, he was informed that she was going away for a year. She would be traveling to Memphis when it was safe to travel after the flood had receded. The House of Pharaoh had been busy preparing for the festivals and ceremonies celebrating the New Year associated with the beginning of the flood. There would be no more meetings, she must attend the events with her family. Senenmut tried not to show his disappointment, Pharaoh's Daughter was to be in Memphis for a year.

Slave Quarters, Memphis Palace

Shiphrah, a Hebrew midwife, opened the door and looked outside. In the darkness she could see men standing together but could not recognize anyone, "Amram!"

"Yes, is Jochebed alright?"

"She is fine, come see your new son." The men with Amram congratulated him and patted him on the back as he made his way into his house. Inside he saw his wife with the newborn baby asleep in her arms.

Jochebed said to him, "He is healthy and his sister thinks he is beautiful."

Miriam was stroking her baby brother's head, "He smells so sweet, father."

Amram was proud, but knew that the future of his son was not good, he was destined to grow up to be a servant for Pharaoh. "I wish we could offer a better life for him," he said to no one, just out loud as he kissed his wife and touched the small hand of his son.

Hannah, Jochebed's grandmother, who lived with them in the small humble house said, "Perhaps God will free him and his family. I have prayed for our people's freedom my whole life."

"Our people have prayed for freedom for many generations!" He replied.

Temple of Ptah in Memphis

High Priest Rewer told Vizier Tinfurer that he was ready to claim the throne. If Egypt had a bad inundation, he could claim that Egypt had to endure it because the gods were not happy with the aging and weak Pharaoh. If the annual flood was good, then he would put in motion the plan they had discussed. It was a vile and cruel plan, one that Vizier Tinfurer would proclaim Pharaoh had ordered and then he could take the throne to stop Pharaoh's cruel command. Vizier Tinfurer was against the plan, but he was easily persuaded by Rewer. Tinfurer would do anything to keep from losing the affection of him and he was also afraid of the High Priest because he knew that people who posed a threat to Rewer's ambition had disappeared.

CHAPTER THREE

Leaving Thebes

Isis smiled on Egypt when her tears started on time, the tears did not start early causing a damaging large flood or late which meant a small harvest and famine. The green wave of plants uprooted far up the River came first followed by the red wave of rich soil deposited annually, keeping the banks of the River fertile. The New Year's celebrations began at the start of the flood, the first season of the year was Akhet, the season of inundation. During these four months, work was resumed on the many construction projects Pharaoh had commissioned throughout Egypt, the families of the workers were supplied food by Pharaoh.

Later when the growing season Peret begins, the workers returned to their homes and fields. The vast wealth of Egypt depended on the abundant crops it produced, these basic foods and grains were traded with other nations. One interesting phenomenon occurred after the men were welcomed back home with festivals in each of the small villages throughout Egypt, nine months later during the next flood season there were many newborn babies. Egypt was renewed and so was Pharaoh's health. But rumors of discontent were increasing from Lower Egypt, the discord in Lower Egypt must be resolved while Pharaoh was alive. After his death, a rebellious Memphis may try and assume the throne, then Hatshepsut's family's dynasty in Thebes could come to an end.

The mosquitoes were present during the flood as always, large floods made them much worse. Hatshepsut developed a fever and became ill, for two days Hatshepsut was delirious and all feared the worse, finally her fever broke and Hatshepsut begin to sleep comfortably. Sitre was with her in the middle of the night when Hatshepsut woke and asked for water, a relieved Sitre brought her water and sent one of the priests to inform her parents.

Senenmut had been assigned a new project in the Temple of Amun that kept him busy during the day, but in the hot evenings, he laid awake on his roof looking toward the palace. He could just make out the roof where he imagined Hatshepsut was sleeping. Disappointed because he had seen her only once during the flood season, he got a fleeting glimpse of her during a parade celebrating the river god Hapi. But he was on the wrong side of the parade route and the future King blocked most of his view of her. Watching the Daughter of Pharaoh go by, he found it difficult to believe that he had spent time with her. Then he received a message from the Queen, she required his audience.

It is the fourth month of Akhet, on the 3rd day, in the twelfth year of the rule of Tuthmose I. Sitre wakes up Hatshepsut while Ra is still deep in the underworld. Today, Hatshepsut starts her three-week journey to Memphis, the River is now safe for her to travel. She will continue her education there and be presented to all of Egypt. With the growing concern that the Vizier of Memphis does not represent Pharaoh, it will be her responsibility to deal with him and his Royal Court. Hatshepsut stretches in bed not wanting to get up while it was still very dark, then she remembers what is happening today and the events of the previous night with her parents.

Pharaoh had surprised her when he informed her that he had made a royal decree which appointed her Co-Regent of Egypt. She was now the most powerful person in Egypt, except for Pharaoh. He told her to quickly form her own Royal Court, he gave her a list of names and their information, "These are people that your mother and I believe can be trusted, you are not obligated to use anyone, but you must choose your Royal Court soon." While Hatshepsut looked at the scroll in her hand, he continued, "I have made all the preparations for my journey to the west, my beautiful daughter will be required to make many decisions, some will be difficult. Be strong and do not hesitate to use this absolute power I have given you." With sadness in his eyes he said, "You will be the Great Wife soon." She held back tears that wanted to flow, she could see the will power it took for her father to control his emotions. He gently kissed her and left her standing with her mother.

The Queen had not said a word during her conversation with her father, she took her daughter's hand, "I will obey your commands and wishes when you become the Great Wife of Egypt." Then with a sigh, "I wish Pharaoh's favorite stone at the Bekheny Quarry was finished so it could be made ready for his sarcophagus." Her mother then left, leaving her alone, Hatshepsut knew of the stone her mother had mentioned. There was only one statue of Pharaoh's father, Prince Sipairi, and it was made of the same stone.

Sitre interrupted her thoughts, "My Lady needs to get out of bed now and dressed for her journey." Sitre was very busy fussing about and giving brusque orders to others as she helped Hatshepsut get dressed. She commented, "You are not well, I wish you did not have to go."

"You must be strong for me today and I am almost well, I only have a slight ear ache. I don't want to be seen today as some young child upset over leaving home for the first time." She opened her arms to Sitre and they embraced for a long time. Princess Hatshepsut, the daughter of Pharaoh and a child of a god, had been raised in a protective and closed environment. For her protection, no one was allowed to get close enough to touch her. Her entire life she had been told by all around her in words and song how beautiful and special she was. Today, she would leave this safe environment and all the people in it.

The paved road from the palace to the royal docks was lined with the Royal Court, officials, noblemen and guests to honor Hatshepsut on her departure. With her were family and Sitre, who had given her a lotus blossom. Her cat Mau came running, he had decided at the last moment to come. Pharaoh looked tired, the Queen was regal and beautiful as always. Prince Tuthmose and Hatshepsut had talked about the trip on several occasions, he wished he was strong enough to make the journey to Memphis. The dock was busy with activity, men were loading items on the Royal Barge, two other large ships and one smaller faster boat.

A few officials, scribes, and palace guards would travel on one of the large ships and the other carried servants, food, and supplies to be used during the journey. The royal barge, "Falcon" was for Hatshepsut with its blue and white Royal Standards. The Falcon was pulled by two large covered row boats, with 20 rowers in each boat, there were only six rowers on the Falcon used to maneuver the barge in and out of the docks. The tall sail on the Falcon would be of little use traveling north down river, against the prevailing winds. These same winds and sail would one day make travel upriver against the current easier and quicker on her eventual return to Thebes.

A smaller faster boat was leaving, it would travel ahead to the next mooring place, announcing the soon arrival of Hatshepsut. Weekly dispatch boats depart from Thebes for Memphis carrying documents, the dispatch boat that departed last week gave advance notice all the way to Memphis of her upcoming travel. This was to ensure that the royal mooring places along the River were prepared. The River was not safe to travel at night, so official overnight stops were maintained along the River.

Ra was just starting his journey across the brilliant

orange morning sky, birds along the banks were starting to make their calls, welcoming another day. As she turned to board the Falcon, little was said between Hatshepsut and her parents, their goodbyes had been said the night before. Looking back at her family, she saw Mau sitting at the foot of Sitre, only the Prince gave a small wave. She quickly turned away to maintain her composure, Admiral Ebana and the captain of the guards were standing at the boarding ramp and both bowed, "It is an honor to command the Falcon with Pharaoh's Daughter on board." Even though Hatshepsut remembered him, she could not greet the Admiral as she quickly walked past him. Her emotions were too close to the surface, she was certain that he thought she was being arrogant.

When she set foot on the gentle rocking Royal Barge, she became very dizzy and a wave of nausea overcame her. Orders and commands were given and the ships started sailing away with the Falcon leading the two other ships. She was surprised by how much the motion of the large elegant barge affected her, she had never had a problem before on any boat, small or large. She tried to ignore her uneasy stomach, even her maids sensed her mood and waited for her command from a distance. There was just the soft swirling sound of the boat gliding through the water. In the distance she could barely hear the soft drum beat for the men manning the oars in the boats pulling her barge. Behind her from the other boats, she could sometimes hear their voices and laughter carry over the water.

When the Royal fleet passed near a small village, the villagers young and old lined up on the banks, with cheers from the men and boys, mixed with the high-pitched shrill call from the women. When she neared a village, she pulled back the sheer curtains so she could be seen, even though she wanted to just be alone. The banks of the River, away from villages, were lined with lush growth of plants. Some birds took to the air while others maintained their watch for fish on long thin legs. The tall palm trees and reeds swayed gently in the breeze while the rigid triangle shaped stems of the papyrus moved less. The River banks were cleared for fields as they approached a village, workers toiled in the hot sun, naked men and boys were fishing along the banks. Occasionally, a curious young boy in a small boat made with bundles of papyrus, would come out from shore for a closer look at the royal procession.

By midmorning Hatshepsut thought that her emotions had settled and, hoping she might feel better walking around, found Admiral Ebana on the bow looking down river. A distinguished looking officer with a great commanding voice who had served with her father when Pharaoh was still a general, she remembered. Walking up to him, "Admiral, are we making good time?" Not really caring, because they would be on the River for at least three weeks.

He was a little surprised when he heard her question from behind. He turned toward her, bowed and then returned facing up the river, "Yes, we are, Pharaoh's Daughter."

"I remember when you took Pharaoh and his Daughter to Memphis five years ago, I was only ten then." She said looking in the same direction as the captain, hoping to make up for not acknowledging him earlier when she boarded the Falcon.

"I remember that trip well also, I am surprised that My Noble Lady remembers me."

"I could never forget you because my father told me that if anything should happen to him, I was to go to you for protection."

Admiral Ebana turned to look directly at her, he was surprised, "I am honored that your father said that."

"Is it still true?"

"Pharaoh's Daughter can always depend on me to serve and protect her family."

"I am pleased that Pharaoh's friend is in command. Where will our first mooring place be today?"

"We will be stopping at General Djoser's estate soon."

Relieved with the idea of getting off the barge soon and on stationary land, but she was not sure why they were stopping there. The General's estate was too close to Thebes to be an official mooring place. She had seen him and her mother together on some occasions, his namesake was a great Pharaoh in Egypt's distant past and he had lived up to his namesake. Pharaoh Djoser had built the first pyramid that looked like a series of steps over a thousand years ago. "Why are we stopping at General Djoser's estate?"

"The Great Wife informed me that General Djoser has requested we stop there. If it pleases Pharaoh's Daughter?"

"I look forward to seeing General Djoser again," with an unsteady walk she returned to her shaded lounge. Ra was directly overhead when they approaced General Djoser's dock with a large gathering of people waiting. The swift advance boat had arrived and already docked at the impressive dock made of large square stones, with steps going down to the water's edge. The different layers of stones and steps allowed a boat to dock safely as the height of the River changed throughout the year. The captain of the palace guards was first to disembark the Falcon, then Hatshepsut, as soon as she touched the ground the dizziness went away.

General Djoser greeted her first with a bow, "Welcome Foremost of Noble Ladies, Daughter of Pharaoh."

"Rise General, I am pleased to see the good friend of Pharaoh and the Great Wife again."

"This way My Noble Lady, I have been looking forward to Pharaoh's Daughter's visit and I hope our accommodations and preparations are suitable." Hatshepsut noticed the military award of "Golden Flies" around his neck, the Honor of Valor was rare and worn with pride all of one's life, most likely he would take it with him into the afterlife. The award represented the persistence that flies have and are associated with a soldiers courage, determination, and aggressiveness during battles. The General was younger than her father, he appeared to be about her mother's age. There were no obvious scars or injuries and he still had a very erect military posture and strong walk.

The activity and noise associated with the arrival of the other boats could be heard in the background. Djoser first introduced his family of two grown sons, a niece, and his sister who he referred to as "The Lady of his House." One of the sons was married, and Djoser explained that he was expecting his first grandchild. The young wife was barely showing, she was about the same age as Hatshepsut, most Egyptian girls their age were married and had families. Hatshepsut offered a blessing, "May the god Bes bless you with a healthy child."

"We are honored by Pharaoh's Daughter."

The main house was large with several immaculate gardens, a lovely pool, several out buildings, circular grain storage buildings, and what appeared to be stables. Hatshepsut was taken to the guest quarters so she could relax, with cool drinks and fresh fruits for her. Abet the older maid, applied cool soothing oils and dressed her in a cool sheer gown. She enjoyed being alone and resting after the morning travel, it was not a long day, just very uncomfortable.

Abet woke a surprised Hatshepsut from a nap, she had not planned on going to sleep, Abet informed her that the evening meal was ready and guests were waiting for her.

The meal was beautifully displayed with music and singing in progress, the food was served by several young servant girls. The conversation with the General and family was pleasant and easy, they would eat first with Hatshepsut before other members of her party. After the meal, they retired to a comfortable cool courtyard with rare large sycamore trees. The pond nearby had many colorful fish coming to the top of the water expecting to be fed, nearby orchards and vineyards offered their fragrant scent of grapes, figs, and date trees. While Hatshepsut visited with the General and his sister, a few of the higher-ranking officials from the other boats came into the courtyard thanking General Djoser for his generous meal.

Later, she thought she recognized a man's voice, turning to see who was speaking to one of the General's sons, it was Senenmut. She was surprised and pleased to see him, he came to her, bowed and then General Djoser said, "Senenmut, what a pleasant surprise to see you!"

"It is an honor to see you again, General," he then returned to the General's son. From her mother's notes about General Djoser's family, Hatshepsut knew that Lady Amenset's husband had been an Army Officer, who had died while on a military campaign. She then became lady of the house to the General who was a widower by then. Hatshepsut discovered that she actually enjoyed the conversation with both Lady Amenset and her daughter, Nafrini. Hatshepsut thought the meaning of her name, "She brings beauty" was appropriate. Nafrini appeared to be a little older and very striking, both were relaxed around her. Hatshepsut surmised that Lady Amenset's husband must have been a Medjay because their daughter had dark complexion and most likely had inherited her tall build from the Medjay, but she had her mother's fine features and beauty. It was a new and pleasant experience to have a casual conversation with someone other than family, she learned that Nafrini was interested in a new form of literature that was becoming popular in Egypt and that she had written some stories.

Most of these stories told of adventures, travel, and brave deeds that kept the listener on edge. Since most Egyptians could not read, the authors read their stories to the audience and acted out the characters. "I have enjoyed performances in the palace by writers. I look forward to hearing one of your stories."

Nafrini answered, "It will be my honor."

Later in the conversation, Lady Amenset spoke of her

son, "My son is the Commanding Officer in charge of the Bekheny Mountain Quarry."

"Does he come home often? I had hoped to meet him in Coptos." Captain Menna was one of the recommended people on her father's list.

"He has been here only once in the last three years," Lady Amenset answered with hesitation.

Hatshepsut looked at General Djoser, unsure if she should ask any more questions. General Djoser explained, "Menna put down a revolt at the quarry by the workers, while there his wife and baby daughter died here shortly after childbirth. He came back for their burial but has not been here since."

"You have not heard from him either?"

Lady Amenset answered, "An occasional letter or message from someone he knows. The last message was before the flood from an officer he knows, he said that Menna is well. He had been hunting a lion that harasses the livestock in the quarry."

"May I deliver a message to him? I will see his commanding officer in Coptos," Hatshepsut asked.

"I could not ask Pharaoh's Daughter to do that, it is kind of you to offer." Lady Amenset replied.

"You did not ask, I offered," Hatshepsut replied with a seldom seen slight smile.

"I am honored by your generous offer, I will write a message tonight."

When the conversations began to slow down, Hatshepsut asked General Djoser if he would show her his stables. "Yes, I would be honored." On the way to the stables, General Djoser asked, "How is my Pharaoh's health?" speaking so that the ever-present palace guard could not hear him.

"He is often in great pain from old wounds received in battles that he fought with you."

"The Pharaoh's heart is light and the scales of his namesake Thoth will balance in his favor." Djoser continued, "How is the Queen?"

Hatshepsut picked up on a change in his voice when he asked about her mother, she replied, "She is well, but concerned for my father." General Djoser just nodded. They continued walking quietly up a freshly swept path to large and well-kept stables that had the pleasant aroma of fresh straw and grain. The horses were being fed by the workers and sparrows were noisily flying around trying to steal a meal.

"Does My Noble Lady like horses?" he asked.

"Yes, I love driving a chariot."

"You drive a chariot?"

"As fast as I can." Hatshepsut answered while looking at a beautiful black stallion and mare. They were the largest horses she had ever seen, "What magnificent animals, they could easily carry a large man, not like the horses we have to pull our chariots."

"I hope to breed a new line of horses that are bigger than our Egyptian horses."

After looking at the stable and his prize horses, the General led Hatshepsut to an area in the courtyard that overlooked the River. It was a lovely shaded area, with a vineyard, a small shrine, and a white granite bench. The cool evening breeze was refreshing and the sweet smell of the grape blossoms made the area very enjoyable. They both were silent for a while enjoying the last rays of Ra before he entered the underworld for the night. General Djoser watched Hatshepsut closely to see her reaction, "You will be a Great Wife, but there will be those that oppose you."

"Your advice and loyalty will always be welcomed by

me." Ra had entered the underworld behind the hills across the River, but there was still an orange glow, with a few purple clouds in the evening sky. She became very quiet and distant.

Djoser noticed the change in Hatshepsut. "What worries my future Queen?"

"I was thinking about my duties and my future with the new king."

"Are you concerned about the responsibilities of the Great Wife or your future with Tuthmose whom you don't love?" Djoser inquired.

Hatshepsut wanted to trust the old friend of her father, but the question caught her off guard, one can never be sure when it comes to politics. "The gods have chosen Tuthmose to be Pharaoh and I will perform my duties as his Great Wife and Queen for Egypt."

"You will serve the future Pharaoh well as his Great Wife and I am certain that Egypt will prosper with your advice and guidance. Tuthmose may be the future Pharaoh, but the future of Egypt is with you, Hatshepsut." Hatshepsut looked at General Djoser and then turned to look at the river and the sunset. She was a little homesick already and overwhelmed with the realization that what had once been in her future was now here, she wanted to change the subject, "How do you know Senenmut?"

"He is a very talented and brilliant young man, whom I have known since he was my scribe. He later left the military and went to serve in the Temple of Amun as a priest and then as an architect. Senenmut always excels at whatever he is doing."

"So, you are the general about whom he has spoken."

From across the courtyard, Senenmut watched Hatshepsut with General Djoser. He was thinking about his meeting with the Queen before they departed Thebes for Memphis and the decision he still had to make concerning his future. When he had received the message from the Great Wife, he was certain that either his career was over, or at the least any association with Pharaoh's Daughter must end. The Queen had to know his feeling for her daughter, foolish for anyone, particularly a commoner.

Arriving at her royal office he saw Ineni, the Royal Architect of Egypt, waiting outside her office. Ineni informed him that he had just recommended him to the Queen, as his replacement when he retired. A guard announced his arrival. The Queen was pleasant, he was pleased when she told him that Hatshepsut enjoyed being with him and trusted him. She stated what he already knew, Hatshepsut could only marry Prince Tuthmose and that Pharaoh would not allow anyone to jeopardize that marriage. She informed him that Hatshepsut probably would ask him to be her personal advisor, she surprised him when she told him that Pharaoh hoped he would choose to be her advisor. They knew he cared for her and would always do what is best for her. Then the Queen had paused and watched him intently, she stated that it may be difficult for him because of his feelings about their daughter. If he preferred to one day be the Royal Architect of Egypt, she would ensure that he got the appointment.

He remembered trying to thank her and rambling on about what an honor either position was for him. Then Queen Ahmose had mercifully stopped him and said that he did not have to decide now, she would send him to Memphis with Pharaoh's Daughter supposedly representing Ineni. He was officially doing inspections on projects in Memphis. Watching Hatshepsut, he realized that he could not be happy unless he was near her, he returned to his quarters.

Hatshepsut and General Djoser walked back to the house in silence, each thinking about what had been said. Entering the house, Lady Amenset and her daughter greeted them, Lady Amenset asked, "Did my brother bore Pharaoh's Daughter with his talk of horses and next year's flood?"

They saw again her seldom smile, "I am glad that we had this time together."

"My brother has been excited for weeks, in the anticipation of seeing his dear friend's daughter again. We are honored that you stopped here on your way to Memphis and will always remember the time we spent with our future Great Wife."

Hatshepsut turned to General Djoser, "I wish to go to my quarters now."

CHAPTER FOUR

Wadi Hammamet

Waking up, it took Hatshepsut a moment to remember where she was, in her half sleep, she first thought she was with her father on the trip they had made together years ago. Then she realized that she was at the estate of General Djoser. After appeasing the local priest by making offerings to their local gods, she arrived at the dock and greeted General Djoser and his family, "I will inform Pharaoh and your dear friend how you honored their daughter."

"The honor is for me and my family to serve the Royal House. The Great Royal Wife is indeed my dear friend."

Lady Amenset gave Hatshepsut a small silk bag containing a message for her son, "I appreciate My Lady's offer."

"You are most welcome." Hatshepsut turned to board the Royal Barge, when her foot touched the barge a wave of nausea came over her again, she stopped and then walked very carefully.

Admiral Ebana bowed as she boarded the barge and noticed her hesitation and unsteady walk, "Is My Lady alright?"

"A little unsteady, but I will be alright." As the Royal Barge sailed away, many swallows were darting around in a bright azure sky. Dogs were barking at the activity and several small boats gave chase, with the people waving to Pharaoh's Daughter.

Once under way, she was feeling sick and called to Abet, "Bring me a bowl." Abet barely returned in time, afterwards she felt better but could not understand what was wrong. If this continued, it was going to be a very miserable journey to Memphis. Mid-morning Hatshepsut sent Abet to determine how long it would be before arriving at Coptos, the next mooring place. She had gotten sick two more times and was relieved when Abet returned stating that they will arrive soon.

It was very hot when the Falcon approached the docks of Coptos, when she saw the large gathering of people and officials waiting in the direct rays of Ra, she was concerned. She did not want to get sick with everyone watching and have their impression of her as being ill or weak. A very nauseous Hatshepsut stepped on the dock, but the moment that her foot touched the ground, she felt much better. When offered a very elegant carrying chair, she declined, concerned about the motion of the chair, "I wish to walk and greet those who came to see Pharaoh's Daughter."

Many had gathered to see and honor her, the only noise that could be heard was that of small children playing and laughing, it pleased the Governor to be seen walking with Pharaoh's Daughter in front of all his constituents. He had not looked forward to the Royal visit because of the expense and there was always the chance that some mistake may offend the Daughter. She was taken to the quarters reserved for Pharaoh where Hatshepsut informed the Governor that she was pleased with the reception and the excellent condition of Pharaoh's Quarters. She also informed him that his son Nehsi would one day hold an important position in her Royal Court. He expressed his pleasure and honor that his son was favored by the future Great Wife. The quarters were clean, well-stocked with food, fresh cut flowers, and palm leaves. After resting and enjoy some food, she sent Abet to have Admiral Ebana come to her quarters.

"Admiral Ebana, I will not be able to continue to Memphis tomorrow," she informed him on his arrival.

"I am not surprised, I saw how ill Pharaoh's Daughter was,

shall I send for a physician?"

A slightly embarrassed Hatshepsut answered, "No, I just get dizzy on the Falcon and then sick."

"Do your ears hurt?" he asked.

"Yes, my right ear hurts, I am getting over a fever I had during the flood. Why do you ask about my ears?"

"It happened to me once, it will be best if we do not sail for a few days," he recommended. "I will make the arrangements, My Lady," he bowed and turned to depart.

But Hatshepsut stopped him, "Admiral will you see if Captain Menna, General Djoser's nephew, is at the fort here or if he is still at the quarry?"

"As My Lady requests."

A rested Hatshepsut was enjoying her meal the following morning when Admiral Ebana arrived to inform her that Captain Menna was still at the Bekheny Quarry. He casually mentioned that there was no recent information about Captain Menna, but that a resupply caravan was scheduled to depart for the Bekheny Quarry the next day. While she listened to him, she decided to go with the caravan to inspect Pharaoh's stone and meet Captain Menna. She was not sure why she decided to make the two-day journey through the desert, maybe the adventure of something new or the idea of spending long boring days in Coptos, whatever the reason, she said, "I will go with the caravan and I will need a chariot, make the arrangements Admiral."

He was slow to replied, "As the Daughter of Pharaoh commands."

"Excellent, I also wish to inspect the horses and chariot later." Admiral Ebana bowed and left her quarters. The real reason for going to the stables was her concern of getting sick while riding the chariot.

Hatshepsut, Admiral Ebana, and two of her palace guards arrived to meet Commander Huni, who was in charge of the garrison. He had been ordered by Admiral Ebana to be in charge of the caravan with the princess. No soldier in the garrison had ever seen anyone from the Royal House and the young beautiful Daughter had their attention. When introduced to Commander Huni, he was formal and gruff, a middle age officer with the weathered skin of a man who had spent his life in the sun. His tunic was not very clean and neither was his head cloth, but he had not expected a royal visit today. Commander Huni commented that he was reluctant for Pharaoh's Daughter to make the march. Hatshepsut spoke directly to Admiral Ebana, "I wish to inspect the progress of my father's sarcophagus at the quarry. If Commander Huni does not want to make the journey, then we should find someone else Admiral."

Commander Huni quickly replied with a slight bow, "I am only concerned for the safety and comfort of Pharaoh's Daughter."

Hatshepsut, who was as tall as the Commander looked directly at him, "I trust the Commander with my safety and Pharaoh's Daughter will require nothing more than what the Commander requires. I wish to see the horses now."

He called to one of the soldiers nearby, "Escort Pharaoh's Daughter to the stables."

Hatshepsut took a small bag from Admiral Ebana, turned and walked with the soldier to the stables. Admiral Ebana smiled, "What do you think of Egypt's future Great Wife?"

"The Daughter is self-assured, but we will see how she does when the rays of Ra get hot and her mouth gets dry in the desert wind."

"You will have no complaints from Egypt's future Queen, just do all you can to protect that future," the Admiral replied as he watched her walk away, "I pray the god Min, protector of the desert, watches over her."

"Watches over all of us," Commander Huni replied under his breath. The soldiers watched the princess as she approached the stables with flies in the air. She was confident in her stride as she walked around piles of dung, her spotless elegant white gown looked completely out of place in the dirty surroundings. Even though she was not dressed formally, she wore more gold than any of the soldiers had ever seen at one time. In addition to the flies, a pungent odor of dung filled the air, the military stable was obviously not maintained as well as those of the palace or General Djoser's.

The chariot was a standard military six spoke chariot that was dirty and the horses were not well groomed, but looked strong and spirited. She spoke gently to the animals in a quiet soft voice for a while, petting them on their noses, then she took some pieces of sweet fruit from the bag and fed the horses. As she led the horses to the chariot, the handler started to help, she looked at him and shook her head ever so slightly. He stopped in his tracks, she wanted all to see that she could take care of the horses and chariot during her travels. She proceeded to harness up the two horses, noticing the pins that held the harnesses to the chariots yoke. During battle if one horse was mortally wounded, the driver could pull the pin and retreat with only one horse pulling the chariot.

The military chariot was lighter and not as lavish as the royal chariots of the palace. When she went to board the chariot, she hesitated as she looked at the floor of the chariot which was made of leather straps. When she stepped on the chariot, she felt fine and rolled the chariot into the compound. The soldiers watched intently because this was the first time, they had seen a woman driving a chariot. Hatshepsut slapped the reigns and drove the chariot as well as any officer, returning to the handler, "The horses will do, feed and water them well. I want the horses groomed and the chariot cleaned," as she gestured to her white gown now stained from the dirty chariot. He bowed to her as she walked back to her quarters with Admiral Ebana.

Before arriving at her quarters, she told Ebana, "Have Senenmut come to my quarters." When he arrived, she dismissed the maids. "What do you know about travel in the desert?" It was late when Senenmut finished telling her what he knew about travel in the desert and what the conditions would be like with the caravan. Hatshepsut then informed him that he would be given the title of Chief Adviser to Pharaoh's Daughter, but with a smile she said, "I will ignore your first advice about not going to the quarry."

Hatshepsut awoke early pleased with the decision about Senenmut and excited about the caravan, she went to the Temple of Min, the local god of Coptos and of the desert. Priests were in the forecourt and bowed to her, she dismissed her palace guard. Entering the open-air inner temple, even in the early morning light she recognized Senenmut. "My Noble Lady, I prayed to the god Min for Pharaoh's Daughter protection." He was really there because he wanted to see her, certain that she would offer prayers to the local god.

"And all who travel with us." Hatshepsut added in a whisper, "Egypt has many gods, but this god I find most obscene. However, I do not want to offend the people or priests of Coptos."

"They will take note that my Lady asked for Min's protection and guidance."

Hatshepsut knelt down on her knees in front of the image of Min and raised her hands asking for protection. After a brief prayer, she stood and was about to leave to join the caravan, when the bark of a baboon startled them. He was nearby on the temple wall, sitting on his hind legs with his raised front paws toward the first rays of Ra warming himself, but he appeared to be looking behind them. Hatshepsut and Senenmut looked but saw no one in the direction the baboon was looking. Senenmut commented on the baboon's posture that was similar to Hatshepsut's posture during her prayers, "I wonder if we chose to worship in such a manner after seeing the monkeys greet the first warm rays of Ra?"

Hatshepsut laughed out loud, "My Senenmut always surprises me with his thoughts." They watched the baboon for a moment, it kept looking behind them. "I must join the caravan," as she hurriedly departed the temple. She knew that the events of the next few days would be told in stories by those traveling with her for the rest of their lives, it was important that she make a good impression for herself and the royal family.

She arrived at the garrison wearing a plain long sleeve white linen tunic that went from her neck to her ankles, her white head cloth had a scarf that would be used to cover her face. The only jewelry she wore was her small gold cobra head band under her head cloth and around her neck was the ever-present half Maat necklace. From a wide woven leather belt hung a sturdy leather scabbard for her dagger, her appearance though fitting for travel still drew everyone's attention, especially the soldiers who had not seen her the day before. Admiral Ebana was standing next to her chariot and Commander Huni was holding the horses. They both bowed and Commander Huni asked, "Is Pharaoh's Daughter ready?"

Her short answer was, "Yes."

A small fat man approached, his tunic was already soaked in sweat. "This is Quarry Inspector Antef, he will be traveling with us," stated Commander Huni. Antef bowed deeply, Hatshepsut nodded slightly, she had seen his kind of official before. He most likely didn't make this trip often, if ever, but he wanted to be seen by her. Commander Huni continued, "If it pleases Pharoah's Daughter, I ask that the chariot be behind the leading group of soldiers, it will be dustier, but safer."

"I will trust you on all matters of my safety." He was surprised at her willingness to do as he requested, not the reply he expected from the young woman who could have anything her heart desired.

The caravan consisted of 25 soldiers, oxen pulling 20 wagons, donkeys carrying supplies, their handlers, and her small entourage of five palace guards and two maids. It was noisy with the animals protesting and men yelling, a lot of dust was already in the air. Admiral Ebana wished her safe travels. She was excited as the caravan started, looking back and in the distance, she recognized Senenmut now standing next to the Admiral.

The caravan followed the ancient dry river bed, called Wadi Hammamet, she knew that this ancient wadi went all the way to the Red Sea. They were soon in the mountains with steep cliffs on both sides, the air was hot, full of dust, and no breeze made its way into the canyon. She could hear the handlers prodding the protesting donkeys and oxen along behind her, the soldiers were talking among themselves ahead. Hatshepsut had to keep reining her horses in, because they wanted to go faster than the slow pace of men walking.

Commander Huni walked up close to her chariot, "I don't expect any problems on our journey because the Bedouins have been peaceful lately. But if there are any problems, I request that My Lady dismount and stay close to me and the soldiers."

"Should the lead soldier be carrying the Royal Standard for all to see?"

"Yes, the standard will cause anyone to think twice about attacking this caravan and bringing the wrath of Pharaohs' army on them."

"As you request Commander." The excitement that Hatshepsut had earlier was starting to wane and boredom had set in. She was leaning against the cane side of the chariot after the horses had settled down to the pace of the soldiers.

Ra was almost directly overhead, when Commander Huni

thankfully called the caravan to a halt in a wide area of the wadi. There was no water well here, but it was a good place for a rest stop. Many rocks were laid out in a large circle, trash and debris was proof that this area was used often by caravans. There were sighs of relief from the men and soldiers. Wiping the sweat from her forehead with her arm, she shaded her eyes with her hand and looked further down the Wadi as the desert shimmered and seemed to wave in the heat. Her maids quickly set up a small tent for her, she was glad to get out of the hot sun and have some privacy.

The older maid was Abet who had served Hatshepsut's mother when she was young. Abet was "Head of Maids" and answered only to Sitre, she made life very comfortable for Hatshepsut in the palace, she was organized and pleasant to be around. Abet knew her position, but Hatshepsut was close to her. The younger maid was a young attractive Hebrew girl named Naomi, they brought her some food and water. The rest was welcomed by everyone, she could not remember ever being this hot before, except maybe when she visited the pyramids years ago with her father.

Living on the River, there was the water and the prevailing wind from the north that gave one some relief from the heat. The total silence of the desert was a new sensation for her. The men and pack animals were resting, there was no noise from wild birds or animals. No vegetation or trees here, just the rays of Ra, sand, and rock. She thought about the effort men and animals had to endure to bring goods into the quarries and the work required under extreme conditions to bring out the beautiful stone to be used by Pharaoh. Her thoughts were interrupted by the sound of men and animals getting ready to continue the march. She hated to leave the shade of the tent and return to the intense hot rays of Ra, Commander Huni asked, "Is the Daughter ready to continue?"

"Yes, how is everyone doing and is the caravan on schedule?"

"There are no problems, we are making good time."

"Inspector Antef, is he OK?"

"He is at the rear of the caravan and complains that we are going too fast, but he will survive."

"I assume he doesn't make this trip often?"

Huni laughed, "Pharoah's Daughter is correct, only once before that I know of and that was when he was first assigned this post. Now he just inspects the number and quality of the stone when they arrive in Coptos against the recorded number that left the quarry."

Hatshepsut nodded and asked, "Will the caravan be leaving the canyon today?"

"Yes, we will make camp in an area that is open and has water, a small compound there will be more comfortable for Pharaoh's Daughter."

With the afternoon rays of Ra to their backs, the march was more comfortable. As Ra was setting, the water well and small soldier compound came into sight. Senenmut had told her that water wells were discovered along the wadi over five hundred years ago, these wells made travel possible for large caravans through the desert. All were relieved that the days' march was over. Commander Huni wanted Hatshepsut to stay in the compound with the soldiers camped around her, but when Abet informed Hatshepsut that the compound was dirty and had fleas, Hatshepsut informed him that she would stay in her tent. He place his soldiers around her tent, the animals were hobbled, watered and fed away from her tent, this helped greatly with the noise and smell.

Hatshepsut stayed in her tent, while the camp was settling down. Her maids removed her dusty tunic, bathed and rubbed oils on her. They were concerned that the food would not be to her satisfaction, but Hatshepsut was relieved to have

DRAWN FROM THE NILE

most of the dust off and be somewhat cooler. The food did not matter to her but she did enjoy her favorite wine that Abet had brought along. "I will not forget your effort to make me comfortable."

61

CHAPTER FIVE

Bekheny Quarry

The howling of jackals kept her from getting a good night's sleep, it was of little comfort that Senenmut had told her that the howling was good for those in camp. If the jackals were quiet that may indicate they were scared off, possibly by someone trying to sneak up on the camp, he had told her. Hatshepsut was up early and the camp was still just beginning to wake up, animals were complaining, they wanted to be fed and watered. The smell of onions cooking in the braziers was in the air.

She could see in the early morning light, writing on the cliffs close to her tent, she decided to inspect the inscriptions and graffiti made by previous caravans. There were many references to how difficult life was in the caravans, they told of losses they had suffered, and often there were derogatory remarks about Pharaoh and his family. A palace guard was standing just a few paces away, but she did not notice Commander Huni when he arrived, she was interested in the inscriptions about the last expedition to the land of Punt. These were more official in appearance, with accounts of days traveled and riches they were bringing back to Egypt, she was startled when Commander Huni spoke, "Men have been writing on these rocks for ages."

"It would appear so. I find the account of the last expedition to Punt very interesting. I would like for Egypt to make another expedition to the mystical land."

"Some of the writings on the rocks are blasphemous to

the Royal House, I am sorry that the Daughter saw them."

"They are the comments of tired and unhappy men, comments that are sometimes justified by the hardships imposed on them. Is it a long march to the quarry today?"

"We should get to the quarry midafternoon making it an easier march today. May I ask why Pharaohs Daughter wanted to make the journey to the quarry in person?"

"I could have sent someone to determine the progress of my father's sarcophagus, but I wanted to see it myself and to insure it is worthy of Pharaoh. Also, this experience is new to me and I wish to learn as much as I can on my trip to Memphis." She did not mention her interest in Captain Menna. Walking back to her tent she said, "I am also interested in seeing how life is at the quarry after the rebellion was put down."

Commander Huni was surprised that she knew of the minor rebellion by the workers there three years ago, "All is well there now and supplies arrive on schedule. The previous officer in charge of the quarry was found guilty of making profit at the expense of the people. Captain Menna is in charge there now, he is the officer who put down the rebellion and he has made sure that the quarry gets the support it is promised."

"Do you know him well?"

"He has been in my command since he recovered from his wounds received in the Cush wars. He is a good officer, he could be in command of his own garrison, but has chosen to stay at the quarry for personal reasons."

"Well, let us be off to meet your Captain Menna and to see my father's stone."

Quarry

Group Captain Menna was in his quarters after he had finished his midday inspections and was making his report in his daily log. He had a scribe that could make these entries but he enjoyed doing it himself and it was a relief to be out of the afternoon heat. The quarry and the village that supported it were in good condition, production was on schedule. There were about 100 people in the village which included the soldiers, the workers, some local mountain people and five skilled stone masons. The majority of the work in the quarry was done by the workers, who were a mix of free and slave laborers. The soldiers were used in peace time on projects like this, it kept them employed and readily available for military action if needed. Plus, at these distant quarries there was always the threat of the "wretched Bedouins of the mountains" or nations farther to the east.

Tomorrow they would perform military training only, the soldiers always looked forward to these military drills because the training got them out of the boring and difficult quarry work. Menna wanted his men to maintain their military skills and not forget that they were fighting men first. It had been a success, their morale was up and production was better, even if they did spend fewer days in the quarry a month. This practice was noted by other officers in charge of different quarries and had become standard procedure, he was proud that his idea had worked well for other quarries.

The soldiers were rotated out every two months so they could go back to the garrisons that supported them. He was expecting a caravan any day now, when a caravan arrived, there would be a day of rest and festival. With normally only one day off out of every ten-day week, the extra day and festivities was always welcomed by the soldiers and villagers.

Menna was talking with one of his junior officers when a soldier came rushing in and came to attention to make a report, he was out of breath after his long run from his outpost. "Make your report soldier!" he commanded.

"A Royal Caravan is coming sir."

"You mean the supply caravan?" Menna corrected.

"The message from the outpost relayed by signal mirror said, royalty, Sir."

Captain Menna dismissed the soldier, he turned to his junior officer, "Have my sergeant report to me."

"Yes sir." The junior officer hurriedly left the Captain's quarters.

Captain Menna knew that Pharaoh was in poor health so it was not him making the journey here. Perhaps Pharaoh had departed this life and needed his sarcophagus now, it must be Pharaohs' son, the prince coming. There was no real reason for Menna to meet the caravan, but he wanted to show respect to the Royal Prince. He wished he had more time to prepare the village, but he had not been informed a royal party was coming, a fresh tunic and clean head cloth would have to do. He buckled his bronze knife on and attached his officer baton to his belt and then he went to his chariot. "When will the Pharaoh's sarcophagus be ready?" he asked the stone mason in charge, who was now waiting by the chariot.

The mason looked at his daughter Tyia, "It will be at least three months, Menna," she answered very seriously. Tyia was always with her father, she had learned the art of seeing the perfect stone in the mountains from her father, it was Tyia who had seen the flaw in the first stone for the Pharaoh and this was the reason for the delay. Menna and Tyia had become close the last few months and he had even thought of getting married and starting a family. But he was not sure it would be a good life for her. After all, he was away when his wife had needed him. Knowing that she had traveled very little, only two trips to Coptos was the extent of her travels. He wondered if she would be happy in strange cities without her father when he was deployed for long periods of time.

Menna smiled at Tyia, "There is nothing we can do about the stone not being ready and we will inform the royal guest truthfully." He mounted his chariot, slapped the reigns and drove off to meet the caravan.

Commander Huni saw the approaching chariot, Captain Menna had not been caught by surprise, he smiled to himself, but Captain Menna is still in for a surprise. The caravan was brought to a halt, Hatshepsut said, "We will meet Captain Menna, get into the chariot Commander!" Commander Huni knew that he wasn't being offered a ride but that it was an order from Pharaoh's Daughter. He had barely gotten into the chariot, when Hatshepsut slapped the horse's reins and headed toward Captain Menna.

Menna saw the officer get into the chariot with the Prince, he stopped his chariot and stepped out to hold his horses. Their chariot came up fast and as it got closer, he recognized Commander Huni and what appeared to be a young slim boy driving the chariot. Hatshepsut could see from a distance the officer waiting for them, his size was imposing and he favored his sister. Captain Menna appeared to be in his early twenties, well-groomed, and a little annoyed at the unannounced visit. She smiled to herself thinking that he is pleasing to the eye, as she brought her chariot to a halt. Captain Menna watched as the dust covered "Prince" and Commander Huni walked up, he bowed to the young Prince.

"I am impressed with your alertness," Hatshepsut said, as she began removing the scarf around her face.

Captain Menna looked up and was surprised to hear a young woman's voice coming from the dust covered face.

"Pharaoh's Daughter, this is Captain Menna."

Captain Menna bowed again, "It is an honor."

Hatshepsut was very impressed at the appearance of the officer, there were scars on his shoulder and arm, his eyes were clear and alert, any enemy opponent would know he was facing an awesome challenge. "Pharaoh will be pleased that his Daughter is well received by one of his officers."

"I pray that my Pharaoh is well?"

"My father is still the Horus Pharaoh," she could see the relief on his face.

Commander Huni turned and waved for the caravan to continue to the Quarry. Captain Menna led Hatshepsut and the caravan back to the village and quarry, the entire village had turned out to see the royal party. There had been visits from officials and palace staff before, but a Royal had never visited before. As much preparation that could be done in a short time, had been done. The soldiers were in formation and the villagers were along the road to the village, waiting. As Captain Menna and Hatshepsut approached, everyone bowed as she passed, she could hear the people call out "Prince of Egypt" in low voices.

When they arrived at his office, he commented, "We assumed that it was the prince that was honoring us with an inspection. I apologize for my error, my Noble Lady. They did not know they are looking at the future Great Wife of Egypt."

Hatshepsut took it all in, "I am impressed at the reception, quickly arranged for Pharaoh's House." The village houses were small and had brightly colored trim, she observed that the houses were made of stone instead of mud bricks as were the houses along the Nile. She realized that stone was in abundance here and that water for making the mud brick was not. The lack of vegetation and trees gave her the same impression she felt in the desolate valley where her father's tomb was.

"Princess Hatshepsut, this is my quarters I hope it will be adequate." Hatshepsut entered the office and quarters of the Captain, she observed that it was clean, with only the faint scent of burnt lamp oil. There was only one room with a bed at one end, the majority of the quarters was used as an office area. There was a desk, two chairs and a woven storage basket, a shelf on one wall behind his desk was filled with long clay cylinders containing rolled documents.

"This will be adequate."

"What will Pharaoh's Daughter require for the night?"

"My maids will make my needs known, if you will see to their wishes and make sure my horses are cared for."

"It will be done," he saluted as he turned to leave the quarters.

"Captain Menna, I wish for a report on the quarry and my father's stone later." He bowed slightly.

Abet asked, "Does my Lady want her bed mat on the floor or shall we use the Captains bed?"

"If the bed appears clean, it will be fine."

The young maid Naomi commented, "There appear to be

DRAWN FROM THE NILE

no fleas in the quarters and there sure aren't any flea bites on Captain Menna." The two maids smiled at each other.

"None that I saw," Hatshepsut replied smiling also.

Once everything was in place the maids started attending to Hatshepsut. She enjoyed having the layers of dust removed and soothing oils applied to her sun-dried skin. Sitting at his desk, she had her meal with wine and noticed a cup made from an ostrich egg sitting in a red stone ring. The inscriptions on it mentioned a victorious campaign at a location called, "Belly of Stones." After her maids had their meal, they dressed Hatshepsut into the one fine sheer linen gown she had brought on the journey. She had a gold and lapis cowrie shell waist band and a broad collar that was small compared to her formal ceremonial collars. It contained many colored stones of lapis, carnelian, and small gold beads. Her gold necklace of Maat with only one wing was not visible under her broad collar.

The coolness of the desert night felt good, she heard Captain Menna approach the Palace Guard at her door. Abet started toward the door, but Hatshepsut said, "I will greet the Captain."

She opened the door while he was talking to the guard and she could see the surprised look on Captain Menna's face. Menna had been impressed with the determined young dust covered Princess who had made the long journey to the quarry. But now, even in the dim evening light, he saw a beautiful young woman. Her eyes, with the green kohl outline, were always watching him, the gold jewelry she wore had a warm glow in the evening light and there was the faint sweet smell of myrrh. He finally spoke, "Princess Hatshepsut requests a report on her father's stone?"

"Yes, come in. Is there anything you need from your quarters?"

"I need nothing and I hope the humble room is acceptable to my sovereign."

"Your quarters are sufficient." The older maid Abet brought two glasses of wine, "Do you enjoy wine, Captain Menna?"

"It has been a long time since I have had wine, but I do enjoy it."

Abet gave him the wine. "This is my favorite wine made from a special blue lotus flower." He took the glass and waited until Hatshepsut started to drink from her glass, he then quickly drank the wine. His plan was to drink the wine, make his report and leave. The wine indeed had a sweet fruit smell, it tasted much sweeter than the beer made here in the village. He soon noticed that the effect was much faster and stronger than beer. It was then that he noticed that the Princess only sipped her wine with her closed lips in a smile. With her almond shaped eyes, she looked like a cat playing with a mouse and he knew who the mouse was. The maid offered to refill his glass but he declined. Hatshepsut sat down, "Have a seat, Captain Menna."

Menna looked around the room as if he had never been in it before, her maids had transformed his quarters with a female touch and with fragrant incense burning. He sat down on a nearby stool, trying not to look at the intense probing eyes of Hatshepsut. "How soon could my father's sarcophagus be ready for shipment to Thebes?"

"The Master Stone Mason informs me that it will be ready in three months. The River will not be rising by then so shipment should be easy."

"That long?" Hatshepsut paused, "You have done well

here the last three years."

He was surprised that she knew how long he had been at this post, Commander Huni must have told her, he thought. "The quarry is producing well and the workers are well taken care of."

"Your mother informed me that the quarry was bothered by a lion."

"My Noble Lady has seen my mother?"

"Yes, I met her, your Uncle, and your lovely sister. My barge stopped at your Uncle's estate our first night from Thebes."

"Hunting the lion, gave my men a diversion from working in the quarry. We must have scared it off, there have had no other attacks on our animals." He now realized how Pharaoh's Daughter knew so much about him.

Menna noticed a small silk sack next to Hatshepsut, when she saw him glance at it, "This is for you," handing it to him, "It is from your mother."

Taking the note, he noticed how small and delicate her hand was, he took out the small papyrus scroll, "May I ask how Princess Hatshepsut found my mother and sister, are they well?"

"They are well and General Djoser speaks highly of you." She was glad to see that he could read, he did not need a scribe. She quietly stood up and went to the other side of the room and motioned for the maids to leave. Menna was still intently reading the letter when he noticed the maids leaving.

"I apologize, I should not have read the letter now," as he stood, ready to leave.

"I wanted you to read it," she said as she walked back toward him. Menna was not accustomed to being this close to royalty, "Please, sit back down." Menna could not believe she had said, please. "Tell me about the quarry, your command here, and about yourself."

Menna talked at length about the amount of stone quarried there, the way he had kept his men trained for military duty and that he would be glad to have the head scribe give her a full and detailed report. He watched the young Princess, careful to not talk about the quarry too long, but she listened and asked the occasional question. He finished and waited to be dismissed. "You did not tell me anything about yourself. Are you happy here, do you desire some other assignment? When you are still at night in your bed, what are your thoughts and dreams?" she asked softly.

Menna was trying to figure out why Pharaoh's Daughter was at this insignificant quarry? Why was she asking about his dreams? What were his dreams? He often thought his dreams had died three years ago. Only recently had he started to think about his future with Tyia. "Your humble officer is honored that my sovereign would be interested in me." He paused and then continued, "My father was a Medjay Officer with my uncle, General Djoser, he met my mother and they were married. We lived close to my uncle's estate. My father died of an illness while on a military campaign."

"Was that at the "Belly of Stones?" she interrupted him, remembering the memorial ostrich egg on his desk.

"Yes, My Lady," surprised that she knew that, "I suffered minor wounds and while recovering, I met my wife and we were to have a baby, but both died. I have kept myself busy here." He finished and felt drained, he had not talked about events in his life to anyone in a long time.

She realized that it was not easy for him to talk about himself and she sensed the guilt he felt. "I think the Captain is too modest about his actions and bravery, we will talk more about your future and how you can best serve Egypt and me," putting the accent on, me. "Tomorrow we will see my father's stone, the village, and the quarry." She stood, Captain Menna started toward the door, "Here is your mother's letter."

Menna took the letter he had forgotten. "Until tomorrow," he bowed and departed. Once outside he walked to a favorite area of his, behind his quarters and on a large rock outcropping, from here he could see a great distance to the east. During the day one could just make out the mountains near the Red Sea. What did she mean, when she said, "serve me"? Probably she meant to serve her in the army, he decided.

The maids came back in after he had left his quarters, Hatshepsut asked Abet if it was pleasant outside, "Yes, it is not too cold."

"Let's go for a walk." They followed what was obviously a well-used path with a Palace Guard just out of hearing distance. "What do you think of our Captain Menna?" Hatshepsut asked.

"He is very handsome."

"Anyone can see that, is he someone that can be trusted and not be influenced by others?" Hatshepsut pressed Abet.

Abet was quiet for a long time as they walked, she too had wished for someone to be Hatshepsut's protector. "If my Lady is looking for someone to be loyal to her, I believe he would be."

"Will he wish to serve a woman?" Hatshepsut asked, as they came upon someone standing alone on the edge of a cleft.

Captain Menna turned and saw Hatshepsut, "This is a lovely spot."

"I will leave my Noble Lady."

"Don't leave. Abet, take the guard back to the quarters, Captain Menna will stay with me." Then she saw lightning in the distant east, "The flashes of light are beautiful."

"Yes, storms have been going on in the east toward the Red Sea for several nights, the tears of Isis are giving someone refreshing rain." They watched the lightning flashing, a very rare sight. She was quiet for a long time before her thoughts returned to Menna. Could she be sure about him? Could she be sure of anything or anybody? Captain Menna was getting a little uncomfortable with the awkward long silence, what was he supposed to say and do now? He decided to just wait quietly and take her back to his quarters when she was ready.

Finally, Hatshepsut asked, "Where do you wish to go for your next assignment?"

"I will go where my Pharaoh and his generals wish, I desire to be close to my family, but the area around Thebes is desired by many."

"Is the Palace a desirable location for you?"

Captain Menna looked at Hatshepsut in the dim light, trying to see the expression on her face, "That is a desired assignment for any soldier."

"Do you have matters here that prevent you from leaving with me when I return to Coptos? I know it is sudden for you."

Menna thought of Tyia, they knew that someday he must leave. To leave with Pharaoh's Daughter without Tyia was something he did not want.

"There is one matter here that I must resolve, before I could leave." He was being forced to make decisions about Tyia he had been putting off. "There is someone here that I need to talk with."

"We should return to your quarters." While walking back, she thought, he is ready to get on with his life. "Captain Menna, I want you to think about the palace assignment, I will make the arrangements with Commander Huni." Hatshepsut turned and walked by the guard at her door into the quarters, he has a lady, good! That is why he has not taken another assignment.

CHAPTER SIX

The Stone

Menna had a restless night, Tyia was very happy when he asked her to marry him, she did express some concern about living in the Royal Palace with royalty and leaving her father. She had many questions that he could not answer. It was still dark when he walked from the soldier's barracks, where he had spent the night, to his quarters.

There he found the palace guard asleep, when the guard realized someone was standing near, he reached for his spear. "Looking for this?" Captain Menna asked quietly, holding the spear. Recognizing the imposing figure holding his spear, he could not come up with an answer for Captain Menna. "Pharaoh's Daughter deserves better protection than this, I will guard her now. You report to your captain that you have lost your weapon." The guard reluctantly left Captain Menna still holding his spear knowing he would pay dearly for this mistake.

Hatshepsut was awake as the first rays of morning light were just starting to come into the quarters. When the maids realized she was awake, they started preparing for the day. Before going to sleep, she thought of far off places in the direction of the lightning flashing, the direction one would travel to the mysterious land of Punt. When Hatshepsut was ready, she sent Abet to get Captain Menna. Abet left the quarters and then immediately returned with him, "Captain Menna is here already My Lady!"

"Good morning, My Noble Lady," as he bowed.

"It is a good morning," she responded, wondering about the spear. "How long have you been at my door?"

"Just a short time, I could not sleep and I did not know how early Pharaoh's Daughter awakes."

"You will discover that my days start early and I burn a lot of oil before going to bed, I do not require much sleep. Shall we see your village and quarry?"

The captain of the palace guard had been watching from a distance, he walked towards them, then Captain Menna tossed the spear to him, "Guard Pharaoh's Daughter better!" The captain took the spear without saying a word, he wanted to challenge Menna and resented him with Pharaoh's Daughter. Hatshepsut watched and listened, she did not know what was taking place, but she sensed that Captain Menna was already protecting her.

There was activity in the village, cooking aroma and smoke was in the air, with children laughing and playing. "I always give everyone a day off after the supply caravan arrives, but today we are honored by the presence of Pharaoh's Daughter. The village was surprised that it was Pharaoh's Daughter and not the Prince." He immediately regretted reminding her that no one recognized her and wanted to change the subject. "With no workers in the quarry, there will be no dust and noise when Pharaoh's Daughter inspects her father's stone."

"I am not surprised no one recognized me yesterday, I almost didn't recognize myself," trying to put him at ease.

On the opposite side of the village they came to an area with larger houses, "This is where the stone masons live." Menna answered, but his attention was at the largest house which was a few houses away.

Hatshepsut saw what was distracting Menna, it was Inspector Antef at the last house and he was in a heated discussion with an older man and a young girl. "Let's go see what Inspector

Antef is upset about." When Antef saw them approaching he became even more animated. "Antef, what is the problem?" Hatshepsut questioned firmly.

"It is of no concern of Pharaoh's Daughter," he replied, and continued to lecture the girl and man.

"Antef, you do not answer Pharaoh's Daughter, with a dismissal!" her voice was as sharp as a sword.

Realizing his serious error, "I apologize to Pharaoh's Daughter, I am upset that Pharaoh's precious stones are being used by these people and not sent to the royal shops for use by real artists." Antef replied, trying to justify his actions.

Hatshepsut looked at the small stone the young girl was holding, who was bowing to Hatshepsut, "Let me see your work." Hatshepsut looked at it closely, it appeared to be an almost completed cat that was lying down, the head was not finished. The stone fragment was beautiful and her work was excellent. Antef still had a look of satisfaction on his face. "Inspector, does Pharaoh have such small pieces of stone, in his Palaces or Temples?"

Antef looked confused, "No, My Noble Lady."

"Do you think that Egypt is so poor that we cannot allow the next generation to learn the skills that will produce the most beautiful statues in the world? I think a man of your position should understand this. If you don't, then perhaps I will appoint someone that can appreciate it." Hatshepsut handed the piece back to the young girl, "This is lovely." Hatshepsut kept her firm gaze on Antef, who was now concerned about his position. "Perhaps you should go inspect the stones that are important to Pharaoh and leave these people alone," giving the arrogant inspector a slight dismissal wave.

"As Pharaoh's Daughter commands." Antef bowed and tried to get away as best he could, while trying to save face.

After he had walked way, Captain Menna made introductions, "Princess Hatshepsut, this is the Master Stone Mason Beni and his daughter Tyia."

"Your Majesty," they replied while bowing again.

"Rise," she commanded. It was the first time that Hatshepsut had really noticed the young girl who appeared to be a little older than she was, there was an exotic look about her. Both her and the Stone Mason were tall and fair, she did not recognize their heritage. Tyia was very slim with a long elegant neck, her hair was the color of wheat and her eyes were the color of lapis. Thinking to herself, this is the person that her Captain is involved with. She thought that Menna's lady is perhaps the most striking and beautiful girl she had ever seen. "I dislike people who use their position of authority to take advantage or abuse others. His behavior is against Maat and my will."

"Pharaoh's Daughter is very kind and protective of her subjects," responded the Master Stone Mason.

"I want to see my father's stone now."

"It will be my honor, this way please." The stone mason led them toward the quarry, Hatshepsut noticed the eye contact between Tyia and Captain Menna. She heard no accent, Tyia and her father had been in Egypt for a long time, she realized. When they arrived at the quarry, Hatshepsut was surprised at its size. It was not only a pit, but a tall rock precipice that had been cut into the mountain, a series of stone ramps had been carved at one side of the mountain of rock so that large pieces of stone could slide down the ramp and not be broken. The mason led them to an area where canvas tents covered the work areas, with many different copper and bronze tools all arranged very orderly. Beneath one tent was a beautiful large dark blue-green stone, work was in the process of taking a section off that would be the lid, "This is my Pharaoh's stone," the mason said proudly.

"It is magnificent, the color and size!" commenting as she walked to the stone and touched it. The stone was smooth, engraving would be done on the outside and inside when it arrived at Thebes, it felt cool and almost alive. "This is worthy of Pharaoh," she stated after walking around it, inspecting and touching all the sides with her hands.

"The top needs to be taken off and then hollowed out, to insure it won't break like the last one. In about three months, it will be ready for the artists in Thebes to finish," he stated.

Hatshepsut hands were dusty from examining the stone, Tyia stepped forward with a small container of water for her to wash her hands. When she finished washing, Tyia offered her the hem of her clean long tunic. Hatshepsut smiled at the young woman, "My hands will dry soon enough." Hatshepsut noticed another large stone in the next tent and went to it, the stone was obviously broken. "Was this my father's first stone?"

The mason answered, "Yes, but as you see it broke while we were cutting the top off. I should have listened to my daughter, she warned me about a flaw."

"Tyia warned you?" Hatshepsut asked looking at a very uncomfortable Tyia.

"Yes, she can read what is in the stone, sometimes better than I can."

"Show me the defect you saw."

Tyia hesitated, but Menna, who was standing by her, nodded encouragement. Tyia walked to the broken stone and took a container of water and rubbed water over it, the deep blue-green color of the stone appeared. Then she wetted an area where there was a gray vein. "There the vein goes too deep," she softly spoke.

Hatshepsut leaned over to look at the gray vein up close, "I don't see any difference, you really can see into the heart of the stone." Tyia bowed slightly and stepped back, Hatshepsut noticed the proud look that Captain Menna had standing by her. Hatshepsut turned and walked back to the stone pit, looking at the ladders, containers of water, tools, and broken stone. She realized the amount of effort spent here for stone to be used by sculptors to make beautiful carvings and statues. "Are there many special stones left in the quarry?" she asked.

Beni answered, "Tyia has one very special stone we hope to remove some day."

"Tyia, show it to me." Menna and Beni, started walking toward the pit. Raising her hand slightly, "I wish for Tyia to show me the stone." They watched as Pharaoh's Daughter followed Tyia, descending down two ladders to the bottom of the pit and crossing to the rock face, there Tyia pointed out an area in the wall of rock. As the two women looked at the rock, Menna and Beni watched, neither one knew what to make of the events.

"This is a wonderful stone, the color is amazing, it appears to be located in a difficult place to remove from the cliff."

"Yes, My Lady, all the stone above will have to be removed first."

"Perhaps someday," Hatshepsut said as she touched it and imagined what it could be used for.

Menna and Beni noticed that Hatshepsut and Tyia had stopped looking at the stone and were talking. Hatshepsut asked, "Tyia are you happy to be leaving with Menna? I know that you will miss your father."

"I do wish to leave and travel, when Menna asked me to marry him last night, I was very happy. But even if he had not asked me to marry him, I was going to leave by myself when he was reassigned to another post."

"You were not sure he was going to ask you to marry him?"

"When Menna came here three years ago, I was fourteen and my father wanted me to marry a local stone mason, but I wanted a different life than living in this quarry. Menna was married then, after Menna lost his wife and baby, he was very withdrawn and unhappy. I waited to see if he would ever care for me."

"I am certain that Menna loves you and is ready to move on with his life, I want you and Menna to be with me in the future."

"Pharaoh's Daughter has offered Menna a wonderful opportunity, but I do not know if My Lady wants someone with her that is not familiar with royal life. I do not want to harm Menna's future," a concerned Tyia answered.

"Menna cannot be happy and serve me well without you with him, you and Menna will get married and leave with me. I look forward to our future together."

After their conversation, they started making their way back to the top of the quarry. Tyia was surer at climbing the rocks and ladders, at one point she held out her hand to Hatshepsut. Menna was shocked that Tyia offered her hand and even more when the Royal Princess took her hand and followed Tyia out of the quarry. Arriving at the top, "Thank you for showing me your favorite stone. I will make sure it is used some day." Tyia smiled slightly and bowed. "We should go back to the village."

The stone mason walked with Hatshepsut, Tyia was next to Menna, he looked at her with questions in the air. Tyia just smiled, nodded, and whispered, "Everything will be fine." When they arrived back at the village, the celebration was in full swing. There were the smells of cooking, music with singing and laughter. Some men were already starting to enjoy their beer.

"Captain we need to talk, is there some place quiet where we can go?"

"Yes, this way My Lady," leading her back to his favorite vantage point, where they had been the night before. No one spoke on the way, when they arrived, he showed her a square cut rock that had been placed there to be use as a bench. The view was still wonderful and the bench was in the cool shade of the mountain, with a very slight breeze.

Finally, Hatshepsut spoke, "Tyia is a lovely and intelligent woman, she will make you a wonderful wife, I want you and Tyia to return with me to Coptos then we will continue on to Memphis. We will be there for about one year before returning to Pharaoh's Palace in Thebes."

"What will I do in Memphis before I become a part of the Royal Palace Guard?"

Realizing that she had not made her plans clear to Menna, "You are not going to be a part of the palace guard. You are going to command my personal guard, my life and safety I will trust to you and you alone, in all matters. I will never go anywhere without you or those you place in your command."

Menna was trying to comprehend what Hatshepsut had said and was wondering why she had chosen him. "My Sovereign honors me with her trust, but why am I right for protecting Egypt's future Great Wife, I do not know her enemies?"

"There are several reasons, Pharaoh recommended you, I know of your bravery and loyalty to Egypt, all the officers around my father and the palace are loyal to him, I need someone who has no other allegiances and owes nothing to anyone. Are you such a person?"

He had seen how loyalties in the military sometimes changed, they were bought with gold or the promise of power. "It will be an honor to serve Pharaoh's Daughter and I will pray to the gods, that I may never fail My Noble Lady!"

"Are there any men that you want to serve with you?"

"There is a Sergeant here that I trust without question and there are two soldiers back in Coptos."

"The Sergeant here, will he want to be with us?"

"I think so, Sergeant Dadu has been with me since I entered the military, he served with my father before me. Sergeant Dadu saved my life after I was injured in the Cush wars."

"I want to meet your Sergeant Dadu and any other men you choose. But now, you and Tyia need to prepare for our return trip to Coptos, go to her." Hatshepsut commanded gently.

CHAPTER SEVEN

Back to Coptos

The last day at the Bekheny Quarry was busy for Captain Menna and Tyia, their marriage was really quite simple even by Egyptian standards. Her father was disappointed that there was no celebration of his only daughter's wedding but was greatly pleased when he received his copy of the wedding contracts from the scribe, dated the fourth month of Akhet, the 10th day, in the 12th year of the rule of Tuthmose I. The official witness was none other than Hatshepsut, Pharaoh's Daughter. Both Tyia and her father proudly displayed their wedding contracts, which became family heirlooms for many generations.

Hatshepsut was a little surprised, when she interviewed Sergeant Dadu, he was everything that Captain Menna wasn't. He was older, shorter, bald, and had the build of a large sycamore tree stump. His movements were slow, but it was obvious from his arms and legs, that he was as strong as a bull. "Sergeant Dadu, what do you think about your change of orders? You do not have to accept these orders, but Captain Menna speaks highly of you."

He answered in a gravelly voice that had been strained from years of shouting orders, "My Captain honors me with his compliments and it has always been a privilege to serve with him." He then hesitated not sure how to best explain his reluctance, "I am an old soldier with no family and as you can see my appearance is not that of my Captain. Pharaoh's Daughter may not wish for me in her Palace Court? I explained this to my Captain." Dadu seemed relieved to have spoken his mind.

"Sergeant Dadu, what I see is a soldier who has served Egypt bravely for a long time. I desire your continued service." Sergeant Dadu returned his eyes to Hatshepsut, no official or officer other than Captain Menna had ever expressed any appreciation to him before. Hatshepsut noticed that he seemed to soften a little.

"If Pharaoh's Daughter believes I can serve her, I am honored to do so."

"Are there any questions you have?" The firmness returned to Sergeant Dadu's voice, "I have no questions, My Noble Lady."

She realized that the Sergeant was not comfortable enough with her to engage in any further conversation, "Before you go, I want you to know that you may have an audience with me anytime on any subject and I will always follow your commands."

Sergeant Dadu seemed surprised at her statement giving him such authority. He quickly got to his feet, bowed and with relief left her quarters. Hatshepsut looked at her maid Abet, "What do you think of the Sergeant?"

Abet answered, "He is not the most handsome man in Egypt, but I'm glad that he is on our side." Hatshepsut smiled and nodded yes.

Later, Sergeant Dadu who was now on duty, announced that the Princess had a guest. Abet went to the door and told Hatshepsut that it was the young woman, Tyia. Hatshepsut smiled, "Let her in."

Tyia entered carrying something, she unwrapped the carving and gave it to Hatshepsut, the head was now finished. It was an excellent likeness of Hatshepsut, "It is a small sphinx of me!" as she examined it closely. "It is a wonderful likeness of me."

Tyia was pleased that Hatshepsut liked it, "The sphinx is

small, but I am sure My Lady will have larger and many more."

"I will always cherish it, when did you find time to finish it? You have much to do, in preparation for leaving tomorrow."

"I could not sleep last night, because I was so excited. After meeting you, I knew that I wanted the statue to be of you. It did not take me long to finish, Menna and I will have tonight," as she smiled shyly.

"You need to go to your Menna, now."

It was still dark when Hatshepsut was awakened the next morning by the activity in the village, dogs were barking, men were talking, and the animals were complaining under their loads of burden. Hatshepsut and the maids were packed and ready by daybreak, when she went outside, Captain Menna and his new wife Tyia were already there standing by her chariot. Captain Menna had his bronze dagger, but no baton, he had passed it to his temporary relief who would be in charge of the village and quarry until a permanent replacement arrived from the garrison at Coptos.

"I trust that My Lady is ready to leave?" he inquired.

"I have enjoyed my visit. I am glad that you and Tyia will be with me." Commander Huni arrived, and said that the caravan was ready, Hatshepsut mounted her chariot. Leaving, she passed all the people of the village, Tyia's father was one of the last people to say goodbye. He and Tyia had one last tearful hug, knowing that most likely they would never see each other again. Everyone was quiet for a long time.

The oxen pulled wagons were loaded with cut stone and donkeys carried just enough supplies and water for the trip back to Coptos, the caravan soon settled into a slow steady pace. After a mid-morning break, Hatshepsut asked Captain Menna to ride with her. "Are there any questions you have?" Hatshepsut was pleased with the many questions he had, she tried to answer them as honest as she could. Some of the questions about the future Tuthmose II were difficult. In the afternoon the questions slowed down, Hatshepsut knew that Captain Menna had much to think about. When he was getting off the chariot, she asked that Tyia ride with her. Riding in a chariot was a new experience and she was surprised that the floor of the chariot was made of leather straps. When she commented on it, Hatshepsut explained that an archer normally stood with the driver in battle, the leather absorbed some of the bumps and aided in his aim. "Are you tired from today's travel?"

"I am a little tired, but I'm so happy I could walk for days!" Tyia paused, "I feel like I have been given the best gift one could ever have."

The caravan stopped for the night at the same place they had stopped before, with the flea infested building. Camp was set up with the usual loud talking and the protests of the livestock. Hatshepsut was alone in her tent with her thoughts after her meal, she was pleased with the events that had happened so far on her journey to Memphis. She didn't know when she went to sleep, but was awakened by a donkey braying loudly, it was still dark and the camp was quiet otherwise. She could not go back to sleep, so she wrapped a blanket around herself and slipped out of the tent. Outside was Menna, "Is everything alright?" he asked.

"Yes, how long have you been on guard?"

"Not long, I could not sleep, so I relieved Sergeant Dadu."

They sat quietly for a long time, both in their thoughts. Menna had stopped thinking of Hatshepsut as only a young girl, when she spoke there was no hesitation and she walked with assurance and confidence. She had made big changes in his and Tyia's life, "I am afraid that I will fail you in some way." Menna finally was able to say to Hatshepsut, while he continued looking ahead and not at her.

Hatshepsut placed her hand on his arm, her touch was soft and warm, "I also have fears, I am afraid I will fail you, my family, and my Egypt. We all have fears, we must overcome."

The caravan was in the mountains shortly before Ra was directly overhead causing the heat to be much more intense in the canyons, Tyia was riding with Hatshepsut, the conversation was relaxed. Hatshepsut smiled when she looked at Tyia covered in red dust, she knew that she looked the same way. There was a disturbance at the rear of the caravan, Menna called to Dadu, "Stay with Pharaoh's Daughter, I am going to see what is going on back there."

Hatshepsut watched Menna run toward the commotion at the far end of the long caravan, Tyia stepped out of the chariot and watched also. Were the Bedouins attacking the rear of the long column, she wondered? Men behind her started pointing and yelling, a female lion was running past the caravan, she was close and paid no attention to them. Hatshepsut looked at the narrow canyon they were in as the lion ran ahead on the ancient river bed, remembering the lightning she had seen in the night sky for days, and wondered what the lioness could be running from? Then she remembered her dream about the lion and suddenly, she knew why, shouting at Commander Huni, "Get your men to safety!"

"Why? The lion is of no threat!"

"Commander, get your men to high ground now, a flash flood is coming." Warning her maids and Tyia, "Run that way," as she pointed to where the soldiers were now running.

Dadu yelled, "Get out of the chariot."

"I am going to warn the others," as she turned her chariot around and quickly headed back down the caravan, warning everyone along the way. Nearing the end of the caravan, the wall of debris and water came into view, Menna was now running toward her. She knew that she had to get to high ground also, but where? She could hear a low rumble as the flash flood came closer to them, Menna was screaming, "Run!"

Most of the handlers had gotten the ox's harness undone from the wagons, and the donkeys were being led up the steep slope, everyone was scrambling as fast as they could to get out of the low area. Hatshepsut knew that the horses and chariot could not go up the steep and unstable incline here. Searching down the wadi, there was an area that was not too steep, she raced toward the area as fast as the horses could run. Dust flying up from the running horses and chariot wheels made it difficult for her to see, Dadu was near as she turned the chariot up the slope, and then he saw the chariot flip over.

Hatshepsut had not seen the large boulder, but felt the chariot start to tilt over, then the tongue of the chariot broke and the horses were free. She put her hand out to help break the fall, then her head hit something and everything went dark for a moment. When she came to, she could hardly breathe because she was pinned under the chariot. Suddenly the chariot flew off of her and she then felt as if she was flying, realizing that Dadu was carrying her she relaxed and darkness came over her again. Dadu slipped and stumbled several times as he ran for high ground with her.

When Menna arrived he found Hatshepsut, Dadu, Tyia, and the maids safe, but Hatshepsut was unconscious, Tyia was holding her head in her lap. Abet was getting their campsite organized, while the younger maid Naomi was standing in shock and disbelief. Menna sat down from exhaustion, Dadu was shaking his head, "She would not get out of the chariot, because she wanted to warn everyone." Then Tyia noticed that Hatshepsut was shivering and that she was bleeding from the back of her head, a blanket was found and put over her.

Commander Huni was getting control of the situation, few supplies had been saved, he came to check on Pharaoh's Daughter. "How is she?" he asked Menna.

"She injured her head and hasn't said a word."

"I don't understand how she knew to warn us about the flash flood?" Commander Huni stated as he returned to his tasks.

With much concern Dadu stated, "I don't think it is good that the Princess is sleeping. I have seen soldiers with head wounds go to sleep and never wake up."

"What should we do?" Tyia asked.

"Get cool wet linen cloths to keep on her head wound and keep her awake as much as possible," he replied.

Menna looked at the very young girl in Tyia's lap, she was not the young woman in control of everything he had seen just a few moments ago. He was dealing with a lot of different emotions, fear for her life, concern for Tyia and everyone, and his failure to protect Hatshepsut. They cleaned her wound and kept a cool wet cloth on her head. Hatshepsut would wake up for a brief moment and then fall back unconscious. Tears were in the eyes of Tyia as they all huddled close together on the side of the mountain. Hatshepsut began to stay awake longer and then go back to sleep, they gave her water and kept her awake as long as possible.

Dadu and the maids got a small campsite set up, a fire was built and some supplies were found. Abet noticed Dadu's legs were bleeding from injuries he had gotten while carrying Hatshepsut and started to tend to his wounds. Dadu insisted that he was alright, Abet gave him a stern look, that even the gruff Dadu did not challenge. Eventually Hatshepsut was awake, she was looking around and trying to comprehend what was going on. "How long have you been holding me Tyia?"

"Not long, how do you feel?"

"My head hurts."

Tyia looked at Menna and smiled in relief. "She will be fine my husband."

The events of the day began to sink in and everyone realized how lucky they were, if they had been deeper into the canyon with steep walls on both sides, no one would have survived. How did Pharaoh's Daughter know to warn them, was the question all were wondering? By nightfall Commander Huni had taken an inventory and discovered that there was water and food enough for only one day. One man was missing, Quarry Inspector Antef and one of the oxen handlers had died, most of the oxen and donkeys were alive, but Hatshepsut's two horses were missing.

A dejected Menna said "I need to check on the camp and men, I will be back soon." He told Dadu to watch Hatshepsut while he was gone. Dadu was watching Menna to see if there was any blame in his eyes, Menna saw the look and responded, "Sergeant you saved our Noble Lady's life, the Princess is very smart but she doesn't listen very well. Perhaps she would have listened to me, if I had been there."

"Perhaps," a relieved Dadu stated.

"I will be back soon," Menna walked off into the dark, he needed to think about all that had happened and what he should have done. The second day that Hatshepsut was in his protection she had almost died, he was so used to being in charge of everything but now he needed to change his priority because he was only responsible for Hatshepsut. Noticing that one of the herdsmen was being attended to by other men even though he didn't appear to be injured, he asked, "What are his injuries?"

The men were surprised by Menna's appearance, one of the men stated, "He is not injured but his father and their two oxen were killed. He doesn't know what he will tell his mother or how he will provide for his family now. One of the oxen was to calve this year and it was to be his, with the calf he had planned to marry and be able to provide for his family, but now?" the man just shook his head.

Menna listened and he knew that life would be hard for the boy's family and his future was bleak. "The gods were not good to you today, but you are lucky to be alive." The boy never looked up but continued to bury his head in his arms, so Menna walked away. He walked around the camp with no real purpose in mind, when he came upon Commander Huni and the captain of the palace guards. "How is Princess Hatshepsut?" the captain of the guards sincerely asked.

"She seems better, she is talking now."

"I am thankful that she is alive, how did Pharaoh's Daughter know to warn us, did the gods tell her?" the captain asked.

Menna did not know the answer for sure, "Perhaps."

"Do you think the she will be able to travel tomorrow?" Commander Huni asked Menna.

Menna quickly answered, "No, she will not be able to travel and will it be safe for anyone to travel tomorrow?"

"Perhaps, you are right, we don't want to get caught by another flood."

CHAPTER EIGHT

Rescue

After Ra had returned victorious from the underworld, the events of the day before were fully revealed, everyone was amazed that more lives were not lost. There was debris everywhere and a red muddy stain had been deposited by the flood water. The debris front of the flash flood contained everything that the water had picked up along the miles of ancient river bed, including snakes and scorpions, there were a few scorpion bites but thankfully no one had been bitten by a snake.

The supplies that were saved allowed for a small morning meal, but the main concern was the limited amount of drinkable water that had been saved. Commander Huni had dispatched five soldiers on to Coptos, they were to clear out the river bed the best they could, in hopes of making the next day's march easier. Only a small trickle of very dirty water was now running down the wadi, a makeshift dam had been made to save as much water as possible for the livestock. Throughout the day, all eyes were on the river bed, but no more water came, in fact, by midafternoon the river bed was dry again.

Menna watched Tyia and Hatshepsut as they talked, he was relieved seeing Hatshepsut beginning to be her normal self again. She asked a lot of questions and was concerned about Inspector Antef and the herdsman that was killed. Hatshepsut then spoke to Sergeant Dadu, "Thank you for saving my life, Pharaoh will never forget." Dadu simply bowed slightly and made no comment. She had noticed that Menna had not said much since the flood and looked away from her when she made eye contact. Tyia went and stood by Menna, "Are you concerned about our continuing to Coptos tomorrow?" Hatshepsut asked, thinking that he was upset with her for not listening to Dadu.

Tyia put her arm around him and looked at him, he glanced at Tyia then at Hatshepsut. "I am worried about you walking tomorrow and I am sorry that I did not keep you from getting hurt."

Hatshepsut then realized what was wrong with Menna, he felt responsible for her injuries, "I should have listened to Sergeant Dadu, he told me to get out of the chariot, and I did not. When the chariot turned over on me, that brave man you chose to protect me risked his life to save me," as she motioned to Sergeant Dadu. "You chose him wisely, because of that wise decision, I am alive today. You cannot be by my side all the time." Menna felt as if the weight of the world had been lifted off of him, he vowed to never make the mistake of not putting her first ever again. Even in the miserable state they were in, everything was much brighter and clearer.

Later in the day there was some commotion and loud talking coming from the direction of Coptos, Menna watched, it could not be another flash flood from that direction. Shortly Dadu reported that there were men and soldiers coming down the canyon from Coptos. They waited until Commander Huni and two men that Menna did not know approached them. Because the men were covered in red mud and dust, Hatshepsut did not recognize them at first, then she called out their names, "Senenmut, Admiral Ebana!"

When they heard her, they both started running toward her, "Thank the gods, Pharaoh's Daughter is safe." Admiral Ebana exclaimed.

Senenmut said, "I was so afraid that I... that Egypt had lost you!"

"How did you know to come so quickly?"

Admiral Ebana spoke, "After the flood came through Coptos, we had no way of knowing if the caravan had started back, we hoped it had not. But Senenmut was not going to take the chance, he got supplies, men, and equipment together and started this way, as soon as the water had receded. When we started seeing supplies from the caravan and found a man's body, we were concerned, then we found two dead horses. That was when we feared the worst My Lady, then we met soldiers from the caravan. Pharaoh's Daughter is safe, the gods were good."

Senenmut saw her rare smile, "I am pleased that you are here." His heart soared because she was pleased with him. When she had asked him to be her Chief Advisor, he did not think he wanted the future Chief Architect position offered by the Queen. Seeing her smile, he was certain now.

"I need to make sure I will be able to travel tomorrow." She stood with Senenmut and Menna by her side, "Menna, this is Senenmut my Chief Advisor, Captain Menna is my Personal Guard and the reason I am alive today."

She asked Abet for her dagger, then took both Menna and Senenmut by the arm and said that she wanted to see the camp and to meet those who had lost so much. Abet expressed regret that Hatshepsut didn't have a clean gown, replying, she was glad to be alive and was not worried about her appearance.

The camp was quiet as they walked, the soldiers and men were in small groups, talking quietly and resting. Most of the preparations had been done for the next day's early departure that would get them back to Coptos tomorrow. All were relieved to see Hatshepsut walking, even if she was helped by Menna and Senenmut. Conversations stopped and even though she was the daughter of a god and normally too bright to look at, she greeted every group of men.

Menna and Senenmut could tell that sometimes they had to carry more weight than at other times, but no one could tell from Hatshepsut's beaming face. When they arrived at the area of the ox men and other herds men, she spoke to each one that had lost so much, telling them that Pharaoh would replace all that they had lost. Speaking directly to the young man who had lost his father and both oxen, "Pharaoh cannot replace the loss of your father, but your family will be taken care of." The men could not believe that the young princess was concerned about their future.

When they returned to the camp, Senenmut commented, "My Lady has touched everyone that saw her today, Pharaoh's Daughter will one day be known and loved by all of her people."

"Not all, I'm afraid, but most I hope," she replied.

As the day turned to evening, they gathered at Hatshepsut's tent. The supplies that Admiral Ebana and Senenmut had brought had been distributed and all were glad to have water and something to eat tonight. Hatshepsut watched them as they warmed their flat bread on stones next to their fire, she never knew how good onions and flat bread could smell and taste. Everyone, herself included, was covered in red from the mud or dust. It was as if they had become a part of the Red Land. Hatshepsut said, "We are all red like the land."

Senenmut replied, "We are honored to be your Red Court tonight." They laughed at his comment. Yes, this is my Red Court of trusted people, she thought to herself. After the simple meal, the conversation increased among the group. The only person not talking was Sergeant Dadu, he was listening, but most of the time he was keeping a watchful eye on what was going on outside their group. Hatshepsut thought that he reminded her of a nervous sparrow, always watching, she realized that it was most likely this trait that had probably enabled him to survive in many threating environments over the years.

When the conversation slowed, Hatshepsut asked a question to different ones in the group, her wish was that everyone become comfortable with each other. Senenmut was the easiest to get to talk, he told of his life in his small hometown, south of Thebes. He described his military time with her father, the "Great Bull" King Tuthmose, and with General Djoser. This surprised Menna, he told Senenmut that the General was his uncle. "I was honored to serve as a lowly scribe to the great General," Senenmut replied. Hatshepsut hoped that a bond was starting to form, it was important, because they would be spending so much time together. Tyia watched Hatshepsut and Senenmut, she could see Senenmut was more than Chief Advisor or at least he wished he was.

Hatshepsut whispered to her maid Abet, who then went into the tent and returned with the small sphinx that Tyia had made. "Look at this, Tyia made it for me," as Hatshepsut handed it to Senenmut. It was admired by Senenmut and Admiral Ebana, no one had to be told that it was a likeness of Hatshepsut, even in the dim light. Menna was obviously very proud and Tyia was just as obviously embarrassed.

Senenmut asked, "Tyia, have you seen the sphinx or statues like this?"

"Only in drawings done by my father."

"Where did your father see them?" Tyia explained how her father was a sculptor, like his father before him. Her grandmother's family were former rulers of Mitanni, the current conquering rulers had made it very dangerous for the old guard to stay in Mitanni. Her father's family came to Egypt when he was just a boy, he later married her mother whose family had also escaped Mitanni. He had worked in the Royal House of Statues in Memphis, but had lost favor with the Vizier in Memphis and was sent to the stone quarry. After her mother died, her father taught her how to work with stone, he also taught her the history, religion, and language of the Mitanni.

"Why did your father want you to learn the language of your ancestors?" Senenmut asked.

"He felt it was important for me to remember and know my heritage. It was a way to maintain our connection with our families, I guess."

"Can you read and write Hurrian, the language of the Mitanni?"

"My father could only teach me to speak Hurrian, he told me stories about my heritage, one night in Egyptian and the next night in Hurrian. Those are some of my most cherished times with my father." A sad expression came over her, "I wish I remembered more about my mother, my father said that she was beautiful and that if I want to see her, all I had to do was look at my reflection."

Senenmut then said, "If that is true, then your mother was indeed beautiful."

This pleased Menna, but Tyia just smiled a little, "I don't know how you can tell because we all look the same, covered in red dust." Everyone laughed, it was so true.

Hatshepsut absent mindedly placed her hand on her dagger and let her fingers tap the handle. She noticed that Sergeant Dadu was watching her, she smiled at him. "Do you like my little dagger?"

"It is beautiful." She pulled the dagger from its leather scabbard and handed it to Dadu. There were gemstones and small gold crocodiles in the blue handle, but he was most interested in the very thin curved blade. It was of a material he had never seen before.

"This was a gift from my mother and it has been in her family for many generations. The dagger was once carried by the great Queen, Sobek the Beauty, who ruled Egypt after her husband the Pharaoh died. It was after her death, that Egypt fell into the time of sadness, shame and chaos. The Hyksos ruled Memphis for a long period of time, Maat was not served."

"Sobek is the crocodile god of strength and patron of

Pharaoh's army," Menna stated.

"Yes, she is and Queen Sobek made many additions to the great temple, called the Labyrinth in the City of Crocodiles," replied Senenmut, "I hope to see it someday."

"What is the blade made of, My Lady?" Dadu asked.

"The blade is made from a very hard material that the gods threw down to Egypt one ancient night. It is said that the night was as bright as day, for a few moments," Hatshepsut stated.

When Dadu heard this, he held it with both hands, as if it might break. "It is made from the bones of the gods!" he exclaimed. Everyone had to see it and touch the sharp thin blade. Hatshepsut enjoyed watching them and sharing her most treasured item. It was then that she knew what the reward from Pharaoh to Sergeant Dadu would be for saving her life. She smiled to herself, looking forward to the day when she could give him his own "Blade" made from the bones of the gods.

Senenmut stated, "I have heard of such things falling from the sky, sometimes at night we see them shoot through the night sky. But I have never held such a gift in my hands." Everyone glanced up in the night sky hoping to catch a glimpse of one of gods' bones shooting across. Senenmut then asked, "I understand that My Lady warned everyone yesterday about the approaching flash flood. How did My Noble Lady know?" All eyes were on her, everyone had the same question, but did not know how to ask Pharaoh's Daughter.

Hatshepsut was reluctant to answer, but felt that it was safe for her little Red Court to hear, "I was warned by the gods or perhaps the Hebrew God in a dream." Everyone looked at each other, not knowing how to reply.

Finally, Senenmut asked, "Does My Lady believe in the Hebrew God?"

"I once had a dream about a lioness running from some

danger. I told Sitre, my Hebrew nanny, about my dream just before I left Thebes. She was certain that it was a warning of some kind from her God."

"Did your dream warn of a flood also?" Menna asked.

"No, I just dreamed about a lion," not really sure herself how she knew, "When I saw the lioness running, I remembered my dream. I looked at the canyon we were in and at the dry riverbed and wondered what danger could there be here, then I remembered watching the lightning every night while in the quarry. The only danger I could think of was a flash flood, because the lion was running without any concern of us, I knew it had to be close." All were quiet and thinking the same thing, how did she put all the pieces together and come up with a quick answer that saved so many lives?

"I would imagine that this story will reach Memphis before we do," Senenmut said with a smile. Hatshepsut just smiled but did not say anything.

It had been two days since the flash flood, and she was ready to leave this place, Hatshepsut waited with Menna, while the maids struck the tent. Senenmut arrived, "Good morning, My Lady, are you ready to continue to Coptos?"

"Yes, I have seen enough of the famous Wadi Hammamet." The three of them smiled a tense uncomfortable smile, but all agreed that it would be good to return to Coptos.

"I have taken the liberty to have a litter made to carry Pharaoh's Daughter," Senenmut stated.

Hatshepsut declined using it, "Let's hope it will not be needed."

Menna and Senenmut just looked at each other, knowing they could say no more. The caravan was soon in the steepest part of the canyon, but now there was no dust, just the fine red mud that covered everything. It was slower travelling this time, because of the mud and debris everywhere. Hatshepsut was weak and her balance was off, even though Senenmut was by her side to help, they seldom spoke but occasionally he asked if she was alright. Then Sergeant Dadu, who had been following and watching, walked in front of the two and stopped them. He spoke as if he was talking to one of his soldiers, "Pharaoh's Daughter will stop walking and use the litter. The soldiers will brag to their grandchildren that they once carried Pharaoh's Daughter." Senenmut was not sure how Hatshepsut would react to the Sergeant's gruff order, he was surprised and relieved when Hatshepsut just weakly nodded yes.

Hatshepsut was embarrassed by all the attention, but being carried in the litter did keep her head from hurting. At one point the soldiers leading the caravan were pointing up into the clefts, the lioness and her two cubs could be seen watching the caravan go by. When Hatshepsut arrived to the area where they were spotted, she asked to stop. So, you were running to protect your cubs, Hatshepsut thought, I am glad you found them in time.

Hatshepsut listened to those around her, keeping her eyes closed because of Ra's bright glare. Everyone was generally in good spirits, Menna and Tyia were happy, even in this miserable environment. As they arrived closer to Coptos, the wadi left the steep canyon, the river bed widened, and travel became easier. When she heard people ahead calling out to the caravan in the distance, she stated that she wished to walk the remainder of the distance. Senenmut and Menna walked by her side, she held on to them tightly.

At Coptos, the road to the Governor's palace was lined with people, they were calling her name and some of the women made shrill cries of happiness. Hatshepsut tried to smile as much as she could, when they were well inside the walls of the palace, she looked back to make sure that they were out of the public view. She stopped walking and began to collapse to her knees, Menna picked her up in his arms and carried her to her quarters. The Governor was very concerned when he saw Hatshepsut being carried. Senenmut tried to relieve the Governor's concerns by telling him that she was just weak from her injuries and that the march to Coptos had been very strenuous. Once in her quarters, Abet stated she would tend to Pharaoh's Daughter and asked to be alone.

Senenmut introduced the Governor to Captain Menna, Tyia, and Sergeant Dadu. Menna informed him that they would be guarding Hatshepsut. The Governor asked about his guards and the palace guards? Menna told him that they could do as they pleased, but that he or Dadu would be with Hatshepsut.

"Captain Menna and Sergeant Dadu have been personally selected by Pharaoh's Daughter to be her personal guards. These two men saved her life and their request is a command from Pharaoh's Daughter." Listening to Senenmut, Menna realized he had been given a huge responsibility and he must use this new authority to ensure her safety.

Sergeant Dadu stayed outside of Hatshepsut's room while everyone else went to their rooms, the Governor's staff showed them where they could bathe and supplied clean clothing. Menna and Tyia both were in awe of Pharaoh's Quarters, there was a center courtyard with a pool, surrounded by flowers, palm trees, and benches made of different colored stone. The rooms surrounded the courtyard with brightly colored columns supporting a covered breezeway. The furnishings consisted of comfortable lounges, a plush bed, and many pieces of art. They especially enjoyed the delicious food and wine.

When Menna went to relieve Dadu, Tyia asked if it would be allowed for her to look around the estate. "You are a friend of Pharaoh's Daughter so you can go and do as you please." He gave her a kiss and left to relieve Dadu. When Menna informed Dadu that his quarters were directly across the courtyard, Dadu said that he would be fine in the soldiers' barracks. Menna shook his head no, "You are no longer just an army sergeant, you are now a part of our Noble Lady's staff and we will be staying together."

"I am uncomfortable around noble men and women."

"You will be fine, do as I or Hatshepsut asks, no one else can imply or command otherwise." Menna chose a bench that was in the shade, across from Hatshepsut's room, it had a clear view of the surroundings. It was a pleasant location that allowed Menna to rest, while maintaining his vigilance. He watched Hatshepsut's maids Abet and the young Naomi come and go several times. Abet saw him in the shade the first time she left Hatshepsut's room, she then acknowledged him and then went on her way.

In his room Senenmut was glad to be clean and have clean clothes and shoes, he was sure the red stain would ever come out of his own things. Definitely, the smell of the mud would be in his memory for the rest of his life. While very tired, he could not sleep and Ra was not ready to enter the underworld, so he went for a walk. He found Tyia standing in the garden holding a white lotus flower, it was the first time he had seen her not covered in dust. Tyia was indeed very beautiful, as he came near, she started to leave, "No, please stay, may I join you?"

"Certainly," she replied. "It is so lovely here, I have never seen anything like this before," as she looked around at the garden grounds. "Growing up in the desert there was so little water, no plants or trees. It is so refreshing to be in the cool shade and surrounded by such beauty."

Senenmut motioned toward a nearby bench and both sat down on the cool stone bench. "Yes, it is very pleasant here, but wait until you see the larger gardens in Memphis."

They sat in the cool evening light, each in their thoughts and thankful that the ordeal was behind them. Senenmut had sent a dispatch to Thebes before he went on the search for Hatshepsut. He thought, I must send another dispatch tomorrow morning, letting Pharaoh and the Great Wife know that their daughter is safe. They both said goodnight and returned to their quarters.

Menna and Dadu took rotating shifts outside of Hatshepsut's quarters where Menna had placed a large cushion and other items to make the watches more comfortable. He planned on adding the two soldiers he had mentioned to Hatshepsut, when she was able to interview and approve their appointment. Hatshepsut had sent for Senenmut, when he arrived, he spoke to Menna briefly, then announced himself and went into Hatshepsut's quarters. "How is My Lady?"

"I am much better. I want your opinion on how to reward Menna and Dadu.

"Are you planning honorary awards, property, or gold?"

Hatshepsut thought for a moment, "Maybe all three."

"Reward them in a way that does them honor, but over their lifetime."

Hatshepsut also asked about Tyia, "What can I do for Tyia?"

Senenmut thought for a moment, "Getting Tyia's father out of the quarry would be the best gift for her."

The next morning, Dadu returned with the two soldiers, they were the best soldiers under the command of Commander Huni. The Nubian twins had proven themselves in battle, they saluted Menna, he could see the excitement on their faces and Dadu had seen to their appearance, they were presentable. After announcing his presence, Abet came to the door. "Is this a convenient time for Pharaoh's Daughter to question the two soldiers?" Shortly, she returned and asked them to enter.

Menna introduced, "Pharaoh's Daughter." They all bowed, he glanced to make sure that the twins were properly respectful.

"Rise," Hatshepsut commanded, as she approached them.

She thought that they were like two identical ebony statues, very large statues. If their abilities were anything like their appearance, Menna had chosen well.

"My Lady, this is Bae and Bek, they are presented for your approval."

Hatshepsut came closer to the two as they watched her. She stood close, looking up at them. They also took notice of her hand on her dagger. "Do you have any concerns that Commander Menna has not answered?"

In unison the two answered, "None, My Noble Lady."

Hatshepsut was expecting them to have a strong Nubian accent, but they did not. Both were wearing a necklace with the likeness of the goddess Satet, carved on a small white stone. "Were your raised near Elephantine?"

The twins looked surprised as did Menna, he had no idea where they had grown up. Bek finally spoke, "Yes, My Lady, our mother brought us to the fort at Elephantine right after we were born."

"I have been to Elephantine once, to watch the River rise on the royal nilometer there. Did your father not come with your mother?"

This time Bae answered, "Our father abandoned our mother when we were born because twins are a bad omen in Nubia."

"I am aware of the Nubian belief that twins are one soul split into two people, with one being good and the other one bad. Which one of you is the bad one?" Hatshepsut asked with a big smile that made both of the twins smile and immediately become more at ease.

Bek answered, "I think that both of us can be bad, My Lady."

Hatshepsut replied, "So can I. I wish to speak to Commander Menna alone," as she motioned dismissal. The twins bowed and saluted as they left her quarters. "How am I going to tell which one is Bae and which one is Bek?" she asked Menna after they had left, "I have never seen two people look so much alike."

"Bae will be the one that answers questions first and talks more. But, Bek will give more thought to questions and he will often be more correct. If I may ask, how did My Lady know they had been raised near Elephantine?"

"I knew from their accent that they had been raised in Egypt and the necklace's they wear are of the goddess Satet, the local deity of Elephantine, it was just a good guess."

A dinner was planned with the Governor and his family for the last night that Hatshepsut was in Coptos. Menna and especially Dadu were not looking forward to the formal occasion, Tyia was nervous but excited, she said we must get use to their new life.

Late afternoon, there was a knock on Menna and Tyia's door, a palace guard announced his presence. When Menna opened the door, he recognized Tyia's father, "Father!" Tyia exclaimed, as he ran to her and they embraced. Her father explained how he could not stay at the quarry and not know what had happened to Tyia and the caravan after the flood. He had come with two soldiers from the quarry. It was an unexpected reunion for both, a few days ago they thought that they would never see each other again.

Naomi had been sent to help Tyia prepare for the formal dinner, Hatshepsut had provided her a gown and jewelry, Menna thanked Naomi, "Tyia looks beautiful." Menna, an ecstatic Tyia, and Dadu announced themselves at Hatshepsut's quarters. Senenmut was there and Abet served wine to everyone, she smiled at Dadu. He was uncomfortable and did not return the smile, this made her smile even more. Tyia looked questionably at Menna because he had also warned her about Hatshepsut's lotus wine. He took a sip and nodded yes to her. Tyia took a small sip and they watched Dadu enjoy his very quickly.

Senenmut commented, "It is good news that your father has arrived."

"I am so glad to see him, when we departed the quarry, I was sure that I would never see him again."

When Hatshepsut entered the room, she was stunning, they all stood but Dadu struggled a little getting up. Her pale green gown came up just below her breasts. A darker green scarf was around her neck and shoulders, that draped to her waist, concealing her. The scarf was held at her waist by a beautiful cowrie gold and jewel belt and her ever present blue handled dagger. She wore a large broad collar consisting of rows of tubular beads made of feldspar, carnelian, and gold. The collar matched her bracelets and anklets. Senenmut commented on how beautiful Pharaoh's Daughter looked, everyone agreed. Abet offered more wine to Dadu, he declined.

"Do you not like my wine?" Hatshepsut asked mischievously.

"I have had enough of My Lady's wine," he growled. They proceeded to the Governor's banquet area, Tyia watched Hatshepsut as she walked with confidence. Her fear was that she would embarrass Menna or Hatshepsut. When they arrived at the banquet room, they heard music and talking, the Governor's Standard Bearer banged his standard on the floor very loudly, three times. The music stopped and all eyes were on Hatshepsut, the Governor stood and announced, "The Foremost of Noble Ladies, Pharaoh's Daughter." When he made the announcement, everyone stood and bowed, Hatshepsut motioned to the Standard Bearer, who again banged the standard one time, all returned to their seats. The musicians began playing and everyone applauded with some of the women using wooden clappers in the shape of hands. They were seated at a large table with the Governor, his family and Admiral Ebana, young servant girls offered flowers to everyone, Tyia took a lotus blossom.

The musicians and servants had small cones of perfumed wax on their heads, the room was filled with many different sweet fragrances. Tyia was not sure what to do in this unfamiliar setting, so she looked around and found a young girl who appeared to be with her parents, Tyia decided to observe her. No one noticed her as she watched and mimicked the girl's every move. Often, she saw other women and men looking at her, when she made eye contact, they would look away. She leaned over and whispered to Menna, "Why is everyone looking at me?"

He smiled, "Because you are the most beautiful woman they have ever seen!" She blushed and smiled at him, "Only in your eyes."

After the meal the music stopped, the dancers left the ballroom, and everyone's attention was on the governor, who stood to speak. He expressed what an honor it is to have Pharaoh's Daughter as his guest, he thanked the gods for her safe return. There was again the sound of applause and that of small sistrums chiming, which some women had. He continued, "There were many who lost their possessions and two who died because of the flood. Because of Pharaoh's generosity, I have been able to replace all that was lost. It has been arranged for the widows of Inspector Antef and the ox man to be cared for. The new Inspector of the quarry will be the highly qualified Chief Stone Mason Beni." No one knew or cared who Chief Stone Mason Beni was, but it was obvious that it meant a lot to the exotic and beautiful lady next to Commander Menna. The Governor then stated that the evening should be one to remember always, he wished everyone happiness and to enjoy being alive."

After the banquet, Hatshepsut asked that everyone return to her quarters, Tyia expressed her appreciation of her father's new assignment. "He deserved the position," Hatshepsut replied.

Back in her quarters, she informed Menna that he now had the rank of Commander and was given a baton by Admiral Ebana, made of ebony, gold, and silver with three red rings, that indicated his rank. Hatshepsut then gave him a scroll, stating that Pharaoh had given Menna and Tyia land, a house, and two servants for the rest of their life and that his pay would be two times his rank for the rest of his and Tyia's life. Before he could collect his thoughts, she placed around Dadu's neck a gold necklace with three large golden flies on it. "Pharaoh gives this, Egypt's highest military award to you. It is for your bravery and it symbolizes your determination and persistence in your actions to carry Pharaoh's Daughter out of harm's way!" After placing the award around his neck, she said, "You are no longer an orphan, we are your family now."

Dadu, the old brusque soldier, was visibly touched. She then gave him a scroll stating he had also been given two times his pay for the rest of his life and a house with a servant. Menna commented, "This is too much, My Lady did not need to give us this." Dadu agreed, "Commander Menna is right, My Lady."

Hatshepsut leaned close to both men, "These are from my father and my mother," she said pointing at the scrolls. "What I give you is my trust and I do not give that often."

Memphis

Vizier Tinfurer ran out of his office with the dispatch he had just received from Thebes in his hand. Arriving at the Temple of Ptah, he burst into the High Priest's office, "Pharaoh's Daughter is coming, Pharaoh knows what we have done."

Rewer quickly dismissed the priests in his office. When they were alone, he went to Tinfurer and slapped him, "How can you be so stupid, do you want everyone in Memphis to know?"

"Pharaoh is sending his daughter, he knows." A sobbing Tinfurer said showing Rewer the dispatch.

Rewer snatched the dispatch out of his hand and read it slowly, "The dispatch simply informs you that she is arriving and to make the proper arrangements."

"But, if she doesn't know, she will find out when she arrives, then we will be arrested and killed."

Rewer thought for a moment, "She has to be alive to arrest us."

CHAPTER NINE

The River

Ra was not up but Menna could tell that people were moving about. Tyia brought him some food and water, "Senenmut is in our quarters, he will take me to the Royal Barge soon, I will be there when you arrive with our Lady."

Menna followed Hatshepsut out of her quarters, she led them to the road lined on both sides by the people of Coptos. There was much excitement as they made their way to the dock, people were talking and straining for a look at the approaching entourage but became quiet as they neared and bowed as they passed. It was an easy short walk down to the dock, Hatshepsut was interacting with the people along the road with many exclaiming, "Long Life for Pharaoh's Daughter."

When Menna noticed that Hatshepsut had not seen the young ox man who had lost his father in the flood, Menna pointed them out to her. The young man was his wife and widowed mother. She stopped and walked back to him. Menna could not hear what she said but the young man and his family were visibly emotional, when she rejoined him, she quietly thanked him for seeing the young man and for pointing him out to her.

The Governor was waiting by the barge, Hatshepsut thanked him for all he had done, she had commanded that today would be a day of festival for all the people of Coptos. She had informed him that he would be repaid for all of his expense by a reduction in next year's tax. Hatshepsut and Menna boarded the Royal Falcon, with relief she did not feel any dizziness or nausea. Glancing at Admiral Ebana, who was watching her closely, she smiled at him. There were no palace guards on the Falcon because she now had Menna and Dadu.

Commands were given that set the barge free and continue her journey to Memphis. Menna joined Tyia, Senenmut, and Dadu on the lower deck, Hatshepsut was on the upper deck setting on the couch with the curtains pulled back. There was much activity on shore and many small boats were in the River, trying to get close for a look at the Royal party. The other ships followed them after the Royal Barge had departed. There was very little conversation until the docks were out of view, and then Tyia said, "Isn't this a magnificent boat? Look at all the different wood inlays of cedar, ivory and ebony, the bright colors, gold trim everywhere and the beautiful large falcon on the bow with its golden eyes and crown."

Menna asked Dadu, "Where are the twins?"

"They are on the other ship with the officials and the unhappy captain of the palace guards, I thought that it would be good to have eyes and ears on that boat."

When the barge was well underway, Hatshepsut looked down and saw her "Red Court" on the lower deck, they were obviously excited by the way they were talking and looking out toward the shore. She called down to them, "Come join me, you are going to get hot in the rays of Ra."

Menna could tell that Dadu looked a little sick, "Are you OK?"

Dadu grumped, "Too much wine and I hate being on the water." They joined Hatshepsut in the shade on comfortable padded seats, Menna didn't notice Abet behind curtains until they were all with Hatshepsut. He was a little upset with himself, it wasn't that he did not trust her, just a lapse on his part. Tyia was enjoying their journey down the River, there was much to see and every turn offered a new and pleasant surprise. The lush shores and large flocks of birds flying along gracefully were a new experience for her. Occasionally, a crocodile slid into the water from the banks, she shivered a little as they disappeared under the water and appeared to be headed for their barge.

Passing one village, they saw a farmer leading his cattle down to the River to get some relief from the midday heat and biting insects. They laughed at a young calf that ran into the river and playfully splashed in the cool water. Hatshepsut was content and enjoyed watching Tyia, who was so excited about everything she saw or heard. Tyia saw Hatshepsut smiling at her and asked, "What pleases my sister?"

"I am enjoying being with my friends." Both young women knew that with each bend in the River, they were getting closer to Memphis and that they were becoming closer also. Hatshepsut saw Senenmut looking off into the distance, "What is my Chief Advisor thinking about?"

Senenmut was startled a little because he was in deep thought. "I was just watching the vultures soaring over there," he pointed to several of the large birds.

"Were you really, why would you find them interesting?"

"I was wondering why the birds can climb higher when they are circling and then they get lower when flying in a straight line. They have to flap their wings a lot more when flying straight," he answered. It was not really a lie because he had wondered it many times before, but he was really wondering what his future was going to be like with Hatshepsut.

"I have never thought about it before, only my Senenmut would notice and question the flight of a vulture. Now I will wonder also, until you can give me an answer."

"I am afraid I have more questions than answers for My Noble Lady," he looked into her beautiful eyes with the blue kohl eyeliner perfectly in place.

"We both have many questions," she stated, turning to

watch the circling birds. The mooring place for the evening was a simple landing dock and modest enclosures to protect the travelers from the night time cold. It was an evening that consisted of a meal, some relaxed conversation, and a much-needed night's rest.

The next day was a typical early departure and another day for the Red Court to be together, getting more familiar and comfortable with each other. They talked and learned more about each other every hour that went by. They would become very close by the end of the journey down the River. The days settled into a relaxing routine, with Tyia always pointing out things that most would have taken for granted. It was a pleasure for Hatshepsut to see things through Tyia's eyes, realizing that she must be careful to not take her privileged life for granted. It was important for her to stay in touch with her subjects.

One unusual event occured when they stopped at one of the remote mooring places for the night. The site was occupied by a small band of Bedouins who refused to leave, the advance boat was manned by only two men and they could not force them out before the arrival of Hatshepsut. They informed the royal party of the problem on their arrival, Sergeant Dadu and the twins went to find out what was going on, Dadu returned with the information. A young Bedouin girl was having a baby and her husband would not leave, the young man had threatened to fight to the death.

When she heard this, Hatshepsut told Dadu to take them some food, supplies, and offer any help if needed, "We will make camp next to the boats for the night." Dadu delivered the items and the message, but only supplies were taken by the Bedouins, they refused any assistance.

Senenmut complimented Hatshepsut for her concern for the Bedouins, who were disliked by the average Egyptian. Hatshepsut informed him and the others that the Bedouins had aided her father during the search for her brother who had been murdered. Her brother and his two guards were watched by the Bedouins as they camped, just in case there was an opportunity to take some items easily or find something that might be left behind.

A young boy was posted for the night watch when the attack occurred. He later told his father that two men dressed in black and who spoke a different language had killed all three men in the middle of the night, the assassins had stolen anything of value and left the bodies exposed. Not knowing who they were, the Bedouins buried them. Later when an Egyptian military search party came looking for them, the Bedouins were questioned. They explained what had happen and took the military to the place where they had been buried.

Pharaoh was able to give his son a proper burial and was thankful for the help given by the Bedouins. The identity of the assassins and who hired them was never determined. Her father was certain they were sent by someone in Memphis, but could not prove it.

Senenmut listened to the information that Hatshepsut shared so easily because they were hearing information that very few knew. Menna was uneasy so he posted extra guards for the night, early the next morning Dadu and Bae went to check on the young girl in the compound. They reported back that there was no one in the compound, Dadu said that one of guards heard a baby cry in the night. Hatshepsut listened to the report and wondered if she would ever have someone who loved her so much that he would be willing to die for her.

Over the next several days of travel, they became aware of a different mood from the villagers they passed on the banks, there was not the usual happy greeting. The villagers watched the Royal Boats pass in silence. Hatshepsut wanted to visit the Great Labyrinth in the City of Crocodiles for Senenmut. The Labyrinth was over 500 years old and construction still continued, it was a site she had not visited with her father and brother five years ago.

The grounds consisted of twelve covered courts with half facing north and the other half facing south, the structure was an immense two-story building with three thousand rooms, with half of the rooms being underground tombs. Above ground were complex passages that led to rooms, courtyards, galleries, and hidden chambers. The walls of each courtyard were made of white marble with beautifully carved figures. A priest guide was needed to lead them through the maze of passages.

After seeing the amazing upper half, they were led to the lower chambers that were restricted to royalty and priests. The lower levels of the Labyrinth contained the burial chambers of many kings, queens, noblemen, and sacred crocodiles. Hatshepsut wanted to see the tomb of her mentor, Queen Sobekneferu, they were guided to her burial chamber, all were amazed at the complex structure. Menna was very uncomfortable, knowing he would have a very difficult time getting out without a guide. Along the way the priest informed them that several would-be thieves had been found totally lost and a few over the centuries had even been found dead. What should have been the high point of her travel down the River soon became one she that would cause her much sorrow and anger.

The Royal Chamber of Queen Sobekneferu was beautiful, carvings told her story and a likeness of her was engraved on each side of a beautiful false cedar door. To no one's surprise, blue and gold carvings in the door matched the handle of Hatshepsut's dagger that had once been carried by the Queen. When Hatshepsut showed the priest the Queen's dagger, he was pleased to see the dagger that had once been carried by the Queen and now by Pharaoh's Daughter. Later when the priest stopped to point out some feature, he asked Hatshepsut if she was going to Memphis to ensure that Pharaoh's decree was being carried out.

"What decree?" The priest was very reluctant to answer, she commanded, "What decree are you talking about?"

"The decree from Pharaoh to have all the newborn male babies of the Hebrews killed."

There was stunned silence from everyone, "My father has never made such a vile decree, how long has this been going on in Memphis?"

"For about two months."

"Take us back to the High Priest." The party worked their way out of the Labyrinth in silence, she could not believe what the priest had said, there must be some mistake. Hatshepsut and Menna went to meet the High Priest, when they returned, it was obvious that the news must be true. Hatshepsut was in a state of shock, disbelief, and fury. Later when asked, Admiral Ebana knew nothing of such a horrible act. Ebana said, "Pharaoh is a warrior, not a murderer of innocent children." The remainder of the trip was completed as fast as possible and the mood on the Royal Barge changed to one of dread and a feeling of darkness, not the true nature of an Egyptian.

As they neared Memphis, the River was growing wider and the banks were more populated. Also, there was the occasional view of a pyramid in the distance and necropolises near the River. Senenmut had stated what Hatshepsut also thought, that the Vizier was behind it. As the Royal Barge "Falcon" made a turn in the River, the enormous gleaming White Walls of the Palace in Memphis came in view. It was a truly impressive sight, with Djoser's pyramid in view as a back drop to the towering fifty-foot white walls. Within the walls were several columned structures above the impenetrable walls with colored pennants flowing in the wind.

Only Hatshepsut and the Admiral had seen the majestic palace before, the palace was meant to impress any arriving foreign king or ambassador with Egypt's riches and power. Without a doubt, Egypt was a great nation and one not to be taken lightly.

The vassal nations under Egypt's rule would do well to stay in line and pay their annual tribute. Even with the gleaming grandeur of the Palace, Hatshepsut felt a feeling of darkness and doom, which had only increased the closer she came to Memphis. Tyia was the first to speak after seeing the city, "What a magnificent sight! It is the most beautiful city I have ever seen, look at the fabulous gardens and pools."

There were many ships in the ancient port city, the ship carrying Pharaoh's Guards preceded to dock before the Falcon. As Admiral Ebana maneuvered toward the dock, officials could be seen waiting for their arrival. The Falcon was expected, it was midday and uncomfortable, the humidity in Lower Egypt was much higher than they were familiar with in Upper Egypt.

When the Royal Barge was secured to the dock, several horns sounded in the dock area and up the ramp to the distant Palace walls. Outside the Palace walls was a small city that served as housing for servants, near was a canal that circled the small city with tents for vendors and merchants, all were needed to support the vast palace complex. Pharaoh's guards were at attention and waiting for Pharaoh's Daughter to depart, Menna and Dadu were with her as she approached the welcoming party. Hatshepsut motioned for all to rise, an official introduced himself and welcomed them, she did not see the Vizier.

"Where is Vizier Tinfurer?" Hatshepsut asked.

"He is away on a hunting trip My Lady, we are thankful that Pharaoh's Daughter has arrived safely, praise to Ptah." The official then turned and started up the long curving ramp to the massive main gates of the Palace. Hatshepsut waited for Admiral Ebana, Senenmut, Tyia, and the twins to join her before she followed him toward the Palace. The agitated overweight official, who was sweating, stopped and waited impatiently for her. After entering the imposing palace gates, they made their way through the lush grounds, a series of stairs, and columned halls with exquisite statues and murals. They entered a courtyard with a fountain and square pillars. A high roof offered shade to the courtyard and the surrounding rooms. The pillars were each brightly decorated with lettering and art from different nations, around the fountain were tall blooming vegetation and flowers.

One room had three servants standing in front of the entrance. Hatshepsut did not know her way around the Palace that well, but when told that these were the quarters for her and her guests, she knew these were not the King's quarters. "This is not Pharaoh's quarters," Hatshepsut said in a low and very controlled voice.

The official bowed and said, "Pharaoh's quarters are not available, these splendid rooms are for honored guests and visiting diplomats. I am certain Pharaoh's Daughter will be comfortable and pleased."

"The King's Quarters should have been made ready, you knew from Pharaoh's dispatch that his daughter was coming, did you not?"

"I'm sorry My Lady," was his only reply.

"Inform Pharaoh's servant, the Vizier, that Pharaoh's Daughter will be here for a year and I will be staying in the Pharaoh's quarters." Before the official could reply, Hatshepsut warned, "I am not pleased."

Admiral Ebana stepped up to the official, "Leave now and make Pharaoh's Daughter wishes known." The official bowed deeply and scurried off.

CHAPTER TEN

Memphis

The quarters consisted of a large main room with several surrounding rooms, at the back of the room, doors opened up to a balcony that was three stories above the white walls. There was a stunning view of the River and large port. The floor in the main room was made of different types of rare wood used only by the wealthy and royalty, the pattern in the floor was an intricate design. The squares were a little larger than one stride with borders of different colored wood. Around the room were columns made to resemble different trees, most of the trees did not grow in Egypt. The most interesting column was in the shape of a sycamore tree that had several holes in the trunk, in one hole was a carved redheaded woodpecker peeking out.

Murals on the walls were of scenes along the river and marshes, couches and tables with food and drinks were arranged near the large sycamore. The guest quarters were elegant and palatial, but no one dared to comment on the luxurious quarters, Pharaoh's Daughter was not pleased. Dadu was sent to position Pharaoh's guards and the twins were posted outside her door. They settled around the table of food and rested on plush couches. Hatshepsut, Admiral Ebana, and Senenmut discussed today's events and their possible meanings. Hatshepsut then asked Abet to get her leather bag, when she returned with the bag, Hatshepsut asked her to take Naomi and the new palace servants to the maids' quarters.

Hatshepsut took out a sealed scroll, she handed the scroll to Admiral Ebana and asked that he and Senenmut read it. While reading it, both men often glanced at Hatshepsut, she made no comment. When they had finished reading it, the Admiral had a smile on his face, "This will not sit well with the Vizier."

But Senenmut was very serious, "The Vizier does not know that Pharaoh has made you his Co-Regent, does he?"

"No one knows but my father and mother, Pharaoh did not think it wise anyone knew until "We" arrived in Memphis. When she accented the royal term "We", they knew that it referred to her and Pharaoh as one. "All in Thebes will soon know," Hatshepsut answered.

Senenmut was shaking his head, "I am certain that My Lady will be in danger when this decree is known."

Hearing what Senenmut said, Menna moved closer, "Is there something I should be aware of, My Lady?" Hatshepsut patted the couch next to her for him and Tyia to sit.

"Pharaoh knows the Vizier has been trying to gain more power, this document," as Hatshepsut pointed to the scroll, "Names me Co-Ruler with Pharaoh. I have control of the military and my wish is my father's command, I am a threat to the Vizier here in Lower Egypt. Admiral, how well do you know the General in charge of the army here?" Hatshepsut asked.

"General Nebi is a good military man and has served your father well."

"We need to determine his involvement in the killing of innocents," Hatshepsut stated. Senenmut noticed her nervous habit of touching her dagger.

"As my Sovereign commands," Admiral saluted his new Commander-in-Chief and departed.

Tyia could not believe what she had just heard, "Are you certain?"

Hatshepsut answered, "Yes." No one said anything as they contemplated their situation.

Menna stated, "Tyia and I will stay in one of the bedrooms with My Lady." Hatshepsut nodded yes and Senenmut agreed.

It was midafternoon when Hatshepsut expressed her desire to go to the pools by the River, she remembered them as being beautiful and she needed to relax. The last few days on the barge were long and no time was wasted for sightseeing. Hatshepsut asked Tyia if she wished to join her, she did. One of the palace servants assigned to Hatshepsut led them through the maze of halls in the grand palace. The servant described in detail the art and it was obvious that she was trained to point out the beautiful art to a foreign dignitary staying in the guest quarters. The talkative servant took them outside through gardens and a large stand of sycamore trees toward the pools by the River.

There were several pools along the River with water from the River entering a distant pool upstream. Each pool had plants and rocks that filtered the water, the water tumbled over a series of steps into the next pool. Eventually the crystal-clear water arrived into the swimming pool. Menna and Sergeant Dadu stood guard by the arched entry into the columned walls secluding the pool. On the river side of the pool were many flowering water plants and tall papyrus plants, one could hear excited voices and laughter traveling across the water when someone caught a fish or greeted someone.

The pool was made of tiered levels of white granite, around the pool were white granite benches, many plants and flowers with dragon flies fluttering around. Birds were singing and calling, there was also the fussing sound of several brightly colored humming birds darting about. The flowers, tall grasses, and reeds swayed back and forth in the cool breeze, in the background was the gentle lapping sounds of water against the shore. Tyia commented that she had never seen a more serene and beautiful place.

Menna sent one of the twins upriver and the other down-river, children were playing in the distance by the upper pools. The palace servant said they were the children of slaves that worked in the Palace complex. One young girl wading in the water's edge was close to them. The servant asked "Shall I send the young girl away?"

"Let her play, the laughter of children sounds pleasant." Abet and Naomi helped Hatshepsut and Tyia undress as they entered the refreshing water. Tyia had never been in such lux-urious cool clear water, Hatshepsut relaxed and was very quiet. Tyia stayed on the shallow levels of the pool because she did not know how to swim. Occasionally Hatshepsut would swim across the pool and return to her resting place. Hatshepsut commented, "The calling of doves is very soothing."

Tyia replied, "I have never heard so many birds in one place before."

A relaxed Hatshepsut eventually asked Abet to bring linen towels, while getting dressed, it suddenly became very quiet except for the chatty servant. She was offering to get food, drink or provide a massage. Hatshepsut held up her hand for her to be quiet, but she continued to talk. Finally, she com-manded in a firm whisper, "Silence!" to quiet the servant.

Menna had noticed the change and came to them, "Did My Lady see anything or anyone that would have scared the birds?"

"Nothing," she replied.

It wasn't just the birds that were now quiet, the men in the boats on the River were silent. The children had stopped playing and laughing, they were now looking at something near them at the river's edge intently. The young girl that had been playing close to them was standing very still and watching them. The breeze had become calm, there were no rustling sounds coming from the trees and vegetation. Menna was un-comfortable as he looked around, the sudden change had happened for a reason.

Then they heard the faint crying of a baby toward the River, but they could not see anyone with a baby. Hatshepsut sent the servant girl to search for it, she soon found a covered basket floating in the water caught in the reeds. She waded to the basket, after retrieving the basket she brought it to Hatshepsut and opened the cover. The basket had started taking on water and the baby had to raise its head out of the water to breathe and cry. Quickly Hatshepsut took the baby and held it close to her, with the baby now in her arms, it went to sleep immediately from fatigue. As they looked at the baby, both Hatshepsut and Tyia were in tears.

One dove began calling and after a few calls, all the birds and previous sounds seemed to return on cue. A very emotional Hatshepsut turned her head away to hide her tears, after drying her eyes, she wrapped the baby in one of the towels by the pool. The servant commented, "It is a Hebrew baby, his mother put him adrift so someone down river might save him."

Hatshepsut questioned her, "Who commanded that the Hebrew babies be killed?"

"It is a command from Pharaoh, My Lady," she answered as she bowed.

Hatshepsut glared at the servant, "Pharaoh would never do such a cowardly thing, this vile order came from within this palace. Anyone involved, I will punish, is that understood?"

The servant bowed again, "Yes, My Lady," as she cautiously backed away from a very angry Hatshepsut.

"What will we do with such a young baby, it appears to be only three or four months old, we must find a nurse?" Tyia asked.

"I will find someone to care for it," Hatshepsut answered, as she held the sleeping baby. The baby was healthy and he had light colored curly hair.

While they were admiring the beautiful baby, Bae came walking up with a young girl. "My Lady, this young girl wishes to speak to you. Is it alright?"

"Yes." The young girl was very nervous, "Don't be afraid, what is your name?" Hatshepsut asked.

"Miriam," she answered timidly.

Hatshepsut inquired, "What do you want?"

"I saw the servant when she found that baby in the reeds, do you have someone that can nurse and care for him?"

Hatshepsut looked at Tyia and then asked Miriam, "Why do you ask, do you know someone?"

"Yes, my baby brother died, perhaps my mother could help." Miriam explained, with her eyes looking down.

Tyia bent down to her, "When did your brother die?"

Miriam looked away and answered uneasily, "He died yesterday."

"Who are your parents?"

"My mother and father are slaves."

"Take my maid and my guard, bring your mother to me."

"Yes, My Lady." Miriam said excitedly and took off quickly in the direction of her home. Naomi and Bae had to almost run to keep up with the little girl.

Hatshepsut and Tyia sat on a granite bench with the baby that was still sleeping but was starting to be restless. "I think that when the baby wakes up, he is going to be hungry, who knows when he last nursed." Tyia stated.

"I cannot believe this is all happening, why would anyone do this?" Hatshepsut wondered out loud.

"I think the Vizier will use the recent events to unite Memphis for him, when he eventually stops the murders and claims that the cruel Pharaoh is unfit to rule Egypt." Menna stated.

"You are probably right." Hatshepsut watched the baby, still trying to comprehend the recent events.

Soon Menna pointed in the direction of Bae and Naomi with the young girl and her mother, "They are returning."

When they came nearer, it was obvious that the woman was injured and appeared to have been beaten, the woman hurried toward them and then fell to her knees and prostrated herself fully on the ground. She pleaded, "Please don't harm the baby!"

Hatshepsut handed the baby to Tyia, and went to the woman, "I am Pharaoh's Daughter and no one is going to harm this child or you." Abet helped her stand and led her to the bench, it was very obvious that the woman was emotionally exhausted. Hatshepsut turned to Bae and Naomi, "Do you know what happened to her?"

Bae told her that two palace guards came this morning looking for her baby, they did not believe her or her husband when they said that they were not hiding a child. So, they proceeded to beat them, and warned them that they will return tomorrow morning, demanding that they have the baby.

"No!" was all Hatshepsut could say. Bae said that he was told that these two guards come to the quarters often looking for newborn babies. They had killed perhaps as many as ten newborns in the last two months. "These men and any other cowards involved will drown. I will do it myself." Hatshepsut said with contempt.

The woman heard her make the threat and asked, "Were these guards not following Pharaoh's command?"

"What is your name?"

"Jochebed."

"Jochebed, I left my father, the Pharaoh, three weeks ago

and arrived in Memphis today, Pharaoh did not command these horrible acts. The Vizier here is doing this in the name of Pharaoh, I will stop those doing this horrible thing."

"Praise God! My people have suffered so much fear and heartache, may I hold the baby?"

Tyia answered, "Yes." She handed the baby to her, the movement caused the baby to wake up, but he did not cry. Jochebed held the baby tenderly as she nursed and rocked the baby gently with tears in her eyes.

"I do not want you to be in your home tomorrow morning when the guards return, you and the baby will stay with me for protection."

"Yes, My Lady."

"What about Miriam, should she stay with us?" Hatshepsut asked.

Jochebed thought for a moment and then said, "She will need to go back to our home because my husband will be worried. She is also needed there to care for my grandmother, who is blind and deaf."

"Miriam," Hatshepsut kneeled down to the little girl, "Go home and tell your father what has happened, your mother will stay with me."

"Yes, My Lady," as she happily skipped away.

"Let's return to my quarters and tend to Jochebed and the baby."

As they made their way to Hatshepsut's quarters, there was much interest in the injured woman and baby, but no questions were asked by guards or staff. When they arrived at her quarters, she saw Admiral Ebana with an army officer that she assumed was General Nebi. They were surprised to see the woman and baby, Hatshepsut told them she would be with them shortly.

While Hatshepsut was in the next room with Jochebed, Menna went to the General, he saluted and introduced himself, Senenmut noticed that Menna never took his eyes off the General. The General may not have known it, but he was a suspect, Menna would have no qualms about relieving this high-ranking officer of his spirit Ka and sending him to the underworld. Pharaoh's Daughter may be in danger and he did not trust anyone. When Hatshepsut came into the room the men stood, "Admiral, I see you have found General Nebi."

"Actually, My Lady he found me, General Nebi heard that Pharaoh's Daughter had arrived and he wished to have an audience with you."

"General Nebi, can you explain to us and to all the gods, what is happening here?" Hatshepsut challenged the General with arms folded.

The General went into great detail about the events leading up to today, how the Vizier was positioning himself for acquiring more power and not just in Lower Egypt. He had been away for four months on a military campaign in the east, it was while he was away that the Vizier claimed Pharaoh had issued a decree. First the Vizier tried to have the palace midwives kill the newborn male babies, but they warned the expecting mothers. Two midwives had suffered for not following the Vizier orders.

The Vizier then ordered the Captain of the Palace Guards to follow Pharaoh's command and he refused without seeing the command from Pharaoh, he was put in prison and may have been killed. A very angry Vizier ordered my officer in charge here to follow Pharaoh's command, but my officer told the Vizier that the military does not answer to the Vizier, he would wait for direct orders from Pharaoh. This infuriated the Vizier and he made all kinds of threats, my officer then sent me a message about what was happening.

I returned about three weeks ago, and sent a dispatch to

Pharaoh, explaining what was going on. I had hoped that was the reason for Pharaoh's Daughter arriving in Memphis. These palace slaves have been doing all they can to save their children, they are not allowed to leave the palace grounds with their babies. They have made contact with Hebrew and even Egyptian families downstream of the palace and have resorted to putting babies in baskets in hopes that they will be rescued.

Hatshepsut listened, trying to control her anger, "I know about the babies in the baskets, I found one today. The woman here will be a wet nurse for him, her baby died yesterday, two palace guards did not believe the woman when she told them her baby had died. You saw the result of their brutality when we arrived, I will ensure that all involved in the death of innocent babies, will pay with their lives." Hatshepsut believed the General, he needed to know her father had named her co-regent. She handed him the scroll, "You need to read this General."

While the General was reading the scroll, she returned to Jochebed and the baby. After he had read the decree he said, "The Vizier will not allow Pharaoh's Daughter to take control."

"We are aware of this and we will do what we can to protect her," Admiral Ebana stated.

Hatshepsut returned to the men, "General, what are our options here?"

The General did not immediately answer, "We are about to commit ourselves to some very serious actions. The Vizier will say that our actions are treasonous, with the appropriate consequences."

"The actions of Pharaoh's Daughter cannot be considered treason," Hatshepsut stated.

"That is true, My Lady, but you must be alive to use your authority," the General warned. "We are making history here tonight, let's hope the gods are with us."

Hatshepsut seemed to relax a little, "Menna, bring Tyia,

Sergeant Dadu, and the twins. I have plans for my Red Court," she said with her cat smile.

CHAPTER ELEVEN

Vizier Tinfurer

Hatshepsut had not slept well, she kept going over the events she and Senenmut had planned, they had set things in motion the night before and she was concerned for her Red Court. The baby in the next room would wake her up just as she dozed off to sleep it seemed, he never cried, but the sounds and movement of Jochebed tending to his needs kept her awake. Senenmut was meeting with the palace staff to try and determine who could be trusted and who was involved with the atrocities that the Vizier had ordered. He also was informing them that Hatshepsut would be holding court the next day, even if the Vizier was absent.

Dadu had spent time with the palace guards, drinking and trying to determind how many were loyal to the Vizier. Before Hatshepsut woke, the twins had gone to Jochebed's home, they told her family to stay with friends. Hopefully the two palace guards would do as they had threatened and return looking for the baby, if they did, they were in for a surprise.

Menna went with Hatshepsut to a shrine that was in the courtyard of the guest quarters, there she said her morning prayers asking for strength, but her familiar gods seemed a long way off. She could not concentrate, perhaps it was because of the distance to her home in Thebes, or maybe it was something else.

In the Hebrew slave compound the morning meals were being finished and preparations were underway for their daily labor, the cooking smells made the twins hungry. "We should have eaten something," Bae said to Bek as they waited.

"We can eat later, the food will be better in the palace," Bek replied.

Just as Ra returned from the underworld, the two guards arrived and barged into Jochebed's home, it was dark inside and it took a moment for their eyes to adjust, they were surprised to see the two large men grinning at them. The leader of the two said, "Well look who we have here, I think we have the two 'nubies' that babysit Pharaoh's little girl. We have heard about you." The other guard laughed a little too much and nervously at the offensive term about the two Nubians. "What are you doing here?"

Bae and Bek moved close to the guards, the guards kept an eye on the twin's swords, still in their sheaths. They did not see the leather wrapped right hands of the twins, which held bronze weights, "Are you the cowards that beat women and murder babies? If so, we are taking you to Pharaoh's Daughter for punishment," Bek stated.

The guards made a move for their swords, but just as they touched the handles, each one was hit by one of the twins. They were on the ground and unconscious, with blooded mouths that had missing teeth. Bae laughed, "That was easy! Let's take them to General Nebi." The two were not moving, Bae threw water on their faces to get them to regain conscious, only one made groaning sounds.

"Is the leader dead?" Bek asked.

Bek checked him, "No, but I think you hit him too hard, you will have to carry him," he answered with a big laugh.

"We will let his partner carry his boisterous friend," Bek stated dryly. Now the alley was full of onlookers near Jochebed's home, the crowd was elated to see the two guards that had caused so much sadness and pain, being led away. One guard could barely walk even with his friend's help, he was not aware of his surroundings, but the other knew their situation all too well. He was scared and his face showed it! There were jeers from the crowd and even some praise to Pharaoh's Daughter, word of Hatshepsut saving the baby had spread. When the twins returned to Hatshepsut quarters with news that the two guards had been taken, she was relieved that they were safe.

"Well done, perhaps they will tell General Nebi who else is involved." Hatshepsut came to them and held their large hands, she had never touched them before, they just looked at her delicate hands. "I am glad that you are safe."

Extra food and water were in the process of being stored in Abet and Naomi's room, Senenmut had suggested they do this the night before, he had concerns about them being poisoned. Bae and Bek saw some food from the morning meal on a table and the stomach of one of them growled, "We haven't eaten yet," Bae stated.

Hatshepsut motioned to the food still on the table, "Of course you haven't eaten, help yourself." She smiled, relieved that their only concern was eating.

There was some nervous conversation, but the mood became lighter when Jochebed brought the baby into the room. The baby was alert, happy, and playful, Jochebed looked much better after Abet had tended to her. She wore a new fine pleated linen gown, her first, "Thank you My Lady for loaning me this lovely gown."

"It is your gown now, are you still willing to take care of the baby for me?"

"Oh yes, My Lady," she answered. With the baby in their presence, everyone was reaffirmed in their actions, this was indeed a just cause and worth the risk. All they had to do was to look at the baby that had been saved and think of the many others that would be because of their actions.

Hatshepsut commented, "I have not heard the baby cry

since he was taken out of the water."

"His mother probably was able to hide him for months because he does not cry." Jochebed sadly stated while looking away.

No one said a word as they contemplated the fear all the Hebrew mothers must have endured. The baby looked at whoever was speaking, as if he understood what they were saying. "He is an amazing baby, so alert," Hatshepsut stated.

While waiting for Senenmut and Dadu to return, there was a knock at the door. Menna and Hatshepsut went to answer the door, expecting Senenmut or Dadu. But when Menna opened the door, they saw two guards, with a very ornate wood chest. Hatshepsut recognized them as personal guards of her father, "Why are you here, is Pharaoh alright?"

"Yes, Horus Pharaoh still rules, My Lady. We were sent by Pharaoh and the Great Wife, with this chest."

"Enter." The two picked up the chest and placed it next to the area of the large cushioned couches. "You look very tired, rest and eat, we will talk later."

"Thank you, Sovereign."

Hatshepsut was surprised when they called her Sovereign, "You have been informed about the title Pharaoh gave me?"

"Yes, Pharaoh wanted us to be aware of the importance of the contents of this chest and of the danger we may face."

"We are grateful for your loyalty to us." Menna led the two guards to a room with food and drink, he also wanted to ask questions about their journey and obtain any news from Thebes.

Hatshepsut opened the chest that had the latch bound in cord and the wax seal of Pharaoh. The first thing Hatshepsut saw was a scroll from her father and mother. She read the letter from her father to Tyia, it stated how thankful they were that she had survived the flash flood. It went on to say that he had received the dispatch from the High Steward Ramose. It was no surprise to her that her father knew nothing of the decree and he was sorry the burden had fallen on her to stop the killings and deal with the removal of the Vizier. He reminded her that she had his full support of any decisions or actions she made and that she must be very careful.

Pharaoh also stated that in the chest is a sealed decree that is to be given to the Memphis Royal Scribe, it was to be read to the Vizier and the Memphis Royal Court. The decree informs the Vizier of Pharaoh's dissatisfaction with him and that he is relieved of his post, he is commanded to report to Pharaoh in person. As she continued to read the letter, she felt more weight on her shoulders. She must act as Vizier until she fills that position, and to carry out the appropriate punishment for all those responsible for the atrocities that have taken place. The letter ended with her father and mother saying they were very proud of her. Tyia could tell that the words of her father and mother had touched their daughter. She placed her hand on Hatshepsut's hand holding the scroll. "You will represent your father well."

Hatshepsut smiled at Tyia, composed herself and started going through the chest. Next, she found a leopard skin sleeve that contained a scabbard and sword. When Hatshepsut removed the sword from the scabbard, Tyia remarked how beautiful it was. It had an ebony and ivory handle with red dots and gold stars inlayed in the ebony. "This is for Sergeant Dadu, it is made from the bones of the gods that fell from the sky."

"Dadu will treasure this, what is the meaning of the red dots?" Tyia asked.

"The dots represent the burning bones of the gods falling from the night sky." She continued looking at the items in the chest, there were some personal items and several gold necklaces that had a cartouche on them. Tyia saw that Hatshepsut seemed very interested in the cartouche and was examining them very closely.

"Is the cartouche of your father?" Tyia asked.

"No, it is my cartouche, my mother had made for me."

"What does it say?"

"Maatkare, it means, Truth is the soul of Ra," Hatshepsut stated, saying the name again, listening to the sound of the words.

"Does this mean that you will be the next Pharaoh?"

"I will be Co-Ruler with my father only, not with my husband, the future Pharaoh Tuthmose II," Hatshepsut answered with disappointment in her voice. "The current problems in Lower Egypt and my father's health require this unusual arrangement."

Hatshepsut continued examining the contents and was just about finished when Sergeant Dadu came in, he looked as if he had not gotten any sleep and appeared to have had plenty to drink. "I have some information, My Lady."

Menna joined Hatshepsut and she asked, "What did you find out?" Dadu explained that he had spent most of the night drinking with the palace guards who wanted to hear about his Golden Flies and they were particularly interested how she had saved the caravan after a lion spoke to her. Everyone thinks that the gods speak to Pharaoh's Daughter. The former captain of the palace guards is alive, most of the guards respect him. There are only two guards and the new captain of the guards who have actually followed the decree, the other palace guards did not want the extra pay and have been making up various excuses for not finding any babies. Some of the guards also think that the Vizier is not on a hunting expedition, but is in fact hiding from Pharaoh's Daughter.

Hatshepsut asked about the current captain of the guard.

"He is not in the palace and is missing after the news of his two guards being taken by the twins, the palace is full of rumors, My Lady."

While listening to Dadu, she was relieved that most of the palace guards still had some honor. When he finished his report, "Oh by the way, something arrived today for you Sergeant," as she handed him the leopard skin cover.

"My Lady, there must be a mistake."

"No mistake Dadu, this is from Pharaoh and the Great Wife, for saving their stubborn daughter's life."

Dadu opened the luxurious leopard skin cover and pulled out the magnificent leather scabbard and belt that held the sword with the beautiful handle with a gold-plated guard, "It is marvelous." When he drew the sword out of its scabbard and saw the thin bright blade, he could not believe his eyes. "Is it made from the bones of the gods, just like My Lady's dagger?"

"Yes," Hatshepsut answered, thoroughly enjoying watching him and knowing what the sword meant to him. The gift could not repay him for saving her life, it was not meant too, but it did make her happy to give him something priceless.

"I will protect My Lady with this weapon from the gods." He was truly humbled and moved by the gift, "I am honored."

She looked forward to future dispatches from Thebes, that arrived weekly. Normally it took about a month to get an answer back from Thebes, but during the flood season correspondence was slower and very erratic. It was midday when Senenmut returned, he had a man with him, accompanied by one of the twins. Senenmut introduced him, "High Steward Ramose this is the Foremost of Noble Ladies, Pharaoh's Daughter." Ramose bowed very low and waited for Hatshepsut's command to rise, Hatshepsut gave Senenmut a puzzled look, but he just nodded OK.

"Rise," she commanded.

"My Noble Lady," Senenmut started, "While meeting with various members of court, High Steward Ramose came to me, he has information about Vizier Tinfurer."

"What information?"

The High Steward was obviously nervous, "It is with great shame that I come to Pharaoh's Daughter."

"Sit here," Hatshepsut said as she pointed to a cushioned couch. The High Steward relaxed a little, but continued to watch the large twin whose hand was still on his sword.

"I do not believe the Vizier is on a hunting expedition, I think he is hiding from Pharaoh's Daughter."

"Hiding because of the vile things he has done using Pharaoh's name?"

"Yes, my Noble Lady."

"He will be found and punished for treason," stated Hatshepsut.

"Pharaoh's Daughter must be careful because he is as dangerous as a cornered hyena."

"I will, I have learned that you informed Pharaoh about the Vizier, your loyalty will not be forgotten."

The relieved Ramose said, "I pray to the gods that I am wrong, My Lady, but I do not trust the Vizier."

"Is there anything we can do to protect you?" Hatshepsut asked.

"No, My Lady, your concern is noble, but no one knows I am here. It would be best if I return alone." Hatshepsut motioned for Senenmut to show the High Steward out. When Senenmut returned, he could see that Hatshepsut was still livid.

"I want the Vizier found and put to death!" she demanded.

Senenmut thought for a few moments, "We will free the

former captain of the guards, perhaps he can find the Vizier."

"Yes, have him report to me, tomorrow will be a long day." Menna asked if she would like for him and Tyia to sleep in their quarters tonight, knowing that Jochebed and the baby were in her bedroom, keeping her awake.

"Stay with me, the couch is comfortable and it is cool by the balcony." The evening was pleasant, after writing a message to her father about the day's events, she and Tyia played with the baby and talked when he was napping. Menna was able to relax some, the first two days in Memphis had been very tense. Sergeant Dadu was on guard outside her door.

CHAPTER TWELVE

Goddess Ammit

Hatshepsut fell asleep quickly because the events of the day had gone well, but in the middle of the night she was awakened from a deep sleep when she heard the baby crying very loudly. This was not normal for the contented baby, Jochebed was trying to satisfy the baby, but there was nothing she could do to console him. Setting up on her couch, she was trying to decide if there was anything she could do to help Jochebed. Then she could not believe her eyes, there appeared to be a black cloud coming up out of the floor in the center of the room. She thought perhaps she was still asleep and dreaming but the form continued to rise.

In the dim light of the oil lamps and the moonlight coming through the balcony doors, she could make out the shape of a man dressed in black. Realizing it was a man, she could not help but gasp at the sight, he quickly turned toward her, she could see his white teeth behind a sinister smile. He started coming toward her, in fear she could only make a weak call, "Menna!"

Both of them heard Menna from the doorway to his room, "I'm here my Noble Lady, I will send this jackal to the underworld." He had also been awakened by the crying baby.

The assassin turned to Menna and in an accent she did not recognize, he challenged, "A bold threat for a man with such a small knife."

Hatshepsut saw that Menna did indeed have just a knife, no match for the large curved sword the assassin had. Menna would not be able to get close enough to use his knife before being cut down by the assassin's sword. The assassin looked at both of them and then he chose to confront Menna first as he started toward him.

Menna yelled, "Dadu!" loud enough to wake all the gods. Hatshepsut had recovered from her initial shock, she grabbed her dagger, leaping off the couch and in just a few quick steps she was behind the assassin. The training she had received from her father took over as she thrust the dagger into the man's right kidney area and twisted the knife as hard as she could. The assassin stopped all movement, his mouth was open but he made no sound, he was frozen from the severe pain caused by her twisting dagger.

Quickly stepping forward, Menna thrust his knife into the man's heart and pulled Hatshepsut away from him, as the assassin fell to the floor. Tyia screamed, "Another assassin!" as another man was coming out of the floor.

Dadu had heard Menna and burst through the door, he saw what was taking place, as Menna stepped between the second assassin and Hatshepsut. Dadu ran to the assassin, who was now attempting to go back down the hole. With a loud yell and one sweeping swing of his new sword from the gods, the man's head rolled across the floor. His body disappeared down into the black hole with a loud dull thud. Tyia took Hatshepsut's arm and was going to lead her away from the ghastly scene, Hatshepsut pulled her arm away. Everyone's eyes were on the hole in the floor, waiting to see if there were any other assassins. Shortly after hearing Dadu and the commotion, the twins, Senenmut and Pharaoh's two guards arrived. Tyia started lighting more lamps, while Dadu looked down into the hole. Nothing was there except the headless body at the bottom of the stairs.

"Are you hurt, My Lady?" Bek asked, as he looked at Hatshepsut with her blooded dagger and blood-stained clothes.

"I am fine," she replied, even though she was shaking.

Menna put his arm around her. "I am not afraid."

"No, My Lady, you are indeed not afraid, you have the "shakes," a normal response after one has been in battle. All warriors have experienced them."

Hatshepsut put her arm around him. Tyia came to her, "You saved my Menna."

"I had no time to think." It was then that everyone noticed Jochebed, holding the now sleeping baby.

"Now the baby sleeps, the assassins may have been successful if he had not cried," Menna stated.

Abet was now by Dadu's side, he said, "We need to find where this spider hole leads and if there are other jackals." Everyone seemed to jump into action, planning what to do next.

Menna told Dadu and the twins, "See where the tunnel goes, don't take any risks." Dadu preceded the twins down the steps into the hole.

"Now we know why I was given this room," Hatshepsut commented looking at the secret trap door, it all made sense to her. They were surprised to hear Dadu's voice coming from the tree shaped column that had the carved woodpecker in one of the holes.

"Can you hear me?"

"Yes, we can, Dadu," Menna spoke near the tree.

"I can hear everything that is being said in the room, there is a listening post down here."

"Be careful Sergeant, no telling what else you may find."

"Yes sir."

Everyone looked at each other, they realized that someone had been listing to all their conversations for the past two days. Menna ordered Pharaoh's guards, "Take your post outside the door, no one is allowed in until we are certain the threat is over."

Abet wanted to put a clean gown on Hatshepsut, "Later," she told Abet. Then she went to Jochebed, "Why was the baby crying?"

"I am sorry, My Lady, I do not know why, he just woke up crying and I could not keep him quiet."

Hatshepsut looked at the sleeping baby, "I need to name this amazing baby, who warned us."

Dadu and the twins were able to follow the tunnel easily which was lit by small lamps, they walked a long way before the tunnel became brighter. They knew they were getting near the end and then they heard two men talking. There were no other sounds, Dadu peaked around the corner, there was only a man and a priest casually sitting and playing a board game. When Dadu and the twins entered the room, the priest asked, "Is it done?" without looking up from his next move. When he did look, the surprised look on his face revealed that he knew the charade was over.

Bek called out from the bottom of the hole, "It is safe and Sergeant Dadu requests that Commander Menna and Pharaoh's Daughter come."

Menna questioned, "Are you sure it is safe for My Lady?"

"Yes sir," Bek answered. Menna turned to Hatshepsut.

"I want some answers, yes, I want to go." Hatshepsut followed Menna down the stairs where Bek had moved the second assassin's body off to the side. "I wonder if my father knew of this tunnel," she commented to herself and Menna. Bek led them quickly through the tunnel, when they arrived at the end, she saw that Dadu and Bae had two men on the floor, both on their knees with their hands tied. One was a priest with his shaved head and wearing the leopard skin tunic of a high-ranking priest. He had several gold necklaces, arm bands, and rings.

To the other man, who she was sure was the Vizier, she asked sarcastically, "Vizier Tinfurer how is your hunting expedition?" He looked up at Hatshepsut and saw the blood on her dagger and clothes, he started begging for his life. "You will pay for the atrocities you did to the innocents in the name of Pharaoh, did you also have my brother murdered?" as she placed her dagger at his throat.

His answer came too quick, "No, I would never do anything like that."

"No? You just tried to kill Pharaoh's Daughter," she replied as she moved the knife across his throat and drew a little blood.

He screamed, "It wasn't my idea, it is Rewer who wants to be Pharaoh," as he nodded toward the priest and began to whimper.

"Is there anyone else in this rat hole?" she asked.

"No one else," Tinfurer answered almost screaming.

"You are no longer Vizier of Lower Egypt. I am Vizier now, both of you will answer for your crimes." When Hatshepsut told Tinfurer she was now the Vizier, Rewer the High Priest of Ptah laughed. She turned and looked at the priest, "Is the power and wealth you desired worth it now?" as she came nearer.

"We should not be governed by ignorant upriver thugs from Thebes who stole our treasure and the throne from my ancestors."

"It looks as if you have stolen a lot from Pharaoh's treasury yourself," she stated as she moved closer to him, Menna was right by her side. Then she saw it! She could not believe what was around his neck, a slight gasp came from her throat and rage coursed through her body. The Priest was wearing the pink gold necklace of her murdered brother.

Hatshepsut pulled her matching necklace out from under

her gown, "Do you recognize this?" holding it in front of his eyes. The priest's eyes grew large when he recognized the necklace. Her voice hissed like a viper, "So, the assassins you sent to murder my brother gave you this as proof that their cowardly deed was completed and you decided to wear it as a trophy, didn't you?"

A look of contempt came back over his face, "Your old weak father sends his little girl to Memphis, what does he expect you to do?"

The priest had barely finished his statement, with two quick movements, she jerked the gold necklace off his neck with her left hand and slit his throat with the other. His look of contempt turned to one of surprise and then horror.

"Pharaoh's little girl sends you to the underworld for the death of my brother. I will feed your body to the crocodiles and your soul will be lost for eternity trying to find your body." She moved closer to his face as he slowly died, with his blood gushing from his throat and on her. His eyes started to close, in a soft voice, "Listen! I can hear the monster Ammit howling for you. Don't make her wait, go now so your heart can be devoured by her." The priest's eyes opened wide in terror, one last time. "You hear Ammit howling, don't you?" He fell face down in the pool of his own blood. Hatshepsut still enraged, turned to the Vizier, "Are you ready to have your vile heart also devoured by Ammit?"

Going for his throat, Dadu grabbed her arm. "No, My Lady, we need him alive!"

Hatshepsut stared at Dadu who had dared to stop her, "You don't give orders to Pharaoh's Daughter!"

Menna came to her, "Dadu is right, we need the Vizier to tell the Royal Court what he has done." There was a long pause with Dadu still holding her arm as she regained control of her anger.

Looking at the Vizier who was in fear for his life, "You will have a very slow and public death on a stake screaming for hours, begging to die." Dadu let go of Hatshepsut's arm, she said nothing. Menna remembered what Senenmut had said once, Hatshepsut is like her father, someday she will show us that she can be like a raging lioness.

"Take this dung to the prison, no food, just water. I will deal with him later and find out all you can about this rat's den and who else is involved in this treason." Hatshepsut commanded, as she started back to her quarters through the tunnel. Menna followed her, leaving Dadu and the twins with the former Vizier and the dead High Priest.

As they climbed back into the room, Senenmut asked, "What did you find?"

Menna answered, "We found the men responsible for the attack tonight."

"Is it the Vizier?"

"Yes, and the High Priest of Ptah," Hatshepsut said coldly. Senenmut looked at Menna who made no comment, he just shook his head, no. He knew that there was more to be told, but did not ask even though he saw more blood on Hatshepsut's tunic. She appeared to be totally detached and unemotional as a statue. "I need to clean up, I will display the bodies and the Vizier tomorrow when I hold court." Looking around at the carnage, she stated, "I am going to Senenmut's quarters. High Steward Ramose may be in danger, send someone to protect him."

Menna could not believe that he had not thought about the High Steward, of course the Vizier knew that the High Steward had warned them. She looked at Senenmut, "Have these quarters cleaned and move me into Pharaoh's quarters, no one is there now." Menna searched Senenmut's quarters to ensure it was safe before resuming his guard outside.

When Senenmut and Tyia asked Menna what had happened, he told them, leaving out no details which shocked Tyia, but Senenmut was not surprised by anything Menna told him. He did ask, "What are Hatshepsut's plans for the Vizier?" Menna stated that she wanted to publicly execute the Vizier on a stake.

"I need to talk to her about the Vizier."

Menna cautiously advised, now would not be a good time to speak with Hatshepsut. Abet then opened the door, "My Lady wants to see Dadu." Menna, Senenmut, and Tyia looked at each other, wondering what Dadu's fate would be.

Senenmut returned with Dadu, he entered her quarters without saying a word to anyone. Once inside, he saw that Hatshepsut was wearing a clean gown and holding her brother's broken necklace, Naomi was brushing her hair. Hatshepsut did not acknowledge him, so he sat down on a couch and waited. Hatshepsut eventually looked at him without saying a word, if she allowed him, he would try and justify his actions.

She finally spoke, "Did I act as Pharaoh or an angry spoiled child seeking revenge?"

"The priest had your brother murdered and he tried to do the same to you, all for greed and power. Your actions will be justified by the gods and Pharaoh will be proud of his daughter."

When Hatshepsut heard Dadu say that her father would be proud, tears ran down her face, she came to him and curled up by his side, "I told you once that you could always say anything to me, I am sorry," she whispered and snuggled closer to him. Dadu took her in his arms and held her until she went to sleep, he was certain that her father would be proud, just as he was.

Hidden in the courtyard outside of the guest quarters, Foreign Ambassador Ipi had watched all the activity in the dark early hours of the morning. He had hoped their plan was successful, but when he caught a glimpse of Pharaoh's Daughter alive going from one room to another, he knew the plan had failed. He did not know what had happened to High Priest Rewer or Vizier Tinfurer but he was sure that his life would soon be in danger.

Before Ra started his daily journey across the sky, Hatshepsut woke up startled, Dadu hugged her slightly. Looking at his arm around her, "You must be exhausted."

"It is an honor to be with Egypt's great leader!" He stood up, stretched his shoulder and back, "I am hungry, how about My Lady?"

"Not really, but I know we have a very busy day planned, so I must eat." She then saw that her dagger had been cleaned, all the memories of last night came flooding back.

"You will be better in time." Dadu commented when he saw her staring at the dagger.

"Yes, perhaps."

Abet prepared food for Hatshepsut and Dadu and then they went to the guest quarters, Senenmut, Menna and the twins were having their morning meal. The room had been cleaned but there remained some stains on the wood floor, they were relieved to see that Dadu was still with Hatshepsut.

"Where are the cursed hyena bodies?" Hatshepsut asked.

Bek answered dryly, "I put them in the cell with the Vizier, I thought he may need some company."

CHAPTER THIRTEEN

Royal Court

Senenmut biggest challenge was changing Hatshepsut's mind on how to handle the recent events, he did not want a public trial and slow execution for the Vizier and Ambassador Ipi if he could be found, Tinfurer had easily given up the ambassador's name to Bek. Senenmut convinced her that the official history should not show any discord between Pharaoh and the Royal Court in Memphis. She had finally agreed, but after today, Tinfurer was to disappear forever even from the gods.

When the Royal Court and guests were assembled, Senenmut returned to inform Hatshepsut that the Royal Court was ready for her. He expected to see Hatshepsut dressed in her royal gown and finest jewelry, but he was surprised at her appearance. She was dressed with a pleated shear linen shift top and a male kilt, the kilt was even tied in the traditional male knot. Seeing the effect her appearance had on a surprised Senenmut, pleased her. She did not want to be perceived as a pampered child or a delicate woman, "What does my Chief Adviser think?"

"Our Noble Lady will make an impression that will be recorded in history by the scribes, everyone in Memphis will note how Pharaoh's Daughter looked today, many will say she was dressed as a Prince." Senenmut answered, not wanting to offend.

The Members of the Royal Court, their wives, and honored guests were anxious to see Pharaoh's Daughter, there had been many rumors since her arrival three days ago and no one knew what to expect. They had become restless when the Standard Bearer struck the Standard three times on the floor and announced, "The Foremost of Noble Ladies, Pharaoh's Daughter," all bowed as Hatshepsut and her "Red Court" entered the Throne Room.

She walked past the members of court and stood by the royal dais, but did not step up to the throne. She nodded to the Standard Bearer who then sounded the standard once and commanded, "Rise." There was a noticeable whispering among the members, all assumed that the beautiful formally dressed Tyia was Pharaoh's Daughter, they hardly noticed the young girl dressed more like a prince.

The silence was broken when a spare writing brush fell from behind one of the scribe's ear to the floor. The chief scribe stood looking at Hatshepsut, waiting for her to reprimand the now prostate scribe.

She stepped forward and slightly motioned for him to sit down. Then she spoke, "Members and guests of Pharaoh's Royal Court in Memphis, I am Pharaoh's Daughter," the members were noticeably surprised that the young girl dressed as a prince was speaking. "I have a sad announcement, it has been learned that the Vizier, the High Priest of Ptah, and all the members of his hunting party have been killed." There was a combined gasp from several members, "An expedition will be sent to their camp and every effort will be made to return any remains for proper burial." There were agreements and acknowledgements from some members, she continued, "Matters of State and Pharaoh's wishes will now be announced, the Chief Royal Scribe will read this dispatch from Pharaoh."

The Royal Scribe left his post with the other scribes who were busy recording the words spoken and events. He bowed slightly as he took the scroll from Hatshepsut, he then raised the scroll and broke the seal in view of all and in a loud and clear voice he stated, "The Royal Seal of Pharaoh Tuthmose has been broken." After reciting the formal titles and five names of Pharaoh, he began to read the declaration that named Hatshepsut his Co-Regent and Commander of the Army.

When the Royal Scribe finished, Pharoah's Daughter announced, "This will end the formal court proceedings, the Chief Royal Scribe will leave with his staff, I wish to meet with only the Members of Court now."

After the guests and scribes had departed, from the side entrance General Nebi and several officers entered with soldiers, several Priests of Ptah, and the Captain of the Royal Guard came in with several palace guards carrying three large sacks that were obviously heavy. Hatshepsut did not think there was a need for the military's presence, but she did want the Members of Court to see that she had the military's support. The Members were very curious about the unusual proceedings, then the guards carrying the large sacks proceeded to open them one at a time in front of the Members of Court. They were surprised to see the first two bodies, but when the last sack was opened and a head of a man rolled across the floor, there were gasps of horror. Hatshepsut was now sitting on the Throne, in a clear and firm voice, "This is how Pharaoh's Daughter was greeted on my arrival in Memphis, by assassins who slipped into my chambers and tried to kill me last night."

There was a collective, hushed, "No" from the members.

Stepping down from the Throne, she walked near the severed head lying on the floor and kicked it in the general direction of its torso. She preceded to the body of Rewer the High Priest, knelling down, she raised his bald head with both hands. "High Priest Rewer is responsible for the murder of my brother, Prince Amenmose, and the attempt on Pharaoh's Daughter's life. I personally slit his throat and sent him to the underworld, I will feed all three of these traitors to the crocodiles so their souls will wander lost in the underworld forever, trying to find their bodies." Hatshepsut dropped his bald head to the tile floor with a loud thud and stood looking at them with her hand on her dagger.

She nodded toward the side entrance, "The Vizier did not go on a hunting expedition and is not dead, the conspirator is here." The guards led him into the court, his hands were bound, and he kept an eye on Hatshepsut. He still had his blood-stained clothes on, he looked very tired and was certain that he was going to be killed, he was recognized by the surprised members of court. "This jackal plotted with the High Priest to murder Pharaoh's Daughter and is responsible for the murder of innocents in the name of Pharaoh. Their hopes were that their various schemes would eventually allow the High Priest to one day become Pharaoh."

There was much discussion among the members, someone asked, "Is that true, Vizier Tinfurer?"

Everyone looked at the Vizier, but he still had his blood shot eyes on Hatshepsut, she came near him and he flinched away, "Speak so all will know the truth." Hatshepsut leaned close to him and hissed, "Speak the truth or all of your family and their generations will die with you."

"It is true," barely loud enough for Hatshepsut to hear.

"Speak up so all can hear, you coward!" she commanded.

"Yes, yes, it is true."

"What is true?" she demanded.

"Rewer came to me with his plan to become Pharaoh, I had no choice but to go along with him, he would have killed me too." Tinfurer said as he dropped to his knees and sobbed.

"Don't blame anyone but yourself for your actions and I am not going to listen to your crying, you did not hear the mothers and their babies when they cried. Get this despicable dung out of my sight, I will deal with him later and Foreign Ambassador Ipi when I find him." When she mentioned Ambassador Ipi's name, the members of the Royal Court, looked around, they seemed to notice for the first time that the Ambassador was not with them.

As the guards led him away, Hatshepsut approached the Members of Court, "These are the members of my personal court," as she pointed to each. "This is my Chief Advisor Senenmut, Commander Menna, Sergeant Dadu, guards Bae and Bek, and my Sister and Sole Ornament, Tyia. Any request from anyone in my personal court, from the military, or from the Palace Captain of the Guards is a command from Pharaoh.

I will assume the responsibility and duties of Vizier in Lower Egypt until a new Vizier is appointed." After a long and uncomfortable pause for the members, she continued. "If any harm comes to any loyal servants of Pharaoh or my personal court, I will personally send the traitor straight to the bottom of the River in a sack to drown and be devoured by crocodiles. Their families will watch them die and then I will send them into the Red Land to suffer a slow and miserable death." Hatshepsut stood with her arms folded and watched the court, again not a word was said, "The court is dismissed," they departed quietly. She was exhausted both physically and emotionally, and it showed.

Senenmut said, "Noble Lady, we should go to Pharaoh's quarters now, I pray that it is worthy of Pharaoh's amazing Daughter."

Hatshepsut smiled at Senenmut, "Your council is wise and your compliments are appreciated, what did you find in the tunnels?"

"The tunnels go between the guest quarters, Pharaoh's quarters, and the Viziers quarters. There are three underground rooms, one large room where they were staying," he paused wishing he had not mentioned the room. Hatshepsut did not react to the memories of the previous night. "A second room holds some weapons and records and the last room contains gold and valuables."

Hatshepsut thought for a moment, "I wish to explore the tunnel later, but for now I want to take Jochebed back to her home, it is safe for her and the baby now. Senenmut, meet with the Captain of the Guards, and deal with the former Vizier now."

Tyia was still traumatized from the events of the previous night and asked, "I do not want to be alone in the palace, may I stay with you and Menna?"

Hatshepsut smiled and took her by the hand, "It was a terrible experience, come with us."

The slave complex consisted of the housing, support buildings, stables, grain bins, and vegetable gardens, all to maintain a Royal Palace. When they arrived at the home of Jochebed, they were met by Jochebed's husband, who obviously had been beaten recently, he bowed slightly and introduced himself as Amram and invited them inside. Hatshepsut noticed that he touched the baby's head that Jochebed held in her arms. Menna gestured with his hand for Hatshepsut to remain by the door, he entered with Jochebed and the baby, inside were Mariam the young daughter playing with a toddler and a very old woman sitting on mats. There was the strong smell of fish stew cooking, a few dried stringy vegetables were on a crude table made from what appeared to be scrap wood. There appeared to be no threat to his Lady and the old woman did not seem to be aware of his presence. Menna stepped clear of the door allowing Hatshepsut to entered, but as soon as she stepped thru the door, the old woman began to make wailing and excited sounds. He firmly asked Hatshepsut to leave.

Jochebed went to calm her grandmother, explaining to Menna that she must be frightened because she is blind and deaf. Menna heard the old woman asking something in Hebrew. "What is she asking?"

"I don't understand," Jochebed answered, "My grandmother has been blind and deaf for about a month, but she keeps asking about the angel she saw, she keeps pleading for her to return."

"Is the woman talking about me?" Hatshepsut asked as she stepped back into the home.

Before Jochebed could answer, the old woman answered in halting Egyptian, "Angel, I see you and I can hear you, have you come to deliver me from my suffering?"

Jochebed went to her grandmother, the twins and Tyia had moved to the doorway and were watching the old woman. "Grandmother, can you see and hear the Princess?" but the old woman did not acknowledge her granddaughter.

"What is her name?" Hatshepsut asked.

The old woman answered, "I am Hannah."

Hatshepsut then turned and addressed the old woman directly, "Hannah, I am Pharaoh's Daughter, you can see and hear me?"

"Oh yes, you are as gleaming gold and your voice is the sound of many angels speaking at the same time, praise God!"

Tyia saw Menna move toward the woman, but the old woman never took her eyes off of Hatshepsut. Something mysterious was happening, perhaps her sister was having another encounter with the gods. Hatshepsut moved to her left and as she did the old woman followed her movement with her milky colored eyes, then Hatshepsut returned to the door.

As she did, the old woman pleaded, "Please angel, do not leave without me."

Jochebed begin to pray out loud. Menna asked, "Should we leave My Lady, I do not understand what is happening?"

Hatshepsut said no, and moved near the old woman, Hannah asked, "May I touch you?"

Hatshepsut looked at Menna, he went to Hanna and felt around her to see if there was any danger. "Is that you Jochebed?" she asked.

"No, I am Menna, a guard of Pharaoh's Daughter." She did not respond to him.

"Yes Hannah, you may touch me." When she touched Hatshepsut's hand, it felt as if every hair on her body was standing up. She had never had such a sensation before, she could not explain the feeling. She experienced a total emotional release, any fear and guilt she had been feeling was gone. There was a soft sigh from the old woman, as she continued lightly touching the back of Hatshepsut's hand.

"My Lady, do you know what is happening?" Tyia asked softly as she entered the room to be closer to Hatshepsut.

"No, but it is amazing!"

"It truly is amazing that God sent an angel to me," the old woman said.

Menna stated, "She can only see and hear you, My Lady."

Hatshepsut nodded yes, she saw a banner on the wall that was white, black and red like the one Sitre had back in Thebes. "Hannah, are you and your family of the Levite Tribe?"

"Yes, my family came to Egypt when Levi's brother Joseph was Vizier of Egypt. Oh! Your voice is wonderous." Hannah continued, "I have prayed for years to see the person who will free us from slavery."

Menna was surprised by Hatshepsut, how did she know anything about the woman's family history?

"Our Noble Lady is truly a god because the blind woman can see her," Bae whispered to his brother.

"I was not sure about Pharaohs being a god before," Bek replied quietly.

Hatshepsut sat down on the mat close to Hannah. "Hannah, I found a baby in the River floating in a basket," then she saw Jochebed crying and shaking her head no. It was then that she knew for sure that the baby she found was Jochebed's. It was no accident that her daughter Miriam was close by, she was watching her little brother. She motioned for Jochebed to hand her the baby, with the baby in her arms, she leaned close to Hannah and whispered, "Hannah, here is your great grandson, he is the one I found in the river. I will protect him."

Jochebed came to her, saying to her in Hebrew, "Sabta," meaning grandmother, "can you see him?"

But Hannah did not hear her, Hannah touched the soft yellow curly hair of the baby. "Yes, he is moses from the River," then she slowly lay down and appeared to go to sleep.

"What did she mean, when she said moses from the River?" Hatshepsut asked Jochebed.

"Moses in Hebrew means, pull or to take out of water," Jochebed answered.

"Moses! He was drawn from the River, that is what we will name him, what do you think?"

"Yes, Moses is a good name for him My Lady."

Everyone remained quiet for a few moments as they tried to comprehend what they had witnessed and watched Hannah peacefully sleeping. Hatshepsut asked Jochebed, "I do not know of a Hebrew Vizier named Joseph, was your grandmother mistaken?"

"It is said that our people came to Egypt when Joseph was Vizier." Hatshepsut knew of no historical record of a Hebrew Vizier in her studies. It must be a story made up by the Hebrews, she thought. "I do not know how, but Pharaoh's Daughter will be the reason that our people will be free someday."

Hatshepsut holding baby Moses sleeping in her arms did not respond to Jochebed's comment. "I will arrange for you and your family to be cared for, when Moses is weaned, I will bring him to Thebes. He will be raised as my adopted son and given an important position in the house of Pharaoh."

Jochebed was overcome with emotion, her son was safe and the horror was over for her people. "My Lady I am sorry I tried to deceive you."

Hatshepsut handed the baby to her, "You did what you had to do to save your child, I admire your courage."

As she left the home of Jochebed, Tyia took her arm as she walked by, "Do you believe that the Hebrew God was responsible for what happened today?"

Hatshepsut was unsure, "I do not know what to believe."

The following morning Abet and Naomi did not know what to do, Ra had triumphantly returned from the underworld a long time ago and their Lady was still asleep, even with the harsh morning calls of the partridges on the palace grounds. They had quietly checked on her several times, she seemed alright, but was still sound asleep. Finally, Abet woke her with a gentle shake of her shoulder, Hatshepsut slowly stretched and opened her eyes. Then she quickly sat up in bed, sending Abet away from her a few steps, "I'm sorry to wake My Lady, but I was concerned."

Still trying to come out of the fog of a wonderful night's sleep, she asked, "How long has Ra been up?"

"Ra has been traveling in his chariot for a long time, My Lady." Dressed only in a thin sheer gown, she went into the main room of Pharaoh's quarters, and saw Menna and Tyia standing on the balcony enjoying the view. Both were formally dressed for their attendance with Hatshepsut when she planned to meet with the individual members of the Royal Court.

They heard her approaching and turned toward her, they saw a mixture of a little girl with sleepy eyes and tousled hair, but also that of a young woman in the sheer gown. "I hope you slept well?" Tyia asked.

"I should be meeting with the Members of Court, not sleeping like a lazy hippo."

Menna said, "The rest is much needed after the ordeal our Lady has been through."

Tyia added, "We spoke to Senenmut, he is meeting with the members and setting up a schedule for later today."

Standing on the balcony, she could see that Ra was indeed high, and the River was already alive with activity. Most of the boats had gleaming white sails, some had a patch work of repaired sails and a few were brightly colored. There was one small boat with bright colored patches on its faded white sail, sailing toward the palace docks. All were gliding across the water that sparkled with the ripples reflecting morning rays of light. "The little boat with the bright patches on the sail is unusual," commented Menna, "I have seen it before, often in the morning, it comes close to the docks and then sails away."

They saw Captain Kawab walk to the dock and motion the boat in. When it came to the dock, Captain Kawab helped what appeared to be a young boy out. They talked for a while and then the little boat sailed away.

"I wonder who it is?" Hatshepsut thought out loud. Looking down at the activity, there seemed to be a brighter feel in Memphis. "I am concerned for my rekhyt."

Tyia knew that Hatshepsut was talking about all common people of Egypt, not just Egyptians, "I think that the rekhyt of Memphis are much better, since My Noble Lady has arrived," she commented.

Hatshepsut soaked up the morning light and breathed in fresh air, with her eyes closed. She seemed to smile a little, "I hope they are." The three of them enjoyed the peaceful moment, Abet brought Hatshepsut a stool to sit on and something to eat and drink. "I have much to do today." Hatshepsut said with a slight sound of sadness in her voice.

While finishing her morning meal, they noticed a naval boat docking at the palace. It appeared that Admiral Ebana was on the boat, it was hard to tell for sure from their distance. After docking, the naval officer was in a hurry to get to the palace, "It appears I may have a visitor soon," Hatshepsut commented.

Hatshepsut, Tyia, and Menna entered the Vizier's chambers, Senenmut was already there, busy going over some reports from the Royal Court members and dispatches from Thebes. His faced beamed as he looked at Hatshepsut, he could not take his eyes off her. "Yes, I know, my mother would approve also," commenting on her formal appearance.

"I think your mother's approval and Senenmut's are two different things," Tyia corrected jokingly.

Senenmut seemed a little embarrassed, caught staring at her, smiling at Senenmut, "Is everyone ready to help me find loyal servants?"

"Yes, Noble Lady. The Royal Court members are all here to present their pleas for continued service, except of course the Minister of Foreign Affairs, Ambassador Ipi. No one knows where he is."

"Is his family still here?"

"Yes, they have been questioned by the Medjay State Police. His wife said that Ipi told her that he was leaving her, she pleaded for him to stay and then he hit her."

"So, we can assume that she was not involved and really does not know where he is? I want Ambassador Ipi found."

"If anyone can find him, it will be the Medjay, My Lady." After a short pause he stated, "Also, Admiral Ebana is here and wishes to have an audience with you."

"Send in Admiral Ebana." Senenmut bowed slightly and went to retrieve Admiral Ebana.

Tyia stated, "You know that Senenmut has room in his heart for only you."

"We both are aware that I am obligated to marry Prince

Tuthmose."

"I did not mention marriage," Tyia said just before the door opened with Senenmut bringing Admiral Ebana. Hatshepsut smiled at Tyia and held her smile as she turned toward Admiral Ebana.

"My loyal friend, I saw that you were in a hurry when you docked this morning. What is the urgency?"

"I have received a dispatch from one of our outposts on the coast, stating that three Mitanni ships will arrive tomorrow."

Hatshepsut asked, "Are they a threat?"

"No, My Lady, to be a threat there would be many more ships, I believe that they carry diplomats or high-ranking officials and only a few soldiers."

Hatshepsut was quiet, she did not know what the current relationship was with this country but she was certain that her mother would have known. "I have two questions and I should already know the answers to both. What is Egypt's and Mitanni's relationship now? Also, I am curious as to how we got an advanced notice of their arrival?"

Admiral Ebana smiled, "I am not certain about our current relationship with Mitanni, but from what I have seen since we arrived, I think Memphis officials have been keeping information from Pharaoh in Thebes."

Senenmut spoke up, "I will get that information for My Lady and Admiral Ebana."

"Thank you, Senenmut," Hatshepsut responded sincerely. Senenmut departed on his new mission.

Admiral Ebana continued, "We are able to get a day's advance notice on approaching ships because of the route they take through the channels in the Delta. The marked course is a long route that assures deep water, but our small scout boats are faster and can take short cuts on the way to Memphis from the Great Green Sea."

"That makes sense, I should have thought of that."

"Pharaoh's Daughter cannot know everything, that is why she has need of humble servants."

"You are kind to not embarrass me, but I require that you always inform me of what is needed and correct."

Admiral Ebana bowed slightly, "As Pharaoh's Daughter wisely commands."

Scribes were called into the Vizier's Office and they started the meetings with the members of the Royal Court. Hatshepsut was formal but not aggressive toward any of the members, she took their written offers of resignation, they were to be notified later if their resignation was accepted. During the meetings, each member was also asked who they recommended to be the new Vizier. Most suggested Ramose the High Steward, but two members were bold enough to suggest that they were qualified. The meetings went all afternoon, with Senenmut and Tyia by her side. Menna was always close, moving around keeping a constant eye on whoever was with her.

A nervous Royal Treasurer and Assistant to the Foreign Ambassador had the longest meeting with Hatshepsut. The Treasurer was asked by Hatshepsut if his records accounted for all the valuables that were found in the tunnel and missing from the Pharaoh's Treasury. He replied, "The former Vizier demanded that the official records not show anything missing. My personal private records will account for all that was taken by the Vizier." Hatshepsut complimented him on maintaining his own records, but admonished him for not letting Pharaoh know what was going on in Memphis. The Treasurer replied, "I was afraid of losing my position and my family was threatened. Many have been threatened by the former Vizier."

The meeting with the Assistant to the Foreign Ambassador was unproductive, Hatshepsut was not able to obtain much information about the missing Foreign Ambassador. The Assistant readily admitted that he did not know where he was, but was positive that the Ambassador would be able to explain when he returned. When questioned about Egypt's current relationship with Mitanni, it was learned that the Foreign Ambassador had made two trips to Mitanni. The Assistant had not been kept informed of the current relations with Mitanni.

When the last meeting was over, the scribes were dismissed, then Senenmut informed Hatshepsut that if it pleased her, he had arranged an evening dinner in the garden with entertainment. She looked forward to a pleasant evening, but she also realized that her days had become more like her mothers, her life had changed forever since arriving in Memphis. Hatshepsut and Senenmut were the last to arrive at the garden, the meal was informal and relaxed. Senenmut had invited Kawab the Captain of the Palace Guards with his wife and Ramose the High Steward, who was also with his wife.

Tyia watched Senenmut, he was always working it seemed, she heard him mention the former Vizier to Captain Kawab. Tyia was certain that the Vizier would never be found, even by the gods. Hatshepsut enjoyed watching the dancers and listening to the music, two cups of her wine helped to relax her. She went to the table where Kawab, Ramose, and their wives were seated. All stood as she approached. "Be seated," but Captain Kawab remained standing and allowed her to use his seat.

Kawab spoke first, "May I introduce my wife, Manoti, we are honored to have been invited to a private audience with Pharaoh's Daughter." Hatshepsut acknowledge Kawab's wife, Manoti with a smile.

High Steward Ramose then introduced his wife, "My Noble Lady this is my wife, Shamise."

"It is a pleasure, Shamise, you must be the oldest child in your family?"

"Yes, My Lady," Shamise was pleased that Pharaoh's Daughter knew the meaning of her name.

Hatshepsut then turned to Captain Kawab, "I wish to visit the pyramids tomorrow and spend the night there."

"Shall I close the pyramids to others?"

"That will not be necessary, will you be able to join us Manoti?"

"I would be honored."

"Excellent." Hatshepsut looked at Ramose with an intense gaze and her mischievous smile, "I interviewed most of the Royal Court today, during the interviews I asked each who they would recommend for the new Vizier. Do you know who most of them recommended?"

Ramose answered with a slight laugh, "I would guess most said themselves."

"A few did, that is true, but most recommended you, I agree with them." Hatshepsut enjoyed the expression of surprise on his and his wife's faces as she watched them.

Ramose quickly regained his composure, "I am honored, but I am not related to the family that has been in that position for many years."

She knew that Ramose had no ties with the family line of many past Viziers, she did not trust them. "That is true and another good reason for you to be Vizier."

Ramose's wife beamed as she placed her arm around him while she thanked Hatshepsut with a nod and smile. "We will make the announcement in a few days, but I do have a request from the future Vizier."

"Yes, My Lady."

"I want to ensure that the two palace midwives who refused to carry out Vizier Tinfurer's order be rewarded and I also want you to protect my adopted son and his family."

"It will be done," Ramose paused, "My Lady has the respect of the Royal Court, we are certain that the lives saved in the desert and that the assassins failed because the gods favor Pharaoh's Daughter."

She was about to leave when Ramose's wife, Shamise, spoke. "Pharaoh's Daughter will be remembered for generations as a brave young woman. When a mother holds her precious baby in the future, they will remember that you saved a baby in the River. Pharaoh's Daughter has earned her immortality."

Hatshepsut was deeply touched by the praises of Shamise. "The Vizier's wife is kind, enjoy the evening," she then returned to her table with Tyia.

"The future Queen of Egypt will be a great ruler!" Shamise stated.

Kawab nodded yes and then after a pause, "I won't get much sleep tonight."

CHAPTER FOURTEEN

The Pyramids

It pleased her to see how excited Senenmut was during the morning meal, they were dressed early for travel and exploring in chariots, Captain Kawab was to be their guide. Hatshepsut allowed Senenmut to drive their chariot, she was not surprised to see that he handled the horses gently. Menna and Tyia were laughing and enjoying their ride in their chariot while Dadu was tense and serious, but his passenger Abet, teased him about his driving. The twins were last in the little caravan and they filled their chariot to the brim. Soon they were out of the city and into the desert, the city backed right up to the Red Land. They slowly made the gentle climb up the plateau while passing other sightseers going up to the monuments. Most had offerings for family members buried there, but some were just tourists. Sadly, some areas had been dishonored in the past with, "We were here" type graffiti written in places.

Later they passed several palace guards with donkeys carrying supplies and tents for them, they had started the trek much earlier. During her first visit Hatshepsut had not noticed the distinct and quick transition from the cool lush palace gardens and the city, alive with activity, to the quiet pyramid complex. It was like a quick passing from life to death, with the promise of eternal life ahead in the mortuary temples with the giant pyramids pointing up to eternity. With Ra to their backs, the rays were directly on the large monuments covered in white stone, the bright reflection made it difficult to look directly at the pyramids. Hatshepsut wondered secretly if the magnificent pyramids had fulfilled their purpose for the Pharaohs buried inside.

As they drew closer, she had a cold chill when she noticed the signs of aging already on the monuments built for eternity. The gold tips had been robbed during Egypt's first period of shame when the Two Lands were not united. During that time, Egypt was divided while the governors of the 40 Nomes or districts along the River had fought for power. Poverty, lawlessness, and hunger existed throughout Egypt, eventually after 125 years, Egypt was reunited by Pharaoh Mentuhotep II. All land then became the property of Pharaoh and there was only one Royal Army under the complete control of Pharaoh. However, the damage had been done to the pyramids and even Egypt could not afford to replace the enormous amount of gold required for the tops of the pyramids.

Seeing all the people here and the damage that had been done over the one thousand years since their construction, Hatshepsut could understand why her father decided to be the first Pharaoh to have his tomb hidden in the valley. His mortuary temple was located near the River where his priests of his cult could honor him daily with prayers and offerings, but the location of his tomb was to remain concealed. She was taken from her thoughts when Senenmut commented, "They are magnificent?"

As they passed a giant head sticking out of the sand, Hatshepsut asked, "Do you know anything about the sphinx?"

"Only that it is much older than the pyramids and that whoever built it has been forgotten. It has been covered in sand for centuries, perhaps if the sand was removed, the mystery would be solved." Then they entered a causeway reserved for royalty, the covered roadway and engraved walls made travel comfortable and pleasant. Hatshepsut smiled at Senenmut as he caught views of the pyramids in the openings of the causeway, his excitement grew, "Just amazing," he said. At the base of the largest pyramid they stopped the chariots in an open-air chapel, everyone was quiet. Senenmut was the first to speak, "Thank you for this opportunity!"

"I wanted to do something for you."

It was as hot as she remembered, with the rays of Ra reflected off the white stones, from her first visit five years earlier with her father. It had been only a quick day trip with her father, she hoped to make new memories and have a greater respect for the immense necropolis. When the palace guards arrived and set up tents for shade, it was much more pleasant. Abet made refreshments for everyone, Tyia offered to stay with her, but Hatshepsut insisted that she and Menna enjoy the day together. Senenmut was gone most of the day exploring the area, when he returned, it was only for a short break and refreshments. She was certain that he would have a lot to talk about tonight and this pleased her.

In Memphis three Mitanni ships could be seen in the distance sailing toward the palace, it was late afternoon when they finally docked. Hidden among the many tents and vendors outside the palace walls was Ambassador Ipi, when he saw the Mitanni ships, he was excited. Perhaps he had found a way to escape the wrath of Pharaoh's Daughter, he wondered if she knew that the Mitanni were involved in their failed plan? Under the old worn and dirty tunic he had stolen, was a rope that dug into his shoulder from the weight of twenty rings of gold. He had taken the gold from the underground storage room, now the gold was all he had. He resented the Vizier and High Priest, after all it was their plan that had failed, now he was a fugitive with no family or prestige. The spoiled and pretentious daughter of the old Pharaoh had taken everything he had worked for his whole life away. He did not believe that the gods were protecting her, despite the rumors, he hated her!

Chief Stewart Ramose, General Nebi, and a battalion of soldiers met the ships, no one knew what to expect. It was not time for the annual tribute from Mitanni and the tribute had never been brought by three ships before. The Egyptian soldiers had been waiting for a long time when General Nebi gave commands to form up. The soldiers assembled into a proper formation from many small groups that had found shelter wherever they could from the intense rays of Ra.

First to disembark were Mitanni soldiers and then a young man with two older men. The young man was obviously royalty with all the gold he was wearing and by his attitude, the Mitanni soldiers gave a very crisp salute as he passed. As he approached Ramose and General Nebi, they could tell he was not pleased that they did not bow or salute, he said nothing but just stood quietly with an intense glare at the two Egyptians. The young man should have known that Egyptians never rendered subservient gestures to any foreign nation, let alone to one of its vassal states. Ramose was first to speak, "I am Ramose, Pharaoh Tuthmose's Chief Stewart in Memphis."

"I am Prince Barattarna, son of the greatest of Mitanni kings, Shuttarna. I should have been met by Minister of Foreign Affairs Ambassador Ipi and the Vizier."

Ramose was not surprised at the young prince's comment, but had a difficult time understanding him because of his poor command of the Egyptian language. "Vizier Tinfurer is missing after going on a hunting expedition."

"Where is the Minister of Foreign Affairs?" he questioned.

Not understanding his question, "I do not understand," replied Ramose.

A flustered Prince motioned to one of his aides. "Most High Prince Barattarna asks why the Minister of Foreign Affairs is not here?" stated one of the aids in much better Egyptian.

"He has left Memphis and it is unknown where he is."

The prince conferred with his two aides, he then asked, "Do you represent Pharaoh?"

Ramose, the future Vizier, was going to enjoy his next reply. "No, Pharaoh's Daughter represents Pharaoh as his Vizier."

The prince gave a laugh under his breath, "Mitanni men do not negotiate with women, not even Pharaoh's Daughter."

Ramose stated in a firm and controlled voice, "I do not know what there is to negotiate, you know the terms of our treaty. If the prince does not wish to have the honor of meeting with Pharaoh's Daughter, then you should get back on your ships and return to your father."

After an exchange between the three men, "We do not wish to insult Pharaoh's Daughter, Mitanni men are not accustomed to being ruled by women. Prince Barattarna requires an audience with Pharaoh's Daughter," stated one of the aides.

"Egypt is blessed by the gods to have Hatshepsut here in Memphis to carry out Pharaoh's wishes. I will inform her of your request and see if the Foremost of Noble Ladies will be available."

When the Prince was told what was said by Ramose, he responded, "I have traveled a great distance and demand an audience today."

"The Foremost of Noble Ladies is busy and your arrival was not expected. It may be several days before you are given an audience," Ramose gladly informed the prince.

After consulting with his aides, "I request accommodations."

"I will escort you to your quarters."

While the ships were being unloaded, Ambassador Ipi approached one of the ship's captains. As he came near, the aloof Captain made a gesture for the dirty peasant to get away. Ipi opened his tunic slightly so the Captain could see the gold, the

Captain's eyes became very wide. "I have important information for Prince Barattarna, he is in danger," stated Ambassador Ipi.

Throughout the day at the pyramids, people came and went, except Captain Kawab, he remained near Hatshepsut. Later during the afternoon heat, his wife joined them in the shade of the tent. Manoti was pleasant and Hatshepsut enjoyed visiting with her, she asked about her family. Manoti stated that they were not able to have children, Hatshepsut could see the sadness in her face and hear it in her voice. Offering her regrets, she suggested that perhaps they could adopt. Manoti answered that they were considering adopting.

As Ra set in the west everyone returned to the camp, they were exhausted, but happy. After a light meal prepared by Abet, they enjoyed talking around the fire. As the chill of the night set in, Hatshepsut thanked Abet when she brought her a warm tunic to put on. The conversation was light and relaxed, Hatshepsut relished the time with her friends. As the fire burnt low, the stars in the night sky seemed to come down to the horizon below their camp on the high plateau. Everyone was quiet, the only sound was when the burning embers made an occasional snapping sound and sent many small sparks into the starry night sky.

Hatshepsut smiled at Dadu and Abet who were talking quietly together. Menna and Tyia were sitting closely to each other and the twins were even quiet, not their normally animated selves. Captain Kawab and his wife had left to be with his guards. Senenmut was near Hatshepsut, he was obviously thinking about the sights he had seen today. She let him be alone in his thoughts but watched him, when he noticed her, she asked, "Did you have a nice day?"

"It was a wonderful day, to see the work of Imhotep, he truly does deserve to be honored as a great builder. Has Pharaoh's Daughter heard stories of the Ancients before the Pharaohs?"

"I know that some believe they existed."

"The Royal Architect Ineni often talked to us at night after working on Pharaoh's tomb, he said that the ancients moved their homes to the River after the rains stopped and their land turned to desert. We listened to him as long as he was willing to talk, he is such a brilliant man and is interested in many subjects."

"Yes. In many ways he reminds me of you," Hatshepsut said as she placed her hand on his arm. Senenmut was sure he blushed, thankful that it was hidden by the night.

It was an early start, the next morning, back to the palace and everyone was busy getting ready to leave. Dadu and Abet seemed to be smiling more than anyone else. Senenmut didn't talk much on the way back to the palace. "I hope you enjoyed your visit to the pyramids?"

"I will never forget seeing them." Senenmut wanted to say more to Pharaoh's Daughter about his feelings toward her, but he dared not. Hatshepsut watched him, had she let him become too close to her? Thankfully Senenmut finally spoke, "I wish only happiness for My Noble Lady and to help her to become the greatest of all Egyptian Queens. I promise to never jeopardize your destiny."

Hatshepsut thought, yes, but will you always be happy with that future? She spoke softly to him, "I know." She took hold of his arm, "My loyal Senenmut." As they neared Memphis, she gently squeezed his arm, and then let go.

After a short rest in her quarters, she informed Menna that she wished to visit the old woman Hannah and asked Senenmut to come with her because he had not seen the blind woman. They made their way through the complex maze of alleyways to the house of Amram and Jochebed, but found the house empty.

Neighbors informed them that the family had moved to a housing area reserved for foremen, Amram had been promoted. When they finally found their house, Menna went in alone and found only Jochebed and the baby. He stood by the door as Hatshepsut and Senenmut entered, it took a moment for their eyes to adjust to the darker room. Jochebed was nursing the baby, she started to get up, but Hatshepsut motioned for her to remain seated, "You are in a different house."

"Yes, it is generous of Pharaoh's Daughter to provide it."

"Where is everyone?"

"Miriam is playing with her brother and my husband, Amram is at work, he is pleased with his new position. I was informed that I am to care for Pharaoh's Daughter's adopted son and that no other work is required of me."

Hatshepsut knew that Vizier Ramose had arranged this all in her name, perhaps she had made a good choice of Ramose, "Where is your grandmother, Hannah?"

Jochebed stood and put the now sleeping baby in his new crib and walked to Hatshepsut, "My grandmother died the night after you were here. She was at peace and praising God, several times she thanked the Lord for answering her prayers."

Hatshepsut did not know what to say, all she could say was, "I'm sorry!"

Jochebed replied, "My Noble Lady has nothing to be sorry about. Because of you, my baby was saved and all future Hebrew babies. Our lives are better because of the kindness of Pharaoh's Daughter, I am sure that God has used My Noble Lady. Pharaoh's Daughter will be remembered in our history." Jochebed had obviously given much thought to what she would say to Hatshepsut.

"I will send for him when he is of age, he will learn of his heritage and brave mother."

Senenmut followed quietly behind Menna and Hatshepsut as they returned to the palace, disappointed that he did not get to see Hatshepsut when she spoke to the blind woman. He had not seen the lion in the desert and he was not with her when she had found the baby, or when the baby warned of the assassins, he did not doubt that the events happened.

Hatshepsut was planning on going through the valuables that former Vizier Tinfurer had stolen from the Royal Treasurer, but Vizier Ramose arrived at Hatshepsut's quarters to brief her on the Mitanni ships. "Who are our Mitanni guests?"

"Prince Barattarna, the very arrogant son of King Shuttarna, and his two aides." Ramose answered and proceeded to inform her of the exchange that he and the prince had. He believed that the paying of their tribute was only a ruse, he was certain they had come to Memphis for other reasons.

Later she asked Tyia, "Perhaps you could listen to our Mitanni guests. If you think it is safe for her, Menna?"

Menna looked at Tyia and saw her hesitation, "It should be safe, will you be able to understand what they say?"

"I am afraid that I will not understand them." Tyia answered not sure about her ability to understand the language her father had taught her.

"My only concern is for your safety, take no chances Menna," Hatshepsut commanded.

It was dark, even with the small oil lamps in the tunnel as Menna, Tyia and Bae went to the secret area beneath the quarters for royal guests. Tyia took a seat and Menna quietly opened the cover in the ceiling that would allow them to hear what was being said in the room above. The ventilation was such that no fumes from their oil lamps entered the room above, it was a well-designed listening post. Tyia could not help but shiver a little when she heard the men talking, Menna placed his hand on her shoulder for support. She was relieved that she could understand most of what was being said, their voices were very faint.

Senenmut had arranged for servants to bring them food and drink, with orders to place the refreshments on the table close to the tree with the bird. After being served, it was much easier to hear the men talking. One man said that the quarters were more elegant than the guest quarters they offered their visiting dignitaries. There was a loud reply, "I am not pleased with the quarters, no place in Egypt is as good as home."

"I apologize, my prince is correct."

The prince was not happy with the situation in Memphis and it was obvious that things had changed. "We were to be given gold by the Vizier to not invade Egypt when the High Priest seized power, now both are dead, we could be in danger."

A concerned aide stated, "People have been killed in this room, look at the blood stains in the floor."

"I brought a small portion of the annual tribute to Egypt in case questions were asked."

"Will Pharaoh's Daughter believe it?"

"I am sure that the young Egyptian princess will be no problem, if she is anything like my sister, we have with us."

"Your sister could be a problem, if it is discovered that she was to be given to Ambassador Ipi."

"I will keep her hidden on the boat, if there is a problem, I will leave orders for the guards to kill her."

"What will the King do to us, if we kill his daughter?"

The Prince laughed, "Father is glad to be rid of her because she has fought off his advances unlike her sisters. Memphis is still vulnerable, an old dying Pharaoh in Thebes and a girl who pretends to be in control in Memphis, it is only a matter of time until we come back and take Memphis.

The Egyptians have become weak, women have too much power and they use 'nubies' as their police and guards. The Hebrew hate their Egyptian masters, they will support us if we tell them we will set them free." Continuing using the insulting term for Nubians, "The "nubies' will go to whoever pays them the most." Then he boasted, "If Pharaoh's little girl is still here when we do come and capture Memphis, I will show her what a real man is like before I kill her."

When Tyia heard the prince, she could not help but gasp. The three men heard her, Prince Barattarna said, "Did you hear someone?" Both men shook their heads yes. They stood and listened very intently but heard nothing else, checking all the rooms and balcony, no reason for the sound could be discovered. The prince opened the door and saw the servant girls flirting with his guards, they were laughing. When the guards saw him, they came to attention and sent the servant girls away. Barattarna returned to the table and continued eating, confident that the sound they heard was from the servants and guards.

The two aides relaxed and enjoyed the fine Egyptian wine. But they would not admit to the prince how good the food and wine was, "Everything is better back home," one whispered to the other with an elbow nudge.

Tyia was glad to not have failed Hatshepsut and relieved to leave. After reporting to Hatshepsut what they had heard, Senenmut and Hatshepsut discussed the information and occasionally confirmed a bit of information with Tyia. What Tyia heard had answered a lot of questions and raised other questions. How had the Mitanni learned about the deaths of the former Vizier and the High Priest?

Senenmut smiled, "I have an idea, but it will take some preparations. My plan will involve women and Nubians, the two things the prince despises. He needs to hear how a lion spoke to you because the lion is very important in the Mitanni religion. They also need to learn what Pharaoh's Daughter does to traitors, and that she can perform magic."

"What magical powers do I possess?"

"My Noble Lady will soon see how powerful she is."

"What about his sister on the ship."

"I will place Palace Guards near the ships with the Mitanni guards, with instructions to protect the girl if needed."

The following morning Hatshepsut went back into the tunnel to inventory the valuables Vizier Tinfurer had stolen from the Royal Treasurer. Memories of the assassins came flooding back when she entered the tunnel from Pharaoh's quarters. The Vizier had stockpiled more gold and valuables than he could ever spend, thanks to Tyia they knew why, it was for the Mitanni. While going through the inventory, Hatshepsut came across an interesting item on the list, a Long Mace and Long Knife of Pharaoh Sekenenre. He was the Pharaoh who had begun the war against the vile Hyksos and had died a violent death in battle. They located the Mace it definitely had the engraved gold cartouche of Pharaoh Sekenenre.

It was as long as a man's arm with a cedar wood grip, above the grip were two gold and silver rings, the remainder of the handle was ebony with an electrum coated on the round club. This was obviously not a ceremonial weapon because there were signs of use and damage. Scuff marks were on the grip and some electrum was missing from the round shaped mace, but the long knife belonging to the first warrior Pharaoh could not be found.

Menna asked to see the mace, he examined it closely and twisted the grip, it turned and unlocked just below the two gold rings. Out of the mace handle he withdrew a long knife, it was two weapons in one, a beautiful and surprisingly deadly weapon.

Hatshepsut observed Menna with the two weapons in his hands, memories of the "night of assassins," when he bravely confronted the assassin with only his short knife came back. She did not want him to ever be in that position again, "That mace and knife are yours."

"No, My Lady, I was just seeing how it came apart," he quickly replied, offering it back to her.

"I never want you to confront someone with just a small knife again, while protecting Pharaoh's Daughter."

All the items were now accounted for, except for twenty rings of gold, a very large fortune. The rings would easily slip on a man's arm, the round shape allowed for easier transporting and storing. The rings were engraved for record keeping, with her father's cartouche and year eleven of his reign, they were part of last year's tribute to Pharaoh. It was decided that someone had taken them for their own use.

CHAPTER FIFTEEN

Magic

The prince was asleep and the two aides were concerned because he had started drinking too much wine and was adding the powder of the "Joy Plant" to his wine. They wanted to leave Egypt, but all they had to do was look out their balcony and see that it was impossible, Egyptian soldiers were between the palace and the dock. All three men felt trapped and were not sleeping well.

The day for the confrontation with the Mitanni Prince arrived, at the appointed time they were summoned to the Royal Court. It was midday and the rays of Ra were very bright as the twins escorted them to the court, Prince Barattarna thought that they were the largest and darkest men he had ever seen. Both were wearing new broad collars that Hatshepsut had made for them, with colored beads, gold clasps, and a gold amulet of the goddess Satet in front. When they arrived, the aids were not allowed to enter the court with the prince and Bek informed the prince that he must remove his dagger. He responded with a challenging statement that he would not remove his dagger. Then Bae, in a low voice that sounded more like distant thunder, "This 'nubie' hopes you try and enter my Noble Ladies court without giving me your dagger."

Prince Barattarna was surprised to hear Bae refer to himself as a 'nubie', knowing that any resistance was hopeless, he reluctantly gave his dagger to Bek. He kept an eye on Bae who had a look of disappointment when he complied with their demand. The twins escorted Barattarna into the Royal Court which was dark because all the windows were covered. They approached Hatshepsut sitting on the throne with a large gold arch behind her, a few dim oil lamps were giving off some light around her. Prince Barattarna could just make out that she was petting a large male lion next to her and she was holding a staff with a large cobra's head in her right hand. Menna was standing on her right side with a covered basket at his feet.

The prince did not notice the strong lion trainer holding the lion from behind or Dadu standing close to the lion, ready to protect Hatshepsut. As he approached Hatshepsut, the lion raised his head and let out a ferocious roar. Hatshepsut raised her hand for him to stop, but the prince had already stopped in his tracks. His eyes began to adjust to the darkness, he could just barely see that there were soldiers on both sides of the room standing at attention. Before he could make out more detail, Hatshepsut asked, "Why is the Prince of Mitanni in Egypt?"

He tried to remain calm and in a very controlled voice, answered in poor Egyptian, "I bring our tribute to Egypt, our protector."

"If you lie to me, it will mean a slow and agonizing death."

"It is true," he quickly replied.

"You did not bring Pharaoh what is required annually, your gifts are of little value or interest except for birds that give birth every day. I will determine if you are truthful."

After Hatshepsut spoke, several things happened very quickly. She struck her staff on the floor and there was the very loud sound as fifty spears struck the shields of the soldiers surrounding the prince. At the same time all the windows were uncovered and the Court was flooded with bright light. The Prince looked around at the commotion, blinking his eyes trying to adjust to the bright light, he saw twenty-five female warriors on his left side wearing battle helmets and were bare breasted with spears and shields. When he looked to his right, he saw twenty-five Nubian soldiers also with spears and shields. Out of the corner of his eye he thought he saw Hatshepsut throw her cobra headed staff on the floor.

What actually happened, she made the throwing motion of the staff, Menna was holding the end of the staff and threw it behind them. When the staff hit the floor behind them, he kicked over the basket at his feet. The warriors and soldiers struck their spears on the floor again while this all took place, causing the prince to flinch and look again at the Nubian and female warriors. When he returned his gaze toward Hatshepsut, he gasped, her staff on the floor appeared to have turned into a serpent at her feet. The prince tried to turn and leave, but the twins took hold of his arms and held him in place. Bae looked at Bek and smiled, Bek shook his head at him.

A snake charmer had come up behind Prince Barattarna, holding a mouse in his hand, the cobra saw his trainer and slithered toward them. Again, the Prince wanted to leave, but was held by the twins. With a hand motion by the charmer, the cobra rose almost as high as the prince's chest. "What are you doing?" he demanded.

"My serpent knows if you lie to Pharaoh's Daughter, be very careful how you answer, your life depends on your answers. Did you come to Egypt to supply soldiers to aid Vizier Tinfurer in an attempt to overthrow Pharaoh?" Hatshepsut asked, knowing that he had not.

"No!" answered the prince.

Hatshepsut nodded her head yes and the charmer moved his hand holding the mouse back and forth, the cobra waved his body with the charmer's hand. "Did you know of the Vizier and the High Priest's plan to overthrow Pharaoh?"

Again, the prince answered, "No."

This time Hatshepsut shook her head no, the charmer made a striking motion with his hand, the serpent made a loud hissing sound and moved slightly toward the prince, appearing to be ready to strike. This time the twins and the prince stepped back, almost on the charmer's feet.

"So, you knew! What was to be your part in their plan? Do not lie again or you will die."

He answered contritely, "Mitanni was to be paid by the Vizier not to invade Egypt when the High Priest came to power."

"What about your sister on your ship?" Hatshepsut asked accusingly.

A very surprised prince wondered how the Egyptian Princess knew about his sister, with his head hanging down, "The Foreign Ambassador Ipi desires her."

"It is a very weak and cowardly king and prince that would not defend an innocent child." Hatshepsut commanded the twins sarcastically, "Remove this brave man from my sight, bring him and his aides back after I decide their fate." When he was gone, the charmer led the cobra back to its basket and threw in the mouse, the serpent went into the basket and the lid was placed on the basket. Menna moved between Hatshepsut and the lion as the trainer led it away.

Senenmut congratulated Hatshepsut, "Pharaoh's Daughter was wonderful, the prince believes My Lady is a goddess and magician."

Hatshepsut smiled, "A goddess that almost jumped off the throne when the lion surprised me with his loud roar. I was about ready to leave with the prince!"

"I think the prince wet himself!" Tyia replied with a laugh, "I was convinced that My Lady did turn her staff into a serpent."

"I think it is time to bring back the prince and aides," Senenmut suggested.

"Yes, bring them back, so we can be rid of them."

Outside the twins let Prince Barattarna confer with his aides in private. Bae laughed when he saw how animated the prince was as he described the events that had happened inside with Hatshepsut. "All of Mitanni will think our Noble Lady has magical powers," Bek commented.

From the palace door, Senenmut motioned for the twins to bring back the prince and his aides. The three men reluctantly followed the twins. They stood very quietly before Hatshepsut. "We have decided to spare your lives, because you were not going to play an active role in the Vizier's attempt at overthrowing Pharaoh. Prince Barattarna, you will inform your father that next year's tribute will be twice what is normally due, because of his actions. We will keep your sister here to guarantee payment, I am sure you wish no harm for her. If you do not pay the amount commanded, Pharaoh's mighty army will march into your land and bring back your head to me. I will have this command given to you in your own language, so there can be no confusion."

Hatshepsut motioned for Tyia to repeat her command in Hurrian. Tyia stepped forward as the three men stared at Tyia, Hatshepsut thought they just admired her beauty. But when she saw the men exchange questioning looks, she knew that it must be something else. As Tyia translated Hatshepsut's command, they listened and made no objections, they did not take their questioning eyes off of Tyia. When she had finished, Hatshepsut asked, "Do you understand?"

All three acknowledged, yes.

"When do you wish to leave?" she sarcastically asked.

"Tomorrow, if it pleases Pharaoh's Daughter," Prince Barattarna replied.

"Excellent, my interpreter and Commander Menna will go with you now to your ship and take your sister. Leave," she commanded. When they arrived at the prince's ship, Menna had Dadu stay with the three Mitanni men. He and Tyia went aboard in search of the girl. When their eyes adjusted to the darkness, they saw her in the back corner of the lower cabin, she was obviously very scared.

"We are not here to harm you," Tyia held out her hand as she spoke to the girl in Hurrian. The young girl came out of the shadows and Tyia could not help but catch her breath, she was surprised how much they favored.

Menna whispered, "The girl could be your little sister."

Tyia replied, "More like me at that age!" The girl came to Tyia as she looked at her closely, she too saw the resemblance. "My name is Tyia and we have come to take you off this boat and to safety." The young girl nodded her head yes. "Is there anything you wish to bring? My husband will help you," as she gestured to Menna. Letting go of Tyia's hand, she went back to retrieve a large leather bag. "Is that all?" Tyia asked, wanting to ensure that they would not have to return to the ship.

The girl spoke for the first time, "Yes," as she took Tyia's hand. Walking past the prince and his aides, Menna said nothing, but he wished he could take his new mace and crush all three men's skulls. The young Mitanni princess did not speak or look at her brother as she walked past him, she continued holding Tyia's hand.

From one of the other Mitanni boats, a hidden Ambassador Ipi watched the young girl he had desired. She was the main reason he had went along with the failed plan of the High Priest. His life had been ruined because of the old Pharaoh's daughter, he vowed to somehow get revenge against the spoiled daughter. He could hear the girl when she asked Tyia where they were going. Tyia answered, "To Pharaoh's Daughter."

"Will I be a slave to Pharaoh's Daughter?" the girl asked as they continued toward the palace.

He could not hear Tyia's answer as they walked farther away, but he hated Hatshepsut even more, now she possessed the girl he lusted for.

Tyia answered softly, "No, she only wishes you to be safe." When they arrived at Hatshepsut's door, she saw Bae, and stopped a short distance from the imposing Bae.

Sensing her concern, he made a big gesture of bowing and smiling, "I am here to protect the little princess." The young girl laughed at his exaggerated motion, he opened the door, "Please enter princess," again he exaggerated his bow. Tyia was not sure if the young girl understood him but she was sure his actions helped relieve some of her concerns.

Hatshepsut was talking with Senenmut, Tyia saw the questioning look on their faces, "This is Pharaoh's Daughter," introducing the girl to Hatshepsut.

The girl walked toward Hatshepsut carrying her leather bag, she bowed and in very broken Egyptian, "I am Princess Istustaya, am I to be given to this man?" as she looked at Senenmut.

Hatshepsut shook her head no, surprised that she knew some Egyptian, "No Princess Istustaya, you are to be given to no one." Hatshepsut answered, with some difficulty pronouncing her strange and foreign name. "I only wish for your safety from your brother and father."

Tyia repeated what Hatshepsut said, Istustaya's reply was a whisper, "Thank you."

Hatshepsut smiled at her, "You may stay in Egypt as long as you wish and you may return to Mitanni at any time." Tyia repeated what Hatshepsut had said.

Istustaya did not understand how Pharaoh's Daughter knew so much about her, "I wish to stay in Egypt forever," she replied.

"I am glad, Tyia will take care of you." Hatshepsut said

with a glance at Tyia to make sure that it was alright.

Tyia smiled, "Come with me Istustaya."

After they had departed, Senenmut said, "There has to be some relationship between Tyia and the girl. Tyia's grandmother must have been related to the girl's family."

"Yes, I am sure that Tyia has many questions also."

It was decided that Tyia would care for her and arrangements were made for Naomi to stay with them. Ramose was presented to the Royal Court as Pharaoh's new Vizier in Lower Egypt, the decree was read by Hatshepsut. Ramose, a loyal friend of Pharaoh, was now Vizier. When Ramose stepped to his new throne, he thanked Pharaoh's Daughter and vowed to fulfil his duties in a manner pleasing to Maat and Pharaoh. The Royal Court members and Temple Priests readily accepted Ramose as the Vizier of Lower Egypt. They were relieved that someone from Thebes had not been chosen to rule as Vizier and punish them for the actions of the former Vizier.

That evening after her meal with her Red Court, Menna said, "I have some information about the small sailboat we saw at the royal dock."

"Yes, what did you learn?"

"After we first saw the boat, I asked Captain Kawab about the boat. It is a young man who lives on the other side of the River who is in love with a girl that was sold as an indentured servant to the palace. He comes with his brightly patched sails so she can recognize him and see he still loves her. Both are on their own, neither has parents."

"How long has he been doing it?"

"The girl was sold by her uncle just before the last inundation. Captain Kawab states that his little boat almost sinks each time he crosses the River."

Everyone was quiet, thinking about the two lovers and

the displayed affection by the young boy. Hatshepsut told Menna, "Have Kawab bring the boy to the palace and find the girl, when he comes again."

"Yes, My Lady."

"We must get these two together before he drowns."

The next days were more like what Hatshepsut had expected when she left her family and home in Thebes. They had settled into a relaxed routine and her Red Court enjoyed the new life they had. Hatshepsut requested that Senenmut help Tyia with Istustaya, the young girl was very eager to learn all she could about Egypt. Her long light-colored hair was very striking because it was almost down to her waist. Hatshepsut and Tyia had short shoulder length hair while most women of Egypt had chosen to shave their heads because of the heat and wore wigs on formal occasions. Tyia offered once to cut her hair, but Istustaya demonstrated how she could pull it up in back. Her hair then reminded them of a horse's tail, she drew much attention from the staff and guards, which pleased her. Senenmut commented to Hatshepsut that she was strong willed and quick to learn, with interest in art and the luxurious life style of the palace.

The responsibilities of Menna, Dadu, and the twins became less stressful because there was no obvious threat to Hatshepsut. The palace was now a safe place for her, the night watch duty was always performed by one of the twins, while either Menna or Dadu were with her during the day. Hatshepsut still occasionally had nightmares about the assassins, so the twin on night duty stayed in her quarters.

One morning when she woke and retrieved her dagger, Bek had polished and oiled the blade. She knew that he had come to her bed, most likely checking on her after one of her dreams. He was still her favorite, although she trusted Bae fully. With only one person required to be with her, this allowed them to have a more relaxed and enjoyable life. They now had free time to rest, explore Memphis, and exercise. The twins found plenty of female entertainment in the palace and city, while Tyia and Menna enjoyed being newlyweds, sightseeing and thanking the gods for their good fortune.

During her morning meals, she always watched for the sail boat, but several days passed before he returned. She was excited as she watched Captain Kawab motion for him to dock. Captain Kawab led the boy toward the Palace, she decided that today's meetings with the members of the Royal Court would be late. She sent Abet to find Tyia, when she arrived, Hatshepsut told her, "The young boy in the sail boat is back."

"What does my Sister plan on doing?"

"I want the two lovers to be together." They waited for what seemed a long time before Captain Kawab was announced at her door by Dadu.

"What have you learned?" Hatshepsut asked as he entered before he could say a word.

"My Lady, the boy's name is Pebes and the girl is Nane, she works in the palace. When I saw the patched sail coming, I sent for her. I was relieved to finally see him because I had told him not to return until he patched the boat."

"So, that is why we have not seen him, I don't know how best to help them."

"My Lady," Captain Kawab hesitated, "I have spoken to my wife about them, if it pleases Pharaoh's Daughter, we wish to bring them into our home."

"I know that you and your wife have no children, but this is the wish of Manoti also?"

Captain Kawab slightly bowed, "Manoti will be honored that Pharaoh's Daughter remembers her name. Yes, My Lady, it is her desire also. I am sure I can find some place in the palace for the boy to work and when the girl has repaid her servitude, she can live with us also."

"I will have the debt removed and arrange for a new boat for him. We cannot allow him to drown, Egypt needs good sailors."

Hatshepsut followed Captain Kawab and stopped a distance from the couple as they sat in the shade. He talked to them for a while, and then gestured toward Hatshepsut. The two young lovers bowed, when they looked again, Pharaoh's Daughter was gone.

Evenings were spent with a meal and conversation shared by her Red Court. One evening Senenmut mentioned that the young princess had shown him several small rolls of parchment that were in her leather bag, they were manuals for training horses. She informed him that her mother's brother, General Kikkuli, was the head horse trainer for her father's army. Her uncle had written the manuals and that she had become very close to him after her mother died. Her uncle had tried to protect her from her father and told her to resist him.

There were many arguments between her uncle and father, Istustaya then related how one morning she went to her uncle's quarters and found him dead and that she suspected her father had murdered him. She took some of her uncle's prized possessions and the manual to remember him. Shortly after her uncle's death, her father, the King announced that she would be given to a visiting Egyptian official as his wife. When Tyia asked her how old she is, she said that she is thirteen, she seemed younger to everyone. Tyia had started calling her Iset, it was much easier to pronounce and she liked the sound of her new Egyptian name.

CHAPTER SIXTEEN

The Royal Library

Correspondence from her parents started arriving in Memphis after a month, the first letters from her parents expressed outrage and disbelief at the attempt on her life. Queen Ahmose told her daughter how proud her father was of her and that he was relieved to finally know who was responsible for his son's assassination, saying that her father seemed to be at peace for the first time since Prince Amenmose's death. Hatshepsut privately cried when she read her mother's words, "Pharaoh's Daughter has given her father a great gift. We are now certain that you will save our family's dynasty."

So much was expected of her and failure was becoming her worst fear. Senenmut and Hatshepsut's relationship had settled into a comfortable and relaxed association between them. He had accepted the life that the gods had deemed for him. Iset was interested in learning all she could about Egypt and she never mentioned her home or family. "It is as if she has accepted her new life in Egypt and is grateful to be away from her family," Tyia once commented.

One afternoon Hatshepsut, Tyia, and Iset were at the garden pools, where they were often joined by Jochebed and baby Moses, they found out how old Iset probably was. During one visit, Iset asked when the baby would be two years old? Her question surprised them, Tyia stated that the baby was just four months old, Iset said that the baby was one year old and would be two on his next birthday. During the following discussion it was discovered that in Mitanni when a person is born, he is said to be one year old and that on his first birthday, he would become two years old. When Iset was asked when she had her last birthday, she said that it was just before she left Mitanni. Hatshepsut and Tyia exchanged glances, this explained a lot and they both realized that Iset was just barely twelve years old. She was only eleven when her father decided to give her to the corrupt Egyptian Ambassador.

They had a new appreciation of just how strong she must be to have endured all the uncertainty and fear. Hatshepsut had a new resolve to make certain that Iset's life in Egypt would be without fear.

One evening when Senenmut was alone with Hatshepsut he told her of a new discovery, it pleased her to see him happy and knew that he was always finding some new subject or interest to challenge him. He explained that in the study time that day with Tyia and Iset, he had learned some information from the text that Iset had brought with her from her home. Her uncle Kikkuli was indeed the Master Horse Trainer for the Mitanni Army. The text contained detailed instructions on caring for, exercising, and the training of horses that were used to pull chariots. It was nothing like the training and care the Egyptians used for their horses, the Mitanni training period for their horses lasted 214 days.

Hatshepsut was still very curious about the Hebrew Vizier of Lower Egypt that Jochebed's grandmother, Hannah, had mentioned. The events that occurred with finding the baby, Jochebed's grandmother, and the baby's warning them of the assassins were often in her thoughts. Did Sitre know of a Hebrew Vizier, she wondered? During previous visits to the Royal House of Books, she found all the usual records, there were even manuscripts on how to appease the gods, drive away lions, and repulse crocodiles and hippos. A section was devoted to medicines and magic, a very large section was for the inventory of items in palaces and temples, of livestock, crop production, and even the number of captured slaves.

But of all the records Hatshepsut found, none mentioned a

Vizier named Joseph. She had questioned the Chief Book Scribe about any records of a Hebrew Vizier named Joseph. He replied that there were no records in this House of any Vizier with the name of Joseph. That was an odd answer, she thought, but did not think more of it.

Hatshepsut asked Tyia to spend the day with her, she planned on searching the House of Books. They visited for a while, talking about what was going on in their lives, while Abet finished her hair. Hatshepsut also wanted to know if Menna was getting bored with palace life, since it had thankfully become routine. Tyia replied that he was happy and relieved that Pharaoh's Daughter was in no apparent danger. "We are happy spending time together and exploring Memphis." She then commented on how she had gained weight since arriving in Memphis. "There are so many different and abundant foods to enjoy," Tyia laughed, "I cannot eat all the sweet cakes I desire." Hatshepsut thought that she was even lovelier than when she first met her, she had a fuller figure, most women would be jealous of such a beautiful woman.

Hatshepsut said that she wanted to do some research at the Royal House of Books. Leaving her quarters, she was pleased to find Bek still on duty, "How is my friend, today?"

He smiled, "The gods favor me with service to Pharaoh's Daughter."

"We will be going to the Royal House of Books again." The Royal House of Books was not attached to the palace, but it was within the large white walls that surrounded the palace complex. The library had a courtyard with a pool surrounded by mature established trees and plants that offered shade. Around the perimeter of the courtyard were many shaded areas where one could sit and read.

They had stopped to admire some yellow lotus blossoms in the pool when a hummingbird flew directly in front of Hatshepsut and stopped. The little bird shimmered with its many iridescent colors reflecting the morning sun as it remained hovering in front of Hatshepsut. She felt chill bumps on her arms as she enjoyed the delightful moment. After a few seconds, the beautiful little bird made a quick dart toward a shaded area in the corner of the courtyard. Before anyone could comment on seeing the hummingbird, it was back and fussing this time at them. Again, it flew in the same direction, but slower this time and stopped after a short distance. Hatshepsut commented, "I think we are supposed to follow him." The little bird led them to a shaded corner where an old man was sitting on a bench holding a small bowl for the hummingbird, that was now on his finger. When the old man noticed them, he quickly stood and bowed. "You seem to have a friend," as the little bird flew away.

"Yes, Noble Lady, I come here often and bring him a bowl of sweet water."

"You know who I am?"

"Yes, I have seen Pharaoh's daughter go into the Royal House of Books before."

Hatshepsut asked that he sit with her, as she sat down on the bench. He looked at Tyia and the large Nubian guard and sat as far away from her as he could on the small bench. Trying to put the old man at ease, "It seems your little friend led me to you. Are you a Book Scribe in the Royal House of Books?"

"I am no longer a Book Scribe because the Vizier did not want Hebrews working in any important positions. Now I come here to just be near the place I love."

"I regret your treatment by the former Vizier who did not serve Pharaoh or Maat well, are you not allowed in the House of Books?"

"No, Noble Lady, not in the House of Books or the quarters I once lived in," he sadly answered.

She took a chance and asked the old librarian, "I have

been looking for any records of a Hebrew Vizier named Joseph. Do you remember ever reading anything about him?"

There was some hesitation by the old librarian, he moved closer to Hatshepsut and looked directly at her, Bek made a step closer to them. "Pharaoh's Daughter is known by my people here." He paused, "The records of Joseph do exist in the Royal House of Books, but they are hidden."

Hatshepsut now angry, asked, "You have seen these records?"

"Yes, Noble Lady, he was a great Vizier."

"Why are they hidden?" Hatshepsut questioned.

"Over the years many Pharaohs and Viziers have commanded that the recorded histories of certain events and their failures be destroyed. The Royal Book Scribes have tried to save all manuscripts they could and have gone against these commands at the risk of their lives. Other records have been hidden to protect secrets that may fall into enemy hands and could be used against Egypt. You must know that I am breaking my oath to my profession by telling you of such a place."

Hatshepsut could not believe what she had just heard, "How can I see these records without betraying you?"

The old book scribe thought for a few moments, "Ask to see the Livestock, Crop and Mine Records of Pharaoh Mentuhotep II, the records will show the name of the Vizier you are looking for. These records tell of the dark times when 70 Kings ruled in 70 days. It is during those years of chaos that the Vizier Joseph lived, but he will be using his Egyptian name and you will need to look for a Vizier named Zaphnath-Paaneah."

"His name means, To Whom Mysteries are Revealed," why such a strange name?

"God have him the ability to interpret dreams, this was how he came to be Vizier," the old man answered.

Hatshepsut placed her hand on his arm, "What is your name?"

"Levi."

"You are named after one of the Hebrew tribes."

"Yes, My Lady," he answered, surprised that an Egyptian Princess would know this.

"Levi, I will not betray your trust," she looked around the courtyard and saw no one, "I will be going inside now, you should leave first." They waited by the pool until they were certain that Levi had left, the hummingbird did not return.

When they entered the Royal House of Books, they were quickly met by the Chief Book Scribe. He bowed and asked, "How may I serve Pharaoh's Daughter today?" She smiled, he noticed her smile, it was the first time she had smiled at him. He did not know that she was playing with her prey, "I would like to see the records of Livestock, Crops, and Mine production during the reign of Pharaoh Mentuhotep II."

"Why would Pharaoh's Daughter want to see such mundane information?" was the confident questioning reply from the Librarian. When he questioned her, Tyia saw Bek move slightly toward him and she tensed waiting for Hatshepsut's reply. The Chief Book Scribe saw the Nubian move and he also saw the smile melt away from her face, he had made a serious mistake in questioning Pharaoh's Daughter.

She had him wait a long time for her reply, he knew that there would be consequences for his actions. The young daughter of Pharaoh had been pleasant in her previous visits to the library and he had forgotten the absolute power she had. Finally, she spoke, "You do not question the reasons or actions of Pharaoh or his Daughter. Find me one of your assistants who can get the information I desire, then you will leave. We will decide if you have a future as Chief Book Scribe tomorrow."

The Chief Book Scribe bowed low, "Yes, Sovereign."

The Chief Book Scribe went to one of his assistants, who reluctantly returned with him. He bowed, "At you service, My Lady."

Hatshepsut glared at the Chief Book Scribe, "Leave!" He bowed low and was glad to leave.

While the Book Scribe was retrieving the records, they waited outside in the cool shade next to the pool, Tyia kept searching for the little bird. "I believe the Chief Book Scribe will give me the information tomorrow about the Vizier Zaphnath-Paaneah," Hatshepsut stated as she let the anger slowly drain away. When the Assistant Book Scribe came and informed Hatshepsut that he had found the records, she returned to the House of Books. Tyia said that she would return with refreshments.

It was midafternoon before Hatshepsut found the record she was looking for. She smiled when she saw his name, Vizier Zaphnath-Paaneah and his statement that he was personally recording this account for his Pharaoh Mentuhotep II. Hatshepsut knew little about the Pharaoh who ruled in Lower Egypt during the first time when the Two Lands were not united and chaos reigned. She did remember that he was the Pharaoh who reunited Egypt into one nation again.

When she touched the pen strokes of the old documents that were almost 500 years old, they seemed almost alive. She motioned to the Book Scribe who was watching her from a distance. When he arrived, she requested information about this Vizier Zaphnath-Paaneah, she could tell that he was not familiar with the name. After a period of time, Hatshepsut was not surprised that he could not find any information about this Vizier. "Inform the Chief Book Scribe to find the records. I will return tomorrow."

On the way back to her quarters, Bek stated with a big grin, "It was a very interesting day to serve my Noble Lady."

"It was indeed," Hatshepsut replied, happy with her discovery, Senenmut would find her new information interesting tonight, it was good to have someone to share things with.

Hatshepsut was awake early, she had slept well, she had discussed the events with Senenmut. He could not believe that there was a place where such ancient documents had been saved by dedicated scribes, who were willing to risk the wrath of Pharaohs and Viziers. He admired their courage to preserve history, but he warned that we must be prepared for disappointment about some things we may learn. There was a reason that the records had been condemned for destruction.

They were met by a very humble Chief Book Scribe, there was a fatigued look on the Librarian's face, he had cleaned up and tried to look his best, but he obviously had not gotten any sleep the night before. She was hoping for the best as he bowed.

"Rise," she commanded. "Your assistant found the records I was looking for yesterday, I discovered the name of the Hebrew Vizier I was looking for." There was no reaction from the Chief Book Scribe. "I want you to consider your answer to my next questions very carefully, have you ever heard of this Vizier?"

"Yes, my Sovereign, I know this name."

Hatshepsut felt great relief, perhaps the Chief Book Scribe would cooperate after all. "Do you know of any records of a Hebrew Vizier anywhere?" Hatshepsut demanded.

"Yes," and with a pause he continued, "I have found some of the records for my Sovereign, they are here," he pointed to a table with several scrolls on it.

She could not let the Chief Librarian know how much she knew, so she asked, "Are there other records and why keep the information from me when I asked for it?"

The Librarian's posture softened a little, he had given in. "What my Sovereign demands of me, requires me to break an oath that I and many others have taken to save records that we were told to destroy."

Hatshepsut pointed to Menna, "This is my personal body guard, Commander Menna and this is my Chief Advisor, Senenmut. We wish to go to the location where the records are kept."

The Chief Librarian knew that her "wish" had to be obeyed, "What my Sovereign requests, I will be honored to do."

She saw the excitement on Senenmut's face, he was like a boy sometimes, he loved discovery. "Take us to this location." she commanded, already knowing the answer.

"It is here in the Royal House of Books, My Lady," was his reply as he led them through the library to his office. The office had a large room off to one side, in it were manuscripts on several tables and the walls were lined with more shelves holding clay cylinders containing manuscripts. The other side of the office led to the living space for the Chief Book Scribe. They were led into the room with tables, the Chief Librarian went to an oil lamp attached to the wall and he blew out the flame and rotated the lamp. The lamp was made in such a manner that the oil did not spill out. He then went to the corner of the room in an area that was not occupied by shelves, he pushed on the wall and the corner opened. Steps led down to a basement area, Hatshepsut followed Menna down the steps, a slight shiver came over her as she entered the basement. The librarian began to light lamps, as the light grew brighter the large size of the area was revealed. There was a strong scent of lamp oil, old linen and cedar, the tables and shelves were made of the rare wood.

After all the lamps were lit, the Chief Book Scribe returned, he waited for Hatshepsut to speak. "How far back in our history do the documents go?"

The librarian thought for a moment, "I am not sure, My Lady, I have read some that tell how and when the pyramids were built."

"Over a thousand years!" she whispered. "I wish to see

the documents about Vizier Zaphnath-Paaneah and the Hebrews first."

The Chief Librarian replied, "I have found some about the Hebrew Vizier, but the Assistant Librarian who knew the most about that subject was dismissed by the former Vizier."

"Is he still alive?" Hatshepsut asked about the assistant he spoke of, knowing that is was most likely Levi.

"Yes, he is My Lady."

"I wish for this assistant to help me and for him to be re-instated to his former position, what is his name?"

"His name is Levi, My Lady."

She was right! "What do you suggest we do for Levi to make up for the injustice he has received from the former Vizier?" She wanted the Chief Librarian to come up with some ideas on his own.

He thought for a moment, "Levi could move back into the scribe quarters and since he is old, he could work only when he wished."

"That is very generous of the Chief Librarian, perhaps you could assure Levi that he has this arrangement for as long as he lives?"

"As My Lady wishes."

Hatshepsut was pleased that the old assistant could come back, work and live in the place he loved. "I will look forward to seeing Levi tomorrow. For now, I wish to see what the Chief Book Scribe has found for me."

The Chief Book Scribe and Levi were waiting for Hatshepsut the following morning, he introduced Levi to her.

Levi bowed, "I am forever grateful to Pharaoh's Daughter."

"It was the Chief Book Scribe who recommended that you return and be rewarded for honorable service to Pharaoh." Hatshepsut answered him with a smile, they both shared a secret.

Senenmut went to the secret library, Levi led Hatshepsut to a table, "I think Pharaoh's Daughter will find this interesting." He showed her a beautiful rich colored dark red leather-bound manuscript. "It is almost 500 years old, written by the Vizier you seek." Hatshepsut touched the manuscript with the leather wrapping that was still amazingly supple. She examined the lettering engraved on the cover, the first part was in Egyptian, "My History, Vizier Zaphnath-Paaneah." Hatshepsut could not believe the second part of the title.

Levi saw her closely examining the writing that was not Egyptian, "I believe the other language is some form of a Semitic language that I am not familiar with. I assume it also tells who the author is."

Hatshepsut slowly answered, "Perhaps," it was as if Joseph was speaking directly to her in the secret language of the architects that Senenmut had taught her, it said, "My People's History is Recorded in this Language." Am I the first person to understand his words since he wrote them? She wondered, as goose bumps rose on her arms. "Are there other manuscripts written in this language," she asked.

"Not that I know of My Lady, but they would not have been saved because no one could read the language."

Levi was very surprised when she whispered, "I can read this language."

"What does it say?"

"Joseph recorded the history of your people in this language somewhere."

Hatshepsut carefully unrolled the manuscript with

Levi's help. Menna took a seat where he could watch Hatshepsut and the entry into the room, he knew that he would be here
all day. Pharaoh's Daughter was happy and excited, this pleased
him. Levi helped Hatshepsut read the document because the
ancient Egyptian language often used, forgotten Lower Egypt
words. Lower and Upper Egypt were indeed two different nations, Hatshepsut knew that she must never forget this. The
story of Joseph unfolded slowly as Ra rode his chariot across the
sky.

She finished the manuscript that Joseph had written and
found no more secret writing in the scroll. There were no clues
as to where the secret manuscript was hidden. Then Levi
brought her another manuscript, it was a record of how the
Hebrew people were punished after the Hyksos were expelled.
They lost all of their possessions, land, and freedom. To de-
crease their influence, many were moved from the Delta and
spread throughout Egypt. Hatshepsut knew this had happened,
that was how Sitre's family had come to live in Thebes. She read
of the cruel things that had happened to them in Lower Egypt,
she could see why the records had been hidden or destroyed. It
was during this time that the first killing of innocents had taken
place, but on a much larger scale than what she had seen on her
arrival in Memphis.

After reading the account, she looked at Levi who had
been watching her closely. "I thought My Lady should know," he
sadly replied.

After the evening meal, Hatshepsut enjoyed her favorite
lotus wine and listened as Senenmut talked about his discover-
ies while Abet and Naomi served them and finished their tasks.
Senenmut said that he had found plans of the Royal Palace, the
plans showed the tunnels they had discovered and no others,
but he was not sure if the plans were complete because they did
not show the secret library. He also discovered a document on
the construction of a canal from the River to the Red Sea that
was never completed, he was intrigued by the idea because it

would be a great benefit to travel and commerce. There was a document that explained when and how the Egyptian triangle sail was made, the date of the record showed that this discovery was over two thousand years ago. He just shook his head, "I had never given it any thought about when and how our sails were designed."

Abet and Naomi had just joined them, Hatshepsut shifted her position on her cushion to be more erect and facing the group, "I would like to tell you what I discovered today about the Hebrew Vizier Joseph." All eyes were on her, she always got their full attention because it was still a huge honor for them to be addressed by the future Queen.

"Vizier Joseph starts with his family's history and ends shortly before his death. He lived when Pharaoh Mentuhotep II, the great Pharaoh from Thebes who defeated rebellious Governors in Lower Egypt, ruled. Upper and Lower Egypt were united after the first period of shame when Egypt was divided. He goes into great detail about his family and events that occurred during his life. I will be brief on some of the details, Joseph wrote about conflict in his family's history, which is typical of rivalries in all families.

Joseph claimed to be his father's favorite son of his ten half-brothers and one brother. He had dreams that were very vivid and one of them told of how his brothers would one day bow down to him, as you can imagine, his older brothers did not like this. They plotted against him, thought of killing him but instead sold him as a slave. He became the property of a high Egyptian official. The brothers told their father that he had been killed by a lion. Joseph was seventeen when this occurred.

Joseph soon was in charge of his master's house, the official's land and possessions grew because of Joseph's gift. It was through his dreams that he knew his current position was God's plan and that one day his family would be saved because of him. He was able to forgive his brothers, not allowing revenge to take charge of his life." Hatshepsut paused, she tried to put herself in his position, she did not know if she could have forgiven his brothers for such a deed. She wished she was as sure as Joseph was about why he was having the dreams.

Hatshepsut continued, "The high Egyptian official who Joseph served was pleased with Joseph, but one day the official's wife wrongly accused Joseph of attempted rape. The official knew his wife was lying, so he did not have him put to death, instead he put him in prison. The Officer in Charge of the prison was the official's friend. There Joseph was given duties and served his new master well and interpreted the dreams of others. When Pharaoh started having dreams that his priests did not understand, he was informed about Joseph. Pharaoh sent for him and Joseph was able to tell Pharaoh the meaning of his dreams. They foretold of a future famine and how Pharaoh should prepare for it. Pharaoh believed Joseph's interpretations of his dreams so he placed Joseph in charge of preparing for the coming famine."

"So, what happened to Joseph next?" Tyia excitedly asked.

"He was made Vizier and he returned to Lunu, the City of Pillars and the Temple of Ra. Eventually, he married the daughter of a priest and was in charge of preparing for the coming famine. It should be no surprise that the dream came true. During the famine all of Egypt, including the former rogue governors, came to Pharaoh for help. It was Joseph's idea for Pharaoh to trade the property held by the governors for food and seed. It was also his idea that a fifth of the future harvests produced on what was now Pharaoh's land be returned to Pharaoh. This is still the required payment today for using Pharaoh's land. Because of these events during the famine, Pharaoh was able to regain ownership of all the land and take power from the local Governors.

It was also during this time of famine that Joseph's

brothers came to Egypt, pleading for food and bowed down to the Vizier. They did not recognize him and did not realize that his boyhood dream was fulfilled. Joseph was able to have his elderly father and family move to Egypt to prosper and grow."

Menna asked, "So he did not seek revenge on his brothers?"

"No, he did not and he was able to save his family, today we have the twelve tribes of the Hebrews and their vast numbers in Egypt today. Joseph told his family to serve both their God and Pharaoh. Because of this, the Hebrew people were accepted by Egyptians and they prospered and grew."

Everyone was quiet as they thought about the Hebrew Vizier who had saved the lives of his family and many people in Egypt. A Hebrew Vizier who had perhaps even saved the Egyptian way of life. Naomi was the first to speak, "Does My Lady believe the story?"

Hatshepsut took her time to answer, she still had many questions, but she wanted to answer truthfully to Naomi about her people. She also knew that Sitre would learn of her answer, "There are several documents that name the Hebrew Vizier, so I do believe he existed and it would take a series of remarkable events for a Hebrew to become Vizier in Egypt. I have been involved in events that I cannot explain."

Menna said, "A dream about a lion that saved many lives from a flash flood, finding the Hebrew baby, how the crying baby probably saved our lives, and even the leading of a tiny hummingbird."

Smiling at him, Dadu and Tyia, "Also an ear ache that prevented me for sailing on the River and send me into the Red Land to find you."

CHAPTER SEVENTEEN

Great Green Sea

Harvest was almost complete in Egypt, it was the third month of Shemu, in a few weeks the tears of Isis would start the annual inundation of the River. Plans were already being made for the five days of feasting, celebrating the harvest and the end of the year. Tax collectors were busy throughout Egypt recording and collecting Pharaoh's share of the year's profits and the reports would soon be completed. Hatshepsut had been busy working with the members of the Royal Court of Memphis and she was pleased with the new appointments, most of the original Members of Court appeared to be loyal to Pharaoh and her.

The uneasy and dangerous time at the beginning of her visit to Memphis was past and now Hatshepsut was accepted and trusted. The Royal Court still remembered her actions toward the corrupt Vizier and the vile High Priest Rewer, Senenmut had recommended that she maintain some distance and remain a threat, "A strong King uses both the crook to guide and the threat of the flail to rule," he said. It had been six months since leaving Thebes and the excitement she had at the beginning was gone, like her father, she enjoyed adventure and action. After an evening meal and time with her Red Court, she asked Senenmut to remain, he was always happy to have some private time with her.

"Have the Medjey discovered any information about the missing Ambassador Ipi or the former Captain of the Palace Guards?"

"No, My Lady, someone is always watching both families,

Ipi's family have been moved out of the Ambassador Quarters into a small house. The State Police believes his wife when she claims no knowledge of his location or actions. The Medjey will not give up their search, My Lady."

"I am tired of Memphis," Hatshepsut stated with a pretend pout.

Senenmut knew she was, she was drinking more of her lotus wine, "What does My Lady desire?"

"I want to see the great Green Sea."

"I would love to see the great sea also, when does My Lady wish to leave?"

"Soon, make the arrangements." She commanded, in a fake royal commanding voice, already feeling better because Senenmut was in charge.

"What route does My Lady wish to take? There are seven major channels through the Delta," he informed her.

She had not given the route any thought, "I wish to take the route closest to the eastern desert, then I can visit Lunu and see if any descendants of Joseph are there."

"A wise choice," he replied.

Hatshepsut leaned over and gave him a hug, he loved her soft touch and sweet fragrance. "How can I reward my friend?"

"My reward is to serve Pharaoh's Daughter."

"Always the same answer," as she leaned back on the large soft cushion, she was quiet for just a moment and soon asleep. Senenmut watched her for a while and wondered if he was being used by her, then decided he did not care. He moved close to her and gently touched her face, she moved slightly, but did not wake up. During the day when Hatshepsut was in charge and fulfilling her duties, she appeared older and aloof. But, now as Senenmut watched her, she looked very young.

Abet came into the room, Senenmut acknowledged her,

"Tell My Lady goodnight," he whispered. Abet smiled and nodded yes. Leaving her quarters, he saw one of the twins in the shadows standing guard. He could not tell if it was Bae or Bek, but pity the person who tried to harm her.

Ra had not started his journey across the sky, but Hatshepsut was awake and ready to sail to the Green Sea. Menna arrived, letting her know that the royal barge, Falcon, was ready for Pharaoh's Daughter. It was decided that Bae and Iset would not go, she did not wish to travel to the Green Sea because that was in the direction of her brother and father. Her Red Court was waiting for her, Captain Kawab was also there, she had asked him about his family.

"We are healthy and are enjoying having Nane and Pebes living with us."

"I have seen Nane and Pebes in a new boat several times. It still has bright colored patches on the sail," Hatshepsut commented.

"It is a new sail, My Lady, but they wanted the patches on the sail so Pharaoh's Daughter could see them together." Captain Kawab bowed slightly.

As they departed, the morning sky was becoming a brilliant orange color, with the birds starting their morning songs. Hatshepsut tried not to show her excitement, she enjoyed watching and listening to everyone as they happily talked and laughed. She smiled as she observed the stoic Sergeant Dadu, who still did not like boats, and was constantly watching like a nervous mouse with stolen food.

Senenmut was his usual self, talking to the Captain and a man she did not recognize. She was sure that he was learning something from both of them. Menna was close and in hearing distance of her, but he was admiring his lovely wife taking in all the sights and sounds around her, she was indeed an artist, she could see beauty in almost anything. Hatshepsut noticed Bek, she had become used to his continuous watchful eye, was he being protective or admiring? She warmly smiled at him and he slightly nodded his head. It was good to be traveling and exploring new places, palace life and performing mundane duties was in her future, but not today. When Senenmut came near she asked, "Who is that with the Admiral?"

"He is our guide, there are many channels in the Delta, Admiral Ebana takes no chances with Pharaoh's Daughter."

"I must thank Admiral Ebana." When Ra was higher in Nut's belly and the sky was bright blue, the River started getting wider. In the distance the River could be seen disappearing into the lush tall growth of trees, papyrus plants, thick reeds, and rushes. The River was completing its long journey to the sea, Hatshepsut felt she was completing her reason for coming to Memphis, it was a good feeling. Holding a lotus blossom close to her face helped overcome the damp odor of the river mud, her thoughts were interrupted by Tyia.

"My sister seems distant, is everything alright?"

Hatshepsut smiled at her, "I enjoy being with my Red Court," Tyia sit down near her in silence. The Falcon neared the selected channel and Hatshepsut noticed that the River flow had slowed down considerably as it divided its waters into the many channels. Traveling deeper into the Delta, a different feeling overcame Hatshepsut. Living her life on the wide river she had always been able to see for great distances, but now in the Delta her vision was obstructed by bends in the narrow channels with tall reeds and grasses on both sides, it was a little uncomfortable for her. The sounds of different animals and birds, the smell of the wet soil and the lush vegetation, all were different.

Just past the tall reeds along the channel were large areas of cultivation that could occasionally be seen. The fields were much larger than those wedged in between the River and the Red Land in Upper Egypt.   Senenmut noticed the two lovely women sitting quietly together, "We are entering deep into Lower Egypt, My Lady."

"Yes, it is different here, does this channel have a name?" Hatshepsut asked to get her mind off the new alien landscape.

"Our guide said that it is called the Right Leg by the locals," he answered with a smile and waited for a comment.

Tyia asked, "Why would they call this channel such an odd name?"

"Egypt's story of the gods, say that Osiris was killed and cut up into fourteen pieces. The upper seven pieces were hidden in Upper Egypt and the lower seven pieces were hidden in Lower Egypt. So, this is his right leg," he stated with a slight laugh.

Hatshepsut asked, "Will we have a long day of sailing?"

"I asked Admiral Ebana a short time ago and he said we will be arriving at the City of Pillars soon." The barge turned and the rays of Ra shown directly in Hatshepsut's eyes, Senenmut quickly adjusted the canopy to protect her from the bright light, she nodded in appreciation.

Tyia stated, "I am sorry but I do not know much about this place." Hatshepsut looked at Senenmut indicating for him to answer Tyia, Menna heard Tyia's question and joined them to hear what Senenmut had to say. He told them about the five ancient Temples, the oldest in Egypt and the first two obelisks erected in Egypt are there. The holy Benben Stone that the god Atum sent into the primeval waters to cause creation is there. He paused, "I wonder if the Benben Stone is like the bones of the gods we see streaking across the night sky?" He continued, "The mythical Phoenix bird landed on the stone on that first dawn, it represented the first life to emerge from the dark waters. The Phoenix is now represented by the heron in art and statues, because the heron can be seen during the annual inundation of the River standing on isolated rocks in the flood plain."

"Joseph the Hebrew Vizier lived in the area of Lunu with his wife, the daughter of a High Priest. I hope there are descendants of Joseph that may still live there, will they remember him and admit their relationship?" Hatshepsut wondered.

Everyone was quiet in their thoughts as they continued through the lush environment, several crocodiles were seen and all got excited at seeing a hippopotamus. The stillness along the channel was occasionally interrupted by the sound of birds taking flight with the passing of the barge. The barge made a turn into a wider part of the River, the temples of Lunu came into view, the temple dock even had pillars, it was easy to see how it got its name, "City of Pillars." Further down the river, the city of Lunu and its large dock with many ships could be seen.

As Admiral Ebana eased the Falcon to the dock, Hatshepsut was welcomed, "Long live The Foremost of Noble Ladies, The beautiful daughter of Pharaoh Tuthmose, Lord of the Two Lands."

The governor and a very elderly High Priest greeted Hatshepsut, the leopard skin draped over one thin shoulder appeared to weigh heavy on the old man. Behind them a wide pillar lined road could be seen that led up to the distant temple complex. After formalities and introductions, the Governor offered his palace for refreshments and rest. Noticing how weak the High Priest appeared, she informed him that she wished to tour and pay homage to the temples later. "As Pharaoh's Daughter wishes," the High Priest stepped onto a large ornate carrying chair and was carried away by eight priests.

It was a short walk to the Governor's Palace during which he explained that the complex was laid out in a circle around the temples and that there were nine major roads radiating out from the center as if they were the rays of the god Atum. The nine roads were named after the nine gods of the ennead,

Hatshepsut noticed that the priests had different colored sashes around their waist, she assumed the different colors represented the different temples.

The palace complex was very organized, the layout was obviously planned, unlike Thebes, all the streets were paved. Arriving at the Governor's Palace during the hottest and most humid time of the day made the cool quarters appreciated, after a brief rest, a maid announced that refreshments were ready. Hatshepsut had changed into more formal attire and led her small entourage to enjoy drinks and food in the cool courtyard. From the courtyard there was a view of the River and dock in one direction and the temple in the other. She enjoyed the music and pleasant conversation with the Governor, "Do you have a family?"

"Yes, I have a wife and daughter and granddaughter. My daughter's husband is away, he is a captain on one of Lunu's ships. He is sailing to Lebanon to trade grain for cedar, to be used by Pharaoh."

Menna stood near Hatshepsut as the others enjoyed the food and drink, Tyia watched Hatshepsut and Senenmut as they visited with their host, she did not envy Hatshepsut always being on display and having to represent her Royal family. This was her first visit here and she must impress and gain the loyalty of these officials. Tyia noticed that all eyes were not on Hatshepsut, some ladies were very impressed with Bek. Once Tyia caught his eyes, she smiled at him, he returned her smile then resumed his watchful duties, she would have to tease him later.

Late afternoon when the heat began to subside, they proceeded to the temples. The tall walls could be seen from a distance and there appeared to be a crown in the center rising above the walls. Arriving at the complex, the Governor led them to the east gate which was much larger and more ornate then the three other gates. They were met by a priest, the Governor bowed and departed, the priest with an orange sash led them inside where the High Priest was sitting in the shade.

Senenmut commented that the walls were taller and thicker than those at Thebes. The High Priest proudly stated that he was correct, the complex was much older and larger than the temple complex in Thebes. When Hatshepsut was asked which temple she wished to see, she replied, "The Mansion of Benben."

The High Priest was not surprised that she wished to see the oldest and largest of temples. They followed the old priest as he walked slowly alone a paved path that was wide and lined by large old sycamore trees, their branches covered the path with the effect of a cool green tunnel. Behind the sycamore trees were many smaller paths that led to areas with several varieties of flowering plants, bushes, smaller trees, and small ponds. The High Priest pointed out some myrrh and frankincense trees.

Hatshepsut stopped to look at the trees she had never seen before, that produced the precious oil and resin that the Egyptians loved. The myrrh trees were small and thorny but the aromatic smell was obvious and sweet. The frankincense trees were scraggy and had no recognizable scent associated to them, she asked questions of the High Priest about their care. While the two talked, Tyia commented to Menna and Senenmut, "I have never been in such a forest of trees before." It was obvious that this was a very ancient site with its worn stone paths and large mature trees. Continuing through the lush setting, they entered a large opening with two red obelisks in view, "These are the first two obelisks erected in Egypt," stated the High Priest.

Hatshepsut informed the High Priest that Senenmut had just erected Egypt's two tallest obelisks in Thebes for Pharaoh, the High Priest acknowledged him with perhaps a little more respect. There were a series of ramps and columned structures on each of the three levels with the top level ringed by columns, this was the crown that could be seen from a distance. Senenmut commented that the ramps and levels reminded him of Pharaoh Mentuhotep II's mortuary complex in Thebes at Deir el-Bahari. The High Priest said that he was correct and that the Pharaoh had built his mortuary temple after visiting Lunu over five hundred years ago.

Hatshepsut stood silently as she looked at the beautiful ancient temple. "I have not seen Mentuhotep II's temple in Thebes," she commented.

"It will be my honor to show Pharaoh's Daughter the temple when we return to Thebes, but it is in need of much repair."

The High Priest led them to the base of the Temple where there was a sacred pool with a bridge over the pool that led to the first ramp. By the bridge were two priests and two priestesses wearing orange sashes, the priests were to take the men to one end of the pool and the priestesses were to lead Hatshepsut and Tyia to the other end. Menna hesitated, Hatshepsut stated, "Bek will stay with me."

Bek stayed close to Hatshepsut as they neared the end of the sacred pool where several nude priestesses were holding folded linen, small offerings, and playing quiet music on lyres.

Hatshepsut approached the pool first because she knew that Tyia would not know the cleansing ceremony required before entering the Holy of Holies in the temples of the gods. She removed her dagger and belt first, handing them to Bek, then she walked toward the pool, two priestesses helped her remove her shoes and tunic. She then stepped into the pool and descended the steps with the help of the two priestesses, the other priestesses offered prayers to Atum in unison asking Atum to accept her offering. After reaching the bottom of the pool, Hatshepsut was about waist deep, then she lowered herself completely underwater. Standing, she turned and started ascending back up the steps out of the pool.

The evening rays of Ra were very low and casting a golden

color over the temple complex, Bek could not keep his eyes off of her wet body as she stepped out of the water. She looked as if she had skin of gold with drops of gold dripping off of her, he bowed, with his eyes remaining on her feet. Priestesses helped Hatshepsut dry and dress in a new long linen tunic and new soft linen shoes. Tyia followed Hatshepsut's example and bathed in the pool, then a priestess gave her and Tyia a small gift of food, for their offerings.

They returned to where Senenmut, Menna, and Dadu were waiting in their new linen tunics, Hatshepsut could tell there was tension between Menna and the High Priest. Hatshepsut told Bek to go bathe and to join them later, she spoke to the High Priest, "Pharaoh's Daughter is ready to make my offering to Atum."

"It is not allowed for those making an offering to Atum to be armed," then he noticed that she was wearing her dagger.

"We will remain armed, the High Priest of Ptah murdered my brother and attempted to kill Pharaoh's Daughter in Memphis."

"No one here wishes harm to the house of Tuthmose," he replied.

Hatshepsut turned and started across the bridge up the first ramp, "The High Priest does not know the hearts of all those in his temples."

Offering no more resistance, he followed her to the shrine where they gave their food offerings to Atum. Climbing to the fourth level, they found a polished black floor entirely circled by two rows of columns supporting a narrow circular roof with white benches underneath. The "Benben Stone" was in the middle, it was about as tall as a man, it became obvious why the priest wore the odd orange colored scarfs, the stone was the same color. While it was not the exact shape of a pyramid, it was larger at the bottom than at the top and it did come to somewhat of a point.

Stepping on the black smooth floor, she noticed the warmth on her feet and her soft linen shoes were very slippery on the flawless floor that had been polished for centuries. The reflection of the Benben Stone in the reflective floor, almost gave the appearance of two stones. She followed the High Priest, who was aided by two priests, toward the stone. He reached out and touched the stone in an area that had obviously been touched often over the centuries because the area was worn smooth and did not have any of the orange color. "One's prayers would be answered by Atum while touching the stone," the priest stated. Hatshepsut was next, she asked for wisdom. Sergeant Dadu was last, as he turned away a loud clanging sound was heard, the tip of his sword had attached itself to the stone. He stood very still looking at the sword and there was a collective gasp from the priests who then dropped to their knees. "He has been chosen by Atum for some special purpose!" exclaimed the High Priest.

Hatshepsut and Senenmut went to Dadu who was still staring at his sword, she took his arm and pulled him away, as he moved farther away the sword fell back to his side. "Take your sword from it sheath," Hatshepsut said, "then place it close to the stone." The stone grabbed the sword again and it remained attached, some priests could be heard praying in the background, Hatshepsut whispered to Senenmut, "What is happening?"

"I am not sure my Lady," when Senenmut removed Dadu's sword, he could feel the pull of the stone. "The stone wants to keep it."

"This has never happened before," the Priest commented, "Where did you obtain such a sword?" he asked Dadu

Dadu answered as he looked at Hatshepsut, "It is a gift from Pharaoh's Daughter."

The High Priest looked at Hatshepsut but Senenmut spoke up quickly, "The sword is a gift from Pharaoh's Daughter, she gave the sword magical powers to protect her brave guard who saved her life."

With Ra setting behind her, the High Priest could not look directly at her, he looked at Dadu with his Golden Flies around his neck. "I now believe the stories I have heard of Pharaoh's Daughter being protected by the gods."

Senenmut was watching her and hoping that she would go along with his story. She smiled at the priest, "The High Priest of Lunu honors Pharaoh Tuthmose and his daughter who are protected by the gods." He asked permission to demonstrate the powers of her sword, each priest came and carefully removed and replaced the sword, feeling the power of Atum.

They all sat on a nearby bench watching the priest, Tyia said, "I believe my sister is having another encounter with the gods."

Hatshepsut replied, "If one is to believe Senenmut." She whispered to Senenmut, "Have you figured out what is happening?"

"I wonder if Dadu's sword and the Benben Stone are like lodestones, My Lady."

"What are lodestones?'

"I have two lodestones in Thebes that I obtained from a trader from the land of the Sea People, the two stones attract each other just as Dadu's sword and the Benben Stone. He then whispered, "They are used by priests to perform miracles in temples."

"Are you telling me the secrets of priests, Senenmut?"

"I keep no secrets from My Lady."

They sat in silence for a while, then Hatshepsut said, "You have two things to show me when we return to Thebes, the lodestones and Mentuhotep II's temple."

"Yes, My Lady." When it was dark, Senenmut pointed to

the polished floor. "Look, you can see the reflection of the stars in the floor." They walked onto the floor and the reflection of the stars made them feel as if they were in space surrounded by stars.

The High Priest came to them, "I was going to show Pharaoh's Daughter the stars in the floor, but she has noticed them already."

"The sensation is wonderful."

"If you lie on the floor the sensation is greater," he stated. Hatshepsut sat on the warm floor and then laid on her back with the chill of the night air being replaced by the warmth of the floor heated by the previous day's rays of Ra. When she moved her head slowly to the side, the night sky was full of stars, she felt as if she was flying! Then came the sensation of spinning, she had to spread her arms to her sides to stop the sensation.

Tyia and Senenmut joined her and enjoyed the unusual and thrilling feeling. Hatshepsut thoughts were of how small she was in this vast expanse of darkness and stars, how far away were the stars she wondered? Did anyone know? She had been told all her life that she was special, but tonight, she felt insignificant.

CHAPTER EIGHTEEN

Prophet

The aroma of fresh baked bread made Hatshepsut realize how hungry she was when she woke, Menna was awake in her room. She wondered how much sleep he actually got, seeing him in the room was comforting, and he reminded her of Sitre always by her bed in the morning.

The morning meal was wonderful with a wide variety of foods that they all enjoyed, the Governor and his wife Sarah had joined them, the conversation was mainly about the events of the previous evening with Dadu's sword. Hatshepsut asked, "Governor, while in Memphis I learned of a forgotten Hebrew Vizier who served Pharaoh, the records state that he married the daughter of a priest here and had two sons." It was very obvious that the Governor was intently listening to what she was saying. "I wish to learn more about this Vizier, do you know of this Hebrew Vizier?"

He did not answer for a very uncomfortably long time, she was about to speak again when he finally answered. "I am surprised that Pharaoh's Daughter knows of this foreign Vizier. Yes, I know of Vizier Joseph, my wife is a descendent of him."

She turned to Sarah, "Are you of the Ephraim or the Manasseh tribe?"

"Pharaoh's Daughter knows of the Hebrew tribes?" a surprised Sarah asked.

Senenmut spoke, "Pharaoh's Daughter wishes to know the history of all her subjects in Egypt and how she can best protect and provide for them."

While the Governor and his wife were looking at Senenmut, Hatshepsut commented, "I know of the Hebrew tribes, my nurse and loyal companion, is a Levite."

Sarah looked at her husband, "I am a descendent of Joseph's son, Ephraim."

The Governor took his wife's hand, "My ancestor was a Cup Bearer for Pharaoh and was accused of trying to poison the Pharaoh. He was put in prison and Joseph was able to answer the meaning of a dream that saved my ancestor's life. When I was young, I went to visit the now empty tomb and statue of Joseph. While there," he smiled at his wife, "Sarah came to visit the tomb that day, also. I thought she was beautiful and we discovered our common history."

"Had you visited the tomb often?" Hatshepsut asked. They both smiled, "No, My Lady, it was our first visit," Sarah answered.

"Why was the tomb empty and does it still exist?" Hatshepsut asked.

"Joseph's sarcophagus was removed from the tomb and hidden after the Hyksos were driven out of Egypt. The small pyramid shaped tomb is still there with his statue, they are on the ancient retirement estate of Joseph, it is still maintained by our people."

Hatshepsut knew that Joseph's mummy was likely hidden to protect it from her ancestors who had treated the Hebrews badly, she did not ask him where it was now hidden. "Were there any artifacts or records in the tomb besides his sarcophagus?" she questioned while looking at Senenmut, she hoped that the history Joseph had written was entombed with him.

"I do not know, My Lady."

"Senenmut, we must visit there today. Do you interpret dreams like the Hebrew Vizier?" she asked Sarah.

Sarah paused and then with a slight shake of her head, "I do not, My Lady." Disappointment was obvious on Hatshepsut's face. "I will let my husband show you Joseph's estate," she bowed and departed.

The governor's boat was comfortable and well furnished, they sailed from the temple dock, past the large city docks, toward many large stone grain silos. The governor pointed out the silos, "These were constructed by Vizier Joseph, My Lady. It is said that he stored grain throughout Egypt in great abundance, like the sand of the sea."

The estate was relatively small and showing its age, only a few men and women were working there, it was maintained by volunteers. The tomb was indeed in the shape of a small pyramid with his statue in front, Joseph had become an Egyptian in many ways, but he had maintained his loyalty to his people and his God. This fact impressed her, he had been able to accomplish both, he had served both Egypt and the Hebrew people.

The Statue was of a handsome middle-aged man with red hair and a multi colored tunic. It was a serene place for one to retire and enjoy his family, he had lived a full life and was remembered. That was all that one could hope for, she thought.

When they returned to the Governor's palace, his daughter and granddaughter were there, he introduced his daughter Rebekah and granddaughter Rachel. His daughter Rebekah favored her father, but the young granddaughter looked just like her grandmother Sarah, except for her beautiful red hair. "You are named after Joseph's mother, is that a popular name?" Hatshepsut asked the young girl.

"It is our way of remembering our history, whoever we are named after, we learn and remember all we can about that person's history. This is how our heritage is remembered," Rachel stated.

"Your hair is so unusual and lovely."

Rachel touched her hair, "It is the same color as the patriarch, Joseph."

"I saw his statue today and the statue did have your color of hair." There was a long pause in the conversation, it seemed as if the Governor's family wanted to say something, Rachel was looking at her grandfather. Hatshepsut waited, when no one said anything, "It was a pleasure meeting you. I plan on returning to Memphis tomorrow, I will return to my quarters."

Hatshepsut thoughts were of Joseph as she drifted off to sleep.

The cobra is looking at me and then it looks to my right, I turn and see a young girl with red hair standing nearby and she is holding something. The cobra moves closer, it appears to bow its head slightly to her. Lowering to the ground it moves away, as it is leaving, it turns and looks at me as if saying goodbye.

I feel a gentle breeze and look back toward where the young girl was, but now she is a grown woman with long flowing red hair. She smiles and motions for me to come to her.

Hatshepsut wakes up from her cobra dream, it is still dark, and she cautiously listens and looks around. Her cobra dream is back after a very long time! Memories of the night that the assassins attacked her, came flooding back, was the dream a warning of danger close by, she calls out, "Bek!"

Bursting through the door, Bek has his sword drawn, "What is it My Lady?" She is out of bed and has her arms around him when Abet enters the room with a lamp, they listen for any sound, but there appears to be no threat of any kind. "I had a dream, I am okay." Abet sees her shiver and gets a robe as Bek stays close, she quickly gets dressed and turns to him, "Let's go wake Senenmut."

Senenmut is trying to get fully awake as Hatshepsut tells him about her dream, "We must go wake the Governor."

"We should wait, My Lady, it is very early," a sleepy Senenmut stated.

"No, I cannot wait until Ra returns."

Arriving at the Governor's residence, they see lite lamps and people moving about, Senenmut announced that Pharaoh's Daughter is here to speak with the girl Rachel.

The Governor and all of his family are awake, "Rachel woke us up and demanded to speak with Pharaoh's Daughter before she leaves for Memphis. She told us weeks ago that when Pharaoh's Daughter arrives, she must talk to My Lady. I was uncertain how we would be accepted by Egypt's beautiful princess, I am sorry for my hesitation." He then bowed and remained in the humble position.

"Rise Governor," turning to Rachel, she saw her holding three scrolls. "You knew that I was coming here weeks ago?".

"Yes, an old Hebrew priest said to give you these when you came."

Hatshepsut took the scrolls which were wrapped in old plain leather, labeled Crop Census. She handed them to Senenmut, "The priest wanted you to give me these?"

"He said it is the history of our people, My Lady," as she motioned to her family.

"I would like to meet this priest."

"I am sorry, My Lady, but he has since died," stated the Governor.

A confused Hatshepsut looked at Senenmut who quickly examined the scrolls, how the priest knew weeks ago that she was coming to Luna, was puzzling? Senenmut said, "It appears to be only ancient records of annual crop production."

A confused Hatshepsut asked if she could have something to drink as she sat on a nearby lounge, Sarah offered Hatshepsut some wine. After a few sips, "Rachel can you interpret dreams like Joseph?"

"No, My Lady, I am called a prophet by some, but I am only a voice for God."

"I don't understand, why are you called a prophet?"

"I can answer questions you have, may I show you?"

"Yes."

When Rachel sat next to Hatshepsut on the lounge, Bek move a little closer. Rachel said, "God will answer questions you have, take my hands and close your eyes." Everyone was standing and watching Hatshepsut as she took her hands, she had the same sensation she had with blind and deaf Hannah. She saw Sarah offering Senenmut some wine, she closed her eyes.

Hatshepsut at first tried to think of a question, but stopped, she felt totally relaxed and at peace. Then she heard a voice and saw an older Rachel and felt a fragrant breeze. The voice was as a choir, speaking in many languages, but she had no trouble understanding her native language, which was pure and clear. The older Rachel began to answer questions without her asking, Rachel would pause after each answer so Hatshepsut could comprehend the answer and how it affected her.

"I knew your name before you were born."

"Sitre was a vessel I used."

"I selected you to find Moses."

"I will protect you."

"You will rule Egypt as Pharaoh."

There were many other answers, most she had never thought about.

"Pharaoh's Daughter will be remembered."

"I have written your story."

The answers kept coming to her.

"I used your dreams."

"Raise Moses as an Egyptian."

Hatshepsut did have one question, who are you?

"I am, who I am."

Sitre's God is real! A feeling of confidence came over her and she had no doubts regarding her future.

The last answer was, *"You will see your father alive again. You must go now."*

Rachel squeezed her hands and Hatshepsut opened her eyes. Surprisingly, it was still dark outside, even after the long conversation. Then she noticed that Sarah was pouring Senenmut another cup of wine, "How many cups of wine have you had?" she asked him.

He seemed confused, "This is my first cup, My Lady."

Now Hatshepsut was confused, she looked at the others in the room, "How long did I have my eyes closed?" she asked Bek.

"My Lady just closed her eyes for a moment and then opened them again."

Hatshepsut asked Rachel, "Is that true?"

"Yes, My Lady."

"Senenmut, did you hear Rachel talking to me?"

Senenmut looked at those around, "No, My Noble Lady, no one heard her talking."

Hatshepsut sat very still trying to comprehend her wonderous experience, could she have learned so much in such a very short time. The Hebrew God had used her dreams, just as Sitre had said. "Did you hear all that I was told?" Hatshepsut quietly asked Rachel.

"Yes, Pharaoh's Daughter will become Pharaoh and be remembered forever."

Finally, accepting what had happened, she spoke to the Governor, "I am honored that you trusted me to meet your amazing granddaughter." Hatshepsut looked at Rachel, "Thank you Rachel, you and your family will always be welcome at Pharaoh's Palace. I will have my scribe write you authorization for passage and a letter of introduction from Pharaoh's Daughter."

Then she told Senenmut, "We must return to Thebes today."

"Return to Thebes or Memphis, My Lady?"

"Thebes, before Pharaoh makes his journey to the west."

There were more people gathered at the dock for Hatshepsut's departure than when she arrived. Pharaoh's Daughter had impressed the priests and people there, their future was going to be influenced by Pharaoh's Daughter and this was most likely the last time that they would see her.

Hatshepsut was quiet as they sailed back to Memphis, strong favorable winds swiftly took her back to Memphis and eventually on to Thebes. Her Red Court could sense a change in her, she had always been confident but perhaps unsure about her future. Now, she had a quiet determination to do what was required to fulfill her destiny. Her commands to all concerned, even Admiral Ebana, were without any hesitation. Admiral Ebana's was concerned about the coming inundation, "We will be in Thebes before the Green Wave appears," she assured him.

Very little time was spent in Memphis, she emphasized to Vizier Ramose her desire for him to care and protect baby Moses and his family and that she would send for the baby when he was weaned in about three years. Vizier Ramose was to continue the search for the former Ambassador Ipi and the former Captain of the Palace Guards. Levi had completed a copy of

Vizier Zaphnath-Paaneah's manuscript she had requested, she thanked him. The Chief Book Scribe was to leave instructions to his successors that her adopted son Moses was to have access to the secret library if he ever expressed the desire.

Once when she was alone with Senenmut she stated, "I believe in the Hebrew God."

"My Lady knows that she must still perform the rituals required by the priests, if you are to maintain their support."

"I will do what is required to become Pharaoh."

The journey back to Thebes was not the relaxed trip she had made to Memphis, thankfully the strong favorable wind made the journey quick. No stops were made during the day to the disappointment of Iset, the only sightseeing was from the Royal Barge.

Iset's interest in Egypt was insatiable with endless questions about what she was seeing. Her command of the Egyptian language was improving each day, she did have an accent that Bae often mocked and teased her about. She was a very self-assured and precocious young girl who stayed close to Bae most of the time. Hatshepsut's thoughts were about how her life was about to change, once she reached Thebes, even the obligation that required her to marry the future Pharaoh did not matter. Everyone still felt as if they were in a race to get to Thebes before the flood, the debris that preceded the flood would made travel on the River dangerous, she tried to reassure them.

Curious about the scrolls she had received from the young prophet, Rachel, she asked Senenmut to examine them again. With much excitement he discovered the scrolls were indeed a history of the Hebrew people. The first part of each scroll was what the title claimed to be, old crop reports supposedly for the governor, then the writing changed to the secret writings of Imhotep.

The author Vizier Zaphnath-Paaneah, now referred to

himself as Joseph, son of Jacob, and that he had chosen the written language of Imhotep for safe keeping and because the Hebrews had no written language. Many hours on the barge were spent by Hatshepsut and Senenmut reading the three scrolls. Often it was difficulty reading the older version of the writings, she was relieved to learn that Joseph had stopped having dreams when, as he said, "He did not require God's continued guidance."

The overnight stop in Coptos was enjoyed by Tyia, her father had settled into his new position as Quarry Inspector. She was surprised and happy to learn the scribe's widowed older sister had moved in with her father. She was shy and uncomfortable around Tyia, because of her association with Pharaoh's Daughter, Tyia was no longer a rekhyt in the eyes of others. Their last stop was at General Djoser's estate, Hatshepsut wanted him to accompany them to Thebes, but he had already gone to Thebes.

Ra was low on the horizon when she arrived in Thebes, her family except Pharaoh, was at the dock to welcome her, including Sitre and even her cat, Mau. Everyone was happy that she had returned earlier than planned, except Mau, he ignored her because she had been gone too long. The Queen could not believe Hatshepsut was home even though the dispatch from Memphis had informed her parents that Hatshepsut was returning to Thebes. Once inside the palace and alone with her mother and Prince Tuthmose, there were questions on why she had returned. She answered, "I was told to return in a dream."

Prince Tuthmose spoke with difficulty, "We have heard how the gods protect my sister in dreams." It was clear that the future King had been consuming the "Joy Plant." When Hatshepsut introduced her Red Court, he was obviously attracted to Tyia and Iset, he asked Tyia if Iset was her sister. Before Tyia could answer him, Iset spoke to him, "The Princess of Mitanni is pleased to meet the future Pharaoh of Egypt."

Three days after her arrival, the Green Wave arrived and Pharaoh's health failed even more. Hatshepsut spent two more days with her father talking to him, sometimes she was not sure he heard her and other times he would answer and ask questions. The last time he was awake, she whispered to her father, "Do you remember the prayer you taught me? You have lived a long good life, your death will be peaceful, many stone monuments will keep your name remembered forever, and your secret resting place is hidden in the sacred valley." Her father closed his eyes and went to sleep, he did not wake up again and the following day his breathing stopped. It is believed that the Horus Pharaoh, at his death, became the Osiris Pharaoh and starts his journey into eternity, she wondered if it is true.

The west is associated with death, after her father became a westerner, the 70 days of preparing for the royal burial began. Just as the star Sirius disappeares and dies in the west for 70 days only to be reborn and rise in the east, so did the Egyptians believe her father would. The rising star signaled rebirth, a new year, and the annual flooding of the River. Final inscriptions in his tomb were completed and his favorite jewelry, weapons, clothes, food, and personal possessions were placed in the tomb for him to enjoy in the next life. Work was stopped on the Temple of Amun even though one side of his two obelisks had still not been finished. Many ceremonies and the coronation of the new Pharaoh would be in the temple, the holy site must be made ready for the hundreds of nobilities arriving from all of Egypt.

CHAPTER NINETEEN

Queen Hatshepsut

The 70 days following Pharaoh's death, Hatshepsut, the future Queen stayed in the Royal Harem with Sitre. Her mother was still the Great Wife and was in charge of the harem, they were able to console and support each other when needed. But, most of all, she looked forward to the visits of Tyia who came often and spent hours with her. A priestess from the Temple of Amun also moved into the harem, her purpose was to assure no man came in contact with Hatshepsut after her moon blood. This insured that the future Great Wife was not carrying a child before her marriage to the new Pharaoh.

The Royal Harem was not a place to keep women locked up, they could come and go as they pleased during the day if they were escorted by a palace guard. The reason the harem was guarded at all times was to keep men out. Sitre visited each day and Hatshepsut would read from the three scrolls, Sitre was able to learned much about the Hebrew history. But both were amazed that the oral history she knew was so close to that contained in the scrolls. The role had reversed for Hatshepsut, now she was the one who read the secret writings to Sitre until she went to sleep.

Hatshepsut learned from Tyia of an earlier confrontation between Menna and the Captain of the Palace Guards. The arrogant captain said that it was his responsibility to guard the Royal Harem, Menna informed him that was fine, but that he or one of his guards would also be at the door protecting Pharaoh's Daughter. The future Pharaoh saw the humor in the situation and ordered the Captain to allow Menna to guard Hatshepsut, as long as she was in the harem, the Captain resented relinquishing any duties to Menna.

The harem was in a state of change and tension, young women in the harem were concerned about their future, they hoped the new Pharaoh would choose them to remain. The mothers of male children were the first to leave the harem, the sons of the old Pharaoh, now had little chance of becoming Pharaoh. Tuthmose II was alive and he was to be the future Pharaoh, unless the new Pharaoh failed to produce an heir. They were destined to live out their lives in a villa far away from the palace. Many haram conspiracies and assassinations had occurred throughout history by minor wives, in hopes that their son would become Pharaoh.

During one of the visits by the future Pharaoh, he and Hatshepsut had a long and interesting conversation. She was pleased to learn that he still looked to her as his older sister and desired her advice. But she could tell he wanted to be perceived as a strong Pharaoh, she must tread lightly to maintain any influence on him and not shatter his fragile confidence. Together they decided that daily reports and correspondence were to be sent to her after he had viewed them. He then mentioned his interest in Iset, she informed him what Iset had been through and how young she actually was. Hatshepsut stated that she did not want Iset taken advantage of and that Iset had seen her brother abuse the drug from the "Joy Plant."

Tuthmose answered defensively that as Pharaoh he could see and be with whoever he wished. Hatshepsut told him firmly that he could have any woman in Egypt in his harem, but that a powerful Pharaoh would not take advantage of a child. "Iset is in my care and I will protect her." Tuthmose started to challenge her, but remembered the stories about her and the gods.

Senenmut was given the additional title as her Chief

Steward and would send her daily reports, she enjoyed reading his reports because of the personal messages he hid in the reports written in the secret language of the architects. She was touched by Senenmut's true concern for her, his admiration of her commitment to her future role as the Great Wife. She planned to fulfill her role as Great Wife and provide an heir for Pharaoh, if Pharaoh could have his harem, then perhaps there was a way she could be with Senenmut.

The day of the final journey of Pharaoh Tuthmose across the River to his Mortuary Temple and then on to his secret burial place arrived. A very long funeral procession was led by Temple Priests, with family and officials following, along the route to the River were hundreds of mourners who loved the Pharaoh. Many boats had preceded the Royal Barge Falcon that carried her father across the River one last time. On the western side of the River were noblemen and their wives from all of Egypt. Paid mourners lined the road to the Temple, but only a select few would go past the Mortuary Temple to the secret location of the tomb. Hatshepsut had the procession remain longer at the Temple, it was obvious the future Pharaoh was having a very difficult time breathing in the heat of the day, he nodded a thank you to her.

At the tomb, the "Opening of the Mouth" ritual was performed so that her father's spirit could eat and drink in the afterlife. After he was safely sealed in his tomb for eternity, Pharaoh Tuthmose II was presented, wearing both the white and red crowns of Upper and Lower Egypt. In the Temple of Amun, the priests began two days of ceremonies transforming Tuthmose II into the new Horus god. His throne name became Akheperenre Tuthmose II, which means "Great is the Form of Ra." A year of festivals and ceremonies were planned to justify the new Pharaoh to his people and win their support.

The Royal wedding of the new Pharaoh and Pharaoh's Daughter followed next, she would assume the new titles of Pharaoh's Great Wife and Pharaoh's Sister and maintained her favorite title of Pharaoh's Daughter. The long day was followed by an uncomfortable night for both, Tuthmose II was exhausted from the many events of the previous days. She informed him that it was not the right time of the month to conceive the future prince and they could just rest and relax.

They made the mutual decision that she was to return to his chambers when it was time for her to conceive. With much relief the exhausted Pharaoh soon went to sleep and the new Great Wife quietly left his quarters, she was pleased to see Menna, with the Captain of the Palace Guards. "I was expecting one of the twins this time of night."

"I was concerned about the safety of my Queen."

She took her friend by the arm and smiled to herself when she saw the look of resentment on the Captain of the Guard's face. Arriving at her quarters for the first time since her father's death, Hatshepsut stopped and gently touched the lotus engraving on her door. "I will have to put this door on my Queen's quarters when I move there." Pausing, "It was good to see you tonight," she told him with a smile. Menna assumed his protective vigilance.

Sitre greeted her with an embrace and even Mau was glad to see her this time. "Are you alright?" a concerned Sitre asked.

"Pharaoh was tired after the events of the past few days, I told him it was not the right time to conceive the Prince of Egypt. He then went to sleep, I do not wish to have his child."

"I have a suggestion, but we will talk later, let me take care of Egypt's new Queen." The exhausted young 16-year-old Queen of Egypt quickly went to sleep.

The following morning, she smiled, because Sitre was there by her bed as always, it was comforting that even as Queen, Sitre was still there. When she stirred, Sitre greeted her, "Good morning, my Queen, I pray God watches over you today."

"God will." Hatshepsut was not accustomed to her new title and Sitre was pleased to hear her new response.

When Sitre called for the maids to help attend to Hatshepsut, she spoke to Abet, they had become much closer after the shared events of the past few months. "Is Sergeant Dadu adjusting to life in Thebes?" she asked Abet.

"Dadu is enjoying his home."

"Are you spending time with him?"

"Yes, as much as I can," as she put her hands to her face, slightly embarrassed.

"I am happy for you! Dadu was given his home and one servant for saving my life. Do you have any suggestions as to who that servant could be?"

"My Lady would do that for me?" questioned a very surprised Abet.

"Go inform Dadu that you will move in with him."

Queen Hatshepsut dressed in her new clothes with blue accents, blue being the royal color of Egypt's King and Queen, Sitre was now wearing a light blue dress. After her morning meal, Hatshepsut asked Sitre to have Senenmut come to her quarters, it did not take long for Senenmut to arrive slightly out of breath. He bowed low and said, "I am honored my Queen called her humble servant."

Hatshepsut led him to her couch, "You are much more than my humble servant, bring me up to date on events in Egypt." They talked all morning about many matters of state, including the annual flood that had occurred, it was not a very good inundation because it was too low. There was no unrest or rebellion from any of the subject nations, he then added that it was probably because the news about a new Pharaoh in Egypt had not been heard by many. She was informed that some members of the Royal Court were anxious for Queen Hatshepsut to assume the leadership role. "We must have patience, how is my friend?"

"I am well."

"Tyia tells me that some of your family came for a visit, I am sorry that I was in seclusion and could not meet them, how is your family?"

"My parents are very proud of my position and titles that My Lady honors me with. They also enjoyed touring the palace, gardens, and temples, I'm sure all my mother's neighbors are tired of her stories by now. She had the same question as always, when am I getting married and having children?" He quickly changed the subject. "I visited Menna and Tyia at their new estate, Iset is staying with them, they cannot believe their good fortune."

Hatshepsut waited a moment, "How are your quarters in the palace? You are entitled to an estate outside the palace."

"I am perfectly satisfied living in the palace because it is convenient and I wish to be close to my Queen."

"Property for you later, perhaps, I hope to work with you every day."

"My Queen's wish is my command!" with a mock bowing gesture and a laugh.

"Do you know of a location for my tomb and Mortuary Chapel?"

Senenmut became silent, he did not like the idea of preparing for her death. Finally he answered, "I know of the perfect place, remember we talked about Pharaoh Mentuhotep II's mortuary complex in Deir el-Bahari?"

"Yes, and the lodestones you talked about."

"I wish to show my Queen this location," he was amazed how Hatshepsut never forgot anything.

"We must see your location soon," Hatshepsut said as she stood.

Knowing it was time to leave, "I will bring the loadstones to our next meeting."

Hatshepsut stopped him by taking his hand, she kissed him on the cheek. He breathed in her sweet fragrance that he remembered and loved. Hatshepsut watched him as he departed, thinking, soon Senenmut.

She spoke to Sergeant Dadu who was outside her door and realized Tyia was probably with Menna at their estate, she did miss seeing Tyia every day. Dadu replied, "My Queen continues to honor me, Abet is very happy."

"It is time for both of you to enjoy your loyal service," Dadu bowed slightly.

Hatshepsut moved into the Queen's quarters, her mother, the dowager Queen had moved to General Djoser's estate for a while. Life had changed for everyone and hopefully for the best.

Her first day in court with the new Pharaoh, she did not speak until Pharaoh asked her a question, it was the proper protocol. Later when they were alone, he informed her that she need not be so formal with him. Hatshepsut responded that when in the presence of others, he was her Pharaoh and that it was proper. He acknowledged that she was correct and that he was having a difficult time assuming his new role. "Being Queen of Egypt is new to me also." They both laughed and relaxed a little. Hatshepsut mentioned that she was going to look into locations for her tomb, did he wish to look with her for his?

Tuthmose said, "Yes, it is important to start the construction of my eternal house but I do not like the idea of needing it."

Hatshepsut asked him, almost whispering, "Do you feel different since the priests and ceremonies made you Pharaoh and a god?"

Tuthmose was silent for a long time and then he answered, "No, I still feel the same."

"Perhaps one's power and transformation take time to grow," she said, knowing that he would only feel more power over time. "I will let my Pharaoh know when it is time to look for the location of our eternal home," she stood and bowed to her brother, he laughed and waved her off.

Pharaoh, Queen Hatshepsut, her Red Court, several of Pharaoh's Palace Guards and what seemed like a small army of servants, staff, and scribes crossed the River. They searched the valley where their father's hidden tomb was for most of the day. Many rest breaks were required because Pharaoh was having difficulty breathing and was weak. Once as they passed where her father's hidden tomb was located, she saw Senenmut make a slight head nod toward its location now covered with rock, she acknowledged the location, no one else noticed. Hopefully, it would remain hidden for eternity. Camp was made early for Pharaoh, after a quick meal he went to his tent for the night. That evening Hatshepsut enjoyed being with her Red Court, Menna expressed concern for Pharaoh, everyone could see that Tuthmose was trying to hide how weak he was. Hatshepsut explained that even as a child, he was not very strong.

Just before everyone retired for the evening, when Tyia and Hatshepsut were alone, Tyia stated, "I am concerned."

"What are you concerned about?"

"Do you want to have Pharaoh's child? Your child may be weak like his father."

Hatshepsut did not answer right away as she looked out into the night. "I have plans that may be dangerous," she eventually said.

"What are you planning?"

"Something soon," Hatshepsut then went to her tent for the night. The following morning Pharaoh announced that the search for his tomb's location would continue another day and that he was returning to the palace. Only a few servants and palace guards remained with Hatshepsut and her Red Court. Senenmut guided them back through the hills to the eastern side of the mountains where they could see Thebes in the distance across the River. They were in a large valley that had ancient ruins, it was the mortuary temple of Pharaoh Mentuhotep II. Even though the temple was over 500 years old and in a state of ruin, Hatshepsut could see how unique it was.

The mountain behind the valley was the shape of a pyramid, "This is perfect! One can see the Palace and Temple of Amun from here," she exclaimed. They then proceeded to explored the ruins, with Menna following behind them. Tyia commented to Dadu and Abet, "I guess our search is over, we will make camp here."

When they returned, Hatshepsut was excited, Senenmut was pleased that she approved of the location and both were very animated in their discussion of what each envisioned there. When the light evening meal of flat bread and vegetables was finished, Hatshepsut and Senenmut sat together still going over his design and plans and listening to her ideas. The servants and palace guards had pitched their tents a distance away from Queen Hatshepsut and her party. Dadu and Abet had been asleep for some time, he had the late watch. It was very late when Hatshepsut and Senenmut became quiet while each were in their own thoughts. Eventually Senenmut stood, "If it pleases My Lady, I will go to my tent now."

Hatshepsut stood and took his hand, "You will sleep in my tent tonight," as she led a very surprised Senenmut to her tent.

Menna whispered, "She is taking a risk!"

"My sister is looking for happiness and I hope there will

soon be a new Prince of Egypt."

Ra was faintly starting to show his rays when Menna came out of his tent while Dadu was standing guard. "Good morning, Commander."

"Sergeant."

"Does the Commander know what I saw last night?"

"Did anyone else see Senenmut leave the Queen's tent?"

"No sir."

"Good, no one needs to know." Dadu just smiled and went to his tent.

The servants arrived soon to Hatshepsut's camp as Ra returned victorious after his nightly battle with the underworld, Senenmut also emerged victorious from his tent. He stood by the campfire as the servants were busy making a morning meal, when Hatshepsut joined Senenmut, he was looking toward Ra over Thebes. Looking at Hatshepsut for a moment, not believing how the gods had blessed him, "I will build a beautiful house here for you and it will last for eternity, as my love for you will."

"We will build it together." Tyia soon joined them, no one said a word for a few moments. Then Hatshepsut spoke first, "Does my sister have a comment?"

"I am glad that she has found happiness," after a brief pause, "Will you tell Sitre?"

Hatshepsut smiled, "This was her idea and she also has plans for Pharaoh."

Senenmut and Tyia looked at each other, surprised, "Sitre, I never would have guessed," replied Tyia.

"Let us pray that no one else does," Hatshepsut hoped.

CHAPTER TWENTY

The Beauty of Ra

Senenmut and Hatshepsut were able to steal away for a few brief encounters in her quarters. After a meeting with Pharaoh's Royal Court, she asked, "If it pleases my Pharaoh, his Great Wife asks for a private audience."

Pharaoh commanded his Court, "Leave Us." His Court quickly left them alone, "You are always so formal." Pharaoh said with a smile, "What does my Queen desire?"

Hatshepsut spoke softly so the guards could not hear, "It is time for Pharaoh to produce a prince."

The smile left his face, "Are you sure?"

"Only as sure as one can be, shall I come to you tonight?"

"Yes," with indecision, then again he said, "Yes, tonight."

"As my Pharaoh commands," Hatshepsut departed the Throne Room.

Sitre and Hatshepsut had planned and prepared for the night. When she arrived with Menna, he handed her two containers of wine and took his post by Pharaoh's door with two of Pharaoh's guards. One of Pharaoh's guards announced the arrival of the Great Wife. When she entered his quarters, it was obvious that he was already under the influence of wine or maybe the "Joy Plant" drug. They talked and drank some of her lotus wine, with much self-control Hatshepsut was pleasant and suggestive. When Hatshepsut thought Pharaoh was aroused, she suggested one more drink to celebrate this night and to the future prince of Egypt, pouring drinks from the second container, she had brought.

Pharaoh drank his while Hatshepsut only pretended to drink, soon, she saw the effect on Pharaoh. While she slowly undressed setting on the side of the bed, Pharaoh became more excited, he stumbled as he came toward her quickly. They both fell back on the bed with his head hitting her on the face, her eye was hurting and she could taste blood from an injured lip. She playfully resisted his advances until he looked around confused, moaned and then passed out.

Hatshepsut lay still for a few moments to make certain that she did not wake him up, moving slowly she got out of bed. Her lip and eye were throbbing as she poured the contents of the container out and sat near the bed. Listening carefully with relief, she heard him still breathing. Thankfully, he had not died from the drink Sitre had made, both were concerned about his health. It was the longest night of her life as she listened to Pharaoh's every breath and watched the water clock. When it was almost time for Ra to start his journey across the sky, she laid down next to Pharaoh. As he was waking up, he moaned and carefully got out of bed, she pretended to be asleep. He went to his chamber bowl, as he was returning to the bedroom, Hatshepsut rolled over sleepily and asked, "How is my Pharaoh this morning?"

He saw her swollen lip and bruised eye and forgot his headache, "Did I hurt my sister?" he asked sincerely.

Setting up in bed, she touched her eye, "My Pharaoh was like a raging bull when he performed his duty last night. May the gods bless us with a strong prince."

Tuthmose watched as she dressed, when she started to leave, he said, "I remember your kindness to me when we were growing up."

Hatshepsut walked back to him, she kissed him on the cheek, "Our father and your mother would be proud of you."

With a catch in his voice, "Do you think so?"

"Yes, rest now, you have earned it."

When she came out of Pharaoh's chambers, the Captain of the Palace Guards, two palace guards, and Menna were there. They noticed her swollen lip and bruised eye, "Pharaoh is resting," she gave a quick smile at Menna. She saw the guards smirking, "Do the guards of Pharaoh not honor his Great Wife?" They quickly bowed and waited for her acknowledgment. "Pharaoh's Daughter, Sister, and Great Wife can arrange a position in some miserable remote outpost in the Red Land for those who do not wish to honor her!" Quickly leading a very angry Menna away, she left them there still bowing. Now spread the sordid details to everyone in the palace, she thought to herself.

Sitre and Tyia were waiting for Hatshepsut and both were visibly upset when they saw her face, "I am fine, our plan went better than expected," going into the details about the events of the evening.

The night was over and their hopes were summed up by Tyia's final comment, "I pray that my sister never endures such a night again."

When Hatshepsut's moon blood did not arrive, she was hopeful and the following month she was ecstatic when she was sure she was with child. Pharaoh was proud and he announced the news to his Royal Court with much celebration in the palace. The real joy was shared by Hatshepsut and Senenmut in private, both certain who the father was. The following months, Hatshepsut worked closely with Pharaoh, gaining more influence every day.

There was only one military campaign, it seemed that Nubia with every new Pharaoh tried to send less tribute and gold. Pharaoh wanted to accept the lesser amount but his Queen convinced him that other nations would learn of Nubia's action and follow suit. It was a quick and minor military action that the generals of the Southern Army of Amun gladly carried out in the name of Pharaoh.

Hatshepsut was becoming more concerned about Pharaoh because he was enjoying the "Joy Plant" too much, again he mentioned that when Iset was older he wanted her. She told him that Iset knew about him using the drug and reiterated that Iset would not be interested in him, no matter his position or power.

With her duties settling into a routine, Hatshepsut wanted Senenmut to design her a new Queen's Quarters, it would be located on the west side of the palace, opposite the traditionally cooler east side. She desired this location because from her bedroom balcony she wanted to have an unobstructed view of the River and the valley where her future mortuary temple was to be built.

The new quarters consisted of her living spaces, a comfortable space for whoever was on guard duty, private rooms for Sitre, a guest room, and a new nursery for the future nanny and baby. She wanted the baby and nanny close by, not in the harem or at some distant estate. The five areas were connected in the front by a large enclosed hall, with only one strong door to the outside, which could only be unlocked from the inside, for night time security. Hatshepsut occasionally had nightmares of the assassins, but no dreams about the cobra. Menna had vivid memories of the night and had worked closely with Senenmut on the security and design of the main door. Senenmut used her old door with the Lotus blossom she loved in her new personal quarters.

Senenmut designed long extending overhangs on the west side to shield the interior rooms from Ra's strong afternoon rays, the steep overhangs also prevented attacks from the roof and he staggered the adjoining windows and balconies so each could catch the prevailing north breeze. When Pharaoh saw the work in progress, he was very impressed with Senenmut's design and workmanship. He requested similar quarters for himself when he finished the Queen's Quarters.   Senenmut assumed another title from Pharaoh, he was now Chief Architect of the Palace.

Most of Senenmut's design work went into his quarters next to the five living quarters of the Queen's complex. His office and living quarters were outside the Queen's complex, but next to her bedroom. He had a separate entrance that entered a formal receiving area, private office and his living space. His living area was one that he personally worked on and allowed limited access to, until it was time to show Hatshepsut. She was curious about his quarters because he was so secretive during its construction and it involved her bedroom. She had seen the main living room with murals of places he had travelled with her, within the paintings were small images of them hidden in the various locations. One section of the wall was left blank for a mural of the future Mortuary Temple he would one day build for her.

Their adjoining bedroom walls had unusually wide pillars and hidden locking mechanisms similar to the secret library in Memphis. On the pillars of Hatshepsut and Senenmut's rooms were copper lamps similar to those in the Memphis House of Books. A secret panel between the pillars could only be moved when she unlocked her side first, he then could rotate his lamp and open the panel. Her room could not be entered from his quarters unless she unlocked her side first, he was very proud of the ingenious design.

Another secret he showed her was a beautiful table made of ebony which held the simple cedar box his mother had given him as a child. He started to tilt the table, but Hatshepsut asked what was in the box, she was deeply touched when she saw the contents. Inside was the first pale green sash she had given him and notes she had written when he was teaching her the secret language. After seeing what Senenmut cherished and had saved, she kissed him, "I have found someone who loves me!"

"You captured my heart like a falcon when we first sat together in the shade," replied Senenmut. He locked the box and proudly showed Hatshepsut how the box was attached to the table and both could be tilted. The section of floor under the table was hinged and rotated open with the table, underneath were steps that went down into a hidden room under the floor. Looking down in the dark space, a slight shiver when down her back, because it was too much like the hidden tunnel in Memphis, "I would not want to be trapped in there."

"Follow me," as he took her hand and a lamp, once in the hidden room, he showed her the back wall, "This is the outside wall of the palace, next to the River." He placed the lamp close and she could see that a lot of the wall had been removed, nearby was a large mallet, "With this, one could be outside quickly." He showed her a rope ladder to be used to climb down the outside wall to the ground.

Hatshepsut was impressed, "Do you think we will ever need to use such a place?"

"I do not think so, but we do not know the future."

Hatshepsut looked at the surroundings, "This is a good place to store the writings of Joseph."

By the time the Queen's new quarters were finished, she was very advanced in her pregnancy. They had secret times together in his quarters, holding each other and looked across the River. One night, Hatshepsut saw a fire burning where her new temple was to be built. "There is a fire at the site of my future temple, I wonder who it is?"

"I asked that a fire be built there tonight, when I am spending many nights in the future there building your temple, you will see our fires burning. Know that my heart will be here with you, like tonight."

Hatshepsut kissed him, Senenmut was completely happy with his work and life. Hatshepsut was glad to have someone to share her life with and knew that he loved her totally, but she was not satisfied. The power behind Pharaoh was not enough for her, she was destined to be Pharaoh, but she was not sure how to fulfill the prophecy.

Dadu was happy living with Abet and had assumed the unspoken role of a father figure to Hatshepsut, he could say things to the Queen that no one dared to say. He once heard a palace guard making a remark about Hatshepsut and Senenmut, Dadu promptly reprimanded him in front of his peers. He then informed his Queen that it was time for her to spend less time with Senenmut, "Pharaoh will soon have suspicions." Realizing that he was right, she convinced Senenmut to accept an estate near Menna and Tyia's estate. His sister, brother, and parents moved into his estate with him and enjoyed the luxurious life style. It was not convenient for him to go to the palace often, so he began work on his parent's tombs, the traditional duty for honored parents by their eldest son.

He also started training horses in accordance with the Mitanni training manual that Iset had brought with her from Mitanni. His father and brother were helpful, but did not see the benefit of the rigorous training and extra work.

Iset was still living with Menna and Tyia, a tutor provided by Hatshepsut was teaching her to write the Egyptian language and the customs of Egypt, her adopted home.

Naomi, Hatshepsut's young maid, had nervously asked to serve only Tyia. Hatshepsut wanted to be certain that Tyia knew of Naomi's romantic feelings toward her, "Does Menna know how Naomi cares for you?"

Tyia answered, "We have discussed Naomi and he is comfortable with Naomi's affection toward me. I do not remember my mother so I enjoy her gentle caresses and attention, when she brushes my hair, she softly hums, it is so soothing." After a long pause, "I do not think I can become pregnant," tears were in her eyes. "Perhaps Naomi could have Menna's child."

A little surprised and saddened Hatshepsut asked, "Do you think she would want to have his child?"

"Oh yes, she would love to be with Menna and have his child, I may be a little jealous."

"I think that Menna should be jealous of her affection toward you," was her reply. Tyia just smiled.

When the day came for Hatshepsut to give birth, Senenmut was not at the palace, he was at his estate. Hatshepsut had sent him a message in the secret writing, that it was time. He wanted to be by her side, but both had decided that it was not wise for him to be there. Tyia was to send a message to him and other officials announcing when the Great Wife had given birth. When the message arrived, it said that the Queen and Pharaoh had a healthy baby girl. He knew that Pharaoh would be disappointed that she had not given birth to the future prince. Then he noticed that Tyia did not mention how Hatshepsut was doing, he then sent a servant with his written congratulations to Pharaoh and the Great Wife, another private message to Tyia asked about Hatshepsut.

Later a very tired and concerned Bek arrived at his estate, he told Senenmut that he should come with him, Hatshepsut was very weak and not improving. Arriving at the palace, he found Menna, Tyia, and Abet outside Hatshepsut's quarters. Tyia eyes were red from fatigue and tears, it appeared she had not slept since the birth. Senenmut was told that Hatshepsut's mother and Sitre were inside her room with the Royal Physician and priests. He anxiously waited until the Royal Physician and the dowager Queen came out of Hatshepsut's room, "I wish to see the Queen."

She answered weakly, the priests are with her now, he then demanded, "I want to see my Noble Lady now!"

Her mother was too tired and emotionally drained to offer much resistance, "As you wish, but be prepared for the worse."

He was overcome with the odor, heat, and the darkness when he entered the room, the smell was from the infection and the assortment of putrid ointments used for treatments. He knew that the standard procedures by the physicians and priests were prayers, magic incantations, and strange concoctions in the form of liquids and pastes. When he gently touched her face, she was burning up with fever, she was awake but did not appear to recognize him. One of the manuscripts he had read in the hidden library in Memphis was a medical journal written my Imhotep, the vizier, architect, writer, and physician who was now worshipped as a god. He knew that she was not getting the treatment that the ancient architect and physician recommended. Senenmut turned to her mother, "Do you want your daughter to live?"

With a shocked look on her face she answered, "Why do you of all people ask such a question?"

"Then get everyone out of here, let me treat My Lady," he stated firmly. The priests looked at him in contempt when they heard him.

The dowager Queen regained her composure and spoke to the priests, "Do you have any other treatments for the Great Wife besides prayers?" There was silence as they each looked at each other. "We thank you for your noble efforts and I ask that you continue your prayers to the gods, I will care for my daughter now," as she dismissed them with a slight wave of her hand. They reluctantly departed Hatshepsut's room.

Senenmut quickly began giving orders, he wanted the room windows opened for fresh air and light. Sitre was to find clean linen sheets and get fresh water and vinegar, when her bedding was removed, he saw that her bed was stained from blood and smelly treatments, Bek was then dispatched to get a new mattress. Sitre and Abet with the help of her mother cleaned her and then vinegar soaked linen gauze was used to stop the internal bleeding. They gave her all the water she could drink and kept cool wet linen sheets on her. This was done all night until the next day, when she finally stopped shaking, everyone thought the worst. But, were deeply relieved to see that she was sleeping peacefully, only cool wet cloths were kept on her head.

Senenmut, Sitre, and her mother stayed with Hatshepsut while she slept, the others left to get some much-needed rest. Later Senenmut went to his quarters with instructions that he was to be awakened if any change in her condition occurred, Bek would not leave. Later, Iset and Naomi came to visit Hatshepsut, they were there when Pharaoh came with the Royal Physician.

Pharaoh seemed truly relieved to see her sleeping peacefully, but the physician appeared to be disappointed. Pharaoh asked his step-mother how she knew what treatment to use, she responded that Senenmut had told them what to do from reading the writings of Imhotep. Pharaoh went to the Great Wife and touched her cheek, "I will return later." As he was leaving, he stopped and spoke to Iset, he obviously still admired her, even more now that she was maturing. Iset was respectful but very cool and it did not go unnoticed by Pharaoh.

Senenmut arrived later, stating that Pharaoh had woke him and thanked him for treating his sister. Bek was standing beside her bed while the others were talking. Hatshepsut woke up briefly when he touched her hand, she smiled at him and went back to sleep. A relieved Bek told them what had happened, her mother shook Hatshepsut's shoulder slightly. She woke again and asked for water, tears of relief and happiness were shed by Sitre and her mother. Senenmut sat down heavily with a sigh of relief as some of the worry and tension left. Bek came to him, "Is my Queen going to be alright?"

"I believe so."

After drinking and speaking to her mother for a moment, she went back to sleep. Her mother came to Senenmut, "Thank you for saving the life of the one we love so much."

"I would not have wanted to live without her."

"I know," she replied.

After many more anxious hours, Hatshepsut was awake most of the time, she was told by her mother that it was Senenmut who treated her. "I am not surprised that my Senenmut knew what to do. I wish to hold my daughter." The sleeping infant was brought to her, "She is beautiful!" Hatshepsut stated with tears in her eyes.

"She looks like my daughter," Queen Ahmose proudly replied.

"Her hair is a lighter color around her face, it is the same color as," Hatshepsut paused and looked at her mother and then Senenmut.

"Yes, it is," Queen Ahmose whispered with a smile. "But it must be kept a secret or she can never be the future Queen." Hearing their discussion, Senenmut came to the bedside and looked at his daughter for the first time. A few days later when alone, they talked about their baby girl, Hatshepsut decided to name her Neferure, meaning "The Beauty of Ra."

"Will Pharaoh like her name?"

"I will make him think it was a name he chose."

Sheriti, the daughter of a nobleman who had lost her child, had been chosen to be the wet nurse of Neferure. The legal papers were drawn up, she would be required to live in the palace and not get pregnant for three years. Her family would be well compensated, there were Royal Decrees, and she was given the title of, Royal Nurse to Princess Neferure.

The future official tutor of Neferure was chosen by Pharaoh, it was to be the elder Pen-Nekhebet who had been Pharaoh's tutor and advisor, when he was young. Hatshepsut thanked Pharaoh for his wise choice and her appreciation of his interest in the education and care of his daughter. She knew that it would be several years before a tutor would be actively involved with Neferure's education and that it was mostly an honorary title for Pen-Nekhebet. There was only one man in Egypt who cared enough and was wise enough to fill that role, it was Neferure's father.

The next year saw Hatshepsut healing, gaining strength and assuming more power, Vizier Hepuseneb and members of the Royal Court were glad to see her assume more control of affairs of state. Pharaoh issued a decree that his Queen had written, titled, Pharaoh's Wish. He had signed it without much interest, he did like it because the decree portrayed him as a wise and kind King. The decree stated that Pharaoh wanted peace and to rule with his crook, the symbol of a good shepherd. His flail would only be used to defend his subjects and to enforce his wish. The Royal Decree stated that Pharaoh's property and subjects should be protected and cared for, Maat would not be served if any of his subjects suffered. Hatshepsut wanted to start the idea of better treatment of all of her rekhyt, even Moses's people.

Her moon blood did not return and the sad realization came to her that she would never have the title of "Pharaoh's Mother." She, like her mother, must watch a son of Pharaoh by another woman become Pharaoh and marry her daughter. The recent months saw a big change in Pharaoh that was noticed by everyone including his Royal Court. It appeared that he had stopped using the "Joy Plant" and was in much better health and spirits. He still had little interest in the day to day affairs of state which he gladly let his Queen and Vizier perform. Iset was soon seen more and more with Pharaoh in the palace, gardens, and zoo, she was enjoying the attention of Pharaoh and being with the Royal family.

Tyia was exploring her interest and skill with stone by studying and working in the Royal Sculptor House near the Palace. The Royal Sculptors, captivated by her charm and beauty, gladly helped her with training and practice. She made a unique small statue of Senenmut and wanted to see what he and Hatshepsut thought of it. The statue was basically a cube with his head and that of Princess Neferure on top. Hatshepsut thought that it was very unique and liked it, but she and Senenmut were being very careful not to raise any suspicions, "A life size statue perhaps later," she stated.

Tyia and Menna were spending more time in the palace, which pleased Hatshepsut. Iset was no longer living with them in their villa, she had moved into the palace. Naomi had become the Lady of the House, a role that she gladly accepted which involved managing the servants and grounds when Menna and Tyia were away.

Hatshepsut and Senenmut had discussed if Iset would be a good choice as a Secondary Wife of Pharaoh, perhaps she could provide a son, a future Pharaoh, and husband to their daughter. Then Iset requested to see Hatshepsut privately, when she arrived, it was obvious that Iset was upset and had been crying. Was the relationship between Iset and Pharaoh over? "Why are you so upset?" dreading to hear the answer.

With much effort Iset blurted out with tears, "I have betrayed your trust, you saved me from a horrible fate and I rewarded you with deceit, please forgive me." Iset was inconsolable and had come to Hatshepsut with outstretched arms.

Hatshepsut held her and wondered if she had learned of her relationship with Senenmut and then told Pharaoh? "Sit, now tell me how you think you have betrayed me," she asked in the calmest voice she could gather.

Iset stopped sobbing, she raised her eyes to Hatshepsut. "I am carrying your husband's child, if you wish, I will return to my father and brother." When she finished speaking, the crying began again.

With much relief Hatshepsut comforted a sincere Iset and tried to think of what to say, she decided to just tell the truth, "Iset, listen to me, I will never have the title of Pharaoh's Mother because I cannot have another child."

Iset stopped crying and looked at Hatshepsut. "I am truly sorry for the Great Wife."

"You did not betray me, Pharaoh can choose any woman he wants, I am happy that you are carrying his child." Iset listened very intently, "Does Pharaoh know?" Iset just shook her head, no. "Do you wish to marry Pharaoh and be his Secondary Wife?"

"Yes, do you think Pharaoh will want to marry me?" Hatshepsut looked at the beautiful young girl and just smiled, Iset saw her smile and then laughed, "I do think he loves me."

"I am certain that you can make Pharaoh happy and we will work together to insure your child continues our dynasty."

Iset was visibly relieved and touched that the woman who had saved her, would allow her to have such a title and honor. "May I go tell Tuthmose?"

"Yes, tell him I sent you." Iset hugged Hatshepsut and quickly ran to find Pharaoh.

Sitre came and saw the stress on Hatshepsut's face, "Is my child alright?"

"Oh yes, but I do need a glass of wine and send for Senenmut."

CHAPTER TWENTY-ONE

Prince of Egypt

Pharaoh was happy and he took every possible opportunity to display his beautiful new wife carrying their child, Iset enjoyed the attention and the many Royal banquets in her honor. Young girls of noblemen throughout Egypt were disappointed that Pharaoh had eyes only for Iset and no desire to increase his harem or acquire other secondary wives, he was completely happy with Iset. Queen Hatshepsut was able to govern as she saw fit, her brother would agree to any plan or desire she had for Egypt. The Royal decrees were in his name and that was all that mattered to him, his Queen had selected most of the Royal Court. One member of Pharaoh's Royal Court she relied on most was Foreign Ambassador Nehsi, longtime friend of Senenmut.

The priests of Egypt were pleased with all the new construction in the temples and they gladly accepted her gifts in return for their support. Many projects were in progress from Thebes to Memphis, tribute continued coming into the coffers of Egypt and no major military actions were needed, Maat was being served in Egypt. Senenmut was busy with the construction of the tombs for Pharaoh and the Queen, he also spent many hours planning the future Mortuary Temple of Hatshepsut. Actual construction would have to wait until the Mortuary Temple for Pharaoh was completed.

When the new Prince of Egypt was born and named Tuthmose III, Hatshepsut and Senenmut were enjoying watching their daughter take her first steps. Her hair had been cut into the "sidelock of youth" at an early age. Senenmut understood why, Pharaoh must not see the color of her hair. Pharaoh and Iset loved their son and spent hours every day together, Hatshepsut had accepted that it would not be her son who was the new prince, she was satisfied with the hopes that her daughter would one day produce a future Pharaoh for her family's dynasty. The baby appeared to be strong and healthy, he favored his mother Iset.

During one of the evenings with Senenmut, Hatshepsut brought up the subject of her adopted son in Memphis, "I think it is time to bring Moses to Thebes." She knew that she was supposed to raise and educate Moses.

For the first time Senenmut disagreed with her, "It would not be fair to the boy, there could be many complications for him. Pharaoh may consider him a threat to his son for the throne, or Moses may be disappointed if he is not allowed to have the throne." Hatshepsut then heard his real concern. "When he is grown, what if he cannot marry the person he loves because he is not royalty?"

She realized Senenmut was expressing his feelings and disappointments, their relationship had to be kept a secret and they could never marry. "I will consider the opinion of my beloved Senenmut." He seemed to soften a little when she mentioned her love of him, but she had not changed her mind.

Events began to unfold that would make the decision to bring the boy to Thebes easy and set Hatshepsut on the course that would fulfill her hopes and the prophecy she had been told.

Iset came to Hatshepsut concerned about the Pharaoh, he had been playing with the baby and had raised him above his head. Pharaoh then dropped to his knees in pain, Hatshepsut found her brother in bed having difficulty breathing and complained of pain in his chest and arm. Pharaoh did not want the Royal Physician but asked that Senenmut treat him, remembering how he had saved his sister's life. Senenmut was summoned and he cared for Pharaoh the best he could, suggesting total rest, he did not remember any treatment mentioned by Imhotep for Pharaoh's condition. Over time Pharaoh did improve but never regained the strength or energy he once had. Any physical exertion caused a shortness of breath.

Eventually Iset told Hatshepsut that Pharaoh had no desire to be with her in bed. Hatshepsut decided it was time for Moses to come to Thebes, Pharaoh was not going to produce another male heir and the fate of her family's dynasty could not depend only on the young Prince Tuthmose. She confided with Senenmut and he could not disagree with her. Preparations were made for Jochebed to bring her son to Thebes, Foreign Ambassador Nehsi was informed about the young boy in Memphis. He was told about all the circumstances of her relationship with baby Moses and all the events that had occured in Memphis, he was honored to be given such personal information. He gladly went to Memphis to bring the boy to his Queen, Tyia went with Nehsi so she could spend time with her father in Coptos.

Two months later, Nehsi arrived in Thebes with the boy and his mother. Hatshepsut watched the ship dock and searched for the boy, when she saw him, she could not believe how he had grown. He was the same exquisitely beautiful child with curly hair, he was watching all that was happening. With Tyia, she saw Menna's sister Nafrini, she had come with them.

Nehsi led Jochebed and Moses off the barge to the small group waiting in a shaded area on the Royal Dock. As they came near the royal party, Moses shyly stopped and stood behind his mother. The young Princess Neferure went to him, took him by the hand and led him to her mother. Hatshepsut watched their precocious daughter and smiled at Senenmut. He just slightly shook his head, he was concerned about the future of the two children.

She knelt down to their level, "You have grown so much since I last saw you."

He smiled and gave her a hug and in very poor Egyptian he said, "Pretty Queen." Moses spoke poor Egyptian which surprised her at first, she then realized that for the past four years he had been raised in an environment where Hebrew was mostly spoken.

"Thank you." He then reached out to touch her broad collar of gold and jewels. "Do you like it?" He just nodded yes. "May I pick you up?" He looked at her not understanding her question, she then held out her arms, he came to her. While holding him, she introduced Sitre to Jochebed.

In Hebrew, Sitre spoke to Jochebed at length and when she had finished, Jochebed smiled in tears and said, "Thank you."

Hatshepsut did not know what Sitre had said, they returned to the palace with Hatshepsut and Neferure holding Moses's hands as they walked together, he did not say anything as he closely observed the wonderous surroundings. In her quarters Jochebed freshened up from her travels while Moses and Neferure played with a wooden toy crocodile, the jaws of the toy moved when it was pulled with a string.

Hatshepsut asked Nehsi about the state of affairs in Memphis. "My Queen would be pleased with how the Vizier of Lower Egypt represents Pharaoh," and then he quickly added, "and my Queen," Hatshepsut smiled. "I do request an audience with my Queen, I have some important information."

"Can it wait?" Not wanting to spoil the arrival of Moses.

"Yes, my Noble Lady," he bowed and left her quarters.

Hatshepsut spoke to Sitre, "Thank you for greeting Jochebed when she arrived."

"I told the boy's mother that I am a Levite and have been with the Queen her entire life. I assured her that My Lady will raise Moses as her own son and that he will learn his ancestry."

Smiling at her dear Sitre, "Thank you."

Moses and Neferure ran into her room excited, using a combination of Egyptian and Hebrew words that caused him to stutter, she could not understand what he was saying. "What are you trying to tell me?" she laughingly asked.

"Moses is excited because I told him that he will be staying with you here in the palace. I had not mentioned this before," replied Jochebed.

Hatshepsut knelt down to Moses's level and spoke to him, mainly for his mother's benefit. "I am glad that you are happy to stay here with me, we will have fun together. One day we will return to Memphis and visit your family."

After the evening meal, she met with Nehsi, he had always impressed her with his language skills, she had plans for him. It seemed like a long time ago that she first met him, Senenmut had brought other architects to their first meetings, but he was her favorite. Tribute was coming into Egypt but Hatshepsut wanted to reestablish distant trade routes that had been disrupted during the time of the Hyksos and she had dreams of an expedition to the mysterious land of Punt. "What news do you have from Memphis?"

"Cousins of your father have been meeting with members of the Royal Court in Memphis, they are trying to convince them that they have a legitimate right to the throne. Their claim is that Prince Tuthmose is the son of a minor wife who is a foreigner and has no Royal Egyptian blood."

"We always knew that this could be a problem," then she saw the look on Nehsi's face as he paused and looked down, there was more he wanted to say but was reluctant, "Speak freely my friend."

"My Queen they are also spreading slanderous lies about you."

Hatshepsut feared the lies were actually the truth, about her and Senenmut, "Tell me what you have heard."

"I know that there is no truth to the lies, but it is being told that my Queen was with child when she left Thebes for Memphis, Moses is said to be a bastard son you had while in Memphis." She had mixed feelings, relief that it was not about Senenmut but mostly outrage about the lies. Nehsi saw her rage, "I am sorry my Queen."

"How did you learn of this lie?"

"Your Vizier in Memphis wanted you to know."

Regaining some control of her anger, "Vizier Ramose is a loyal friend, he and the Royal Court know the truth! You were right to inform me of my enemies and how they may attack me. We will meet again with Senenmut, I am sure he will know how to deal with my cousins."

It had been planned for Jochebed to return to Memphis before the annual inundation, but it was decided that she should stay in Thebes until after the flood. The priests of Hapi had seen a very early and rapid rising River on the official nilometer in Elephantine, the area near the first cataract got the name because the large boulders look like elephants in the River.

A warning was sent to Thebes and down the River all the way to Memphis, the nation must prepare for an early and destructive annual flood. Irrigation ditches, canals, livestock, and homes were in danger and next year's crops would be small. Pharaoh would be expected to use Egypt's store houses to help feed the nation in the coming year.

The first indication of a large flood was the early arrival of the Green Wave which contained large trees that had been uprooted by the excessive tears from Isis, far upriver. Next came the Red

Flow and the River just kept rising, it was one of the worst floods in recorded history. The flood water even reached the palace walls, there was much destruction throughout Egypt. Once the waters began to receded, the smell of decaying organic matter and dead fish was accompanied by flies, followed by enormous swarms of mosquitoes.

The people of Egypt from Thebes to Memphis suffered with fevers, infected sores, and boils causing many deaths. Amazingly, Moses was the only person that had no mosquito bites, the mosquitoes did not even land on him, let alone bite him. Hatshepsut questioned Jochebed about it, her reply was, "Mosquitoes and fleas have never bothered him, I do not know why." Hatshepsut realized that the beautiful boy was being protected by the Hebrew God.

Many living in the palace were sick from infected mosquito bites, those that could, stayed indoors with incense burning to protect themselves.

One evening a concerned Iset informed Hatshepsut that Pharaoh was covered in boils, he was asking for Senenmut. When Hatshepsut arrived with Senenmut to Pharaoh's quarters, they were shocked when they saw him. The Royal Physician had lanced several boils and Senenmut saw red lines running from several of the incisions in his arms, Pharaoh was burning up with fever. The Royal Physician was relieved to see Senenmut and the Queen. Pharaoh had commanded his guards, that if he died, the physician was to be sent to prison and have his hands cut off.

When Hatshepsut was told of the order, she privately assured him that the orders of the delirious Pharaoh who was once kind, would not be carried out. The relieved and thankful physician offered praises to a wise and just Queen.

All Senenmut knew to do was to clean the infected incisions with vinegar and apply cool cloths for the fever, this gave some comfort to the Pharaoh. Two days later Senenmut, Iset, and

Hatshepsut were in his room when a very weak Pharaoh became alert and asked that they come to his bed. The Captain of the Guards came closer for Pharaoh's protection and to hear what he wanted to say. Hatshepsut remembered him, he had smirked at her and her injuries, when she came out of Pharaoh's chamber years ago. Menna also remembered him and stepped between him and his Queen.

Pharaoh asked Hatshepsut, "Will you protect Iset and my son." Hatshepsut knew that he was really asking that no harm come to his son or Iset from her. Often in history, many Queens had taken advantage of an untimely death of a Pharaoh, secondary wives and their sons had disappeared so that the Queen's choice could ascend to the throne. She saw the fear in his eyes and even in those of Iset.

Hatshepsut took Iset's hand and that of her husband, "I will insure within my power that one day Prince Tuthmose becomes Pharaoh, this is my promise," she said with sincerity. Pharaoh became very quiet and calm, he took in a deep breath and placed his hand on his chest. His spirit Ba departed his body and Horus Pharaoh became Osiris Pharaoh at a very young age.

Iset cried and Hatshepsut held her close, when Iset had regained control of her emotions, she asked, "Is my son really safe?"

"I saved you once from your brother, I will always protect you and the future Pharaoh." She held Iset and saw the concerned look on the guard's face. He knew that his future was in jeopardy, Hatshepsut commanded him, "You are now to protect the future Pharaoh, Prince Thutmose."

"As my Noble Queen commands," grateful to continue his service in the palace and with more respect for his Queen. Menna was surprised, but Senenmut nodded approval, she had chosen to not seek revenge but instead had wisely gained his loyalty.

The now Dowager Queen and Regent to Tuthmose III had

full control of Egypt. Most Egyptians loved Queen Hatshepsut and had heard stories of how the gods communicated to her, but they did not know that she had actually been the person who had been responsible for Egypt's prosperity during the three years of Pharaoh Tuthmose's short reign. The priests had taken advantage of the excessive flood and claimed the gods were not happy with the former Pharaoh, it was up to the next ruler of Egypt to obtain their support, by satisfying their desire to remain powerful and rich.

CHAPTER TWENTY-TWO

Regent Queen

Pharaoh's tomb was hastily finished for his burial, his unfinished mortuary temple would have to wait until Egypt had recovered from the devastating flood. Few attended the funeral procession and burial because Egypt was still suffering with many deaths from diseases. Those that could work, were trying to rebuild their lives, uncertainty and fear was throughout Egypt. Much effort and luck would be required for Hatshepsut, as the Dowager Queen, to maintain control and trust of her people and especially the priests of Egypt. The priests had gladly accepted the gifts and aid for building projects throughout Egypt from Pharaoh Tuthmose II, but he had been blamed for the gods being angry and causing his death and destructive flood. Queen Hatshepsut needed to be seen as favored by the gods, capable of rebuilding and controlling Egypt, and appease the priests who would decide if the gods favored her. Her Viziers and Royal Courts of Upper and Lower Egypt knew she was the controlling force behind the former Pharaoh, now she must become a loved and trusted ruler in her own right.

Senenmut had recommended that her control of Egypt must be seen as a gradual acquisition of power. She must be seen as a supportive Regent of Prince Tuthmose and not as a usurper, desiring absolute rule.

Queen Hatshepsut did not collect taxes and she opened the store houses to feed Egypt. She also did something that had never been done before, the military was dispatched throughout Egypt to help rebuild. Hatshepsut was able to work with the supportive members of both Viziers and Royal Courts in Upper and Lower Egypt. Stelae were erected at Egypt's borders showing the Dowager Queen Hatshepsut standing behind the young Thutmose III, her Royal headdress of tall ostrich feathers on top of her crown displayed her active role in ruling Egypt.

Hatshepsut and the nation waited and watched with much anticipation for the next inundation. Her continued role of ruling Egypt depended on the flood because it was important that the gods were perceived to favor her. Hapi, god of the River, saw the tears of Isis start on time and stop when the water was at the perfect level, priests of Upper and Lower Egypt claimed that the goddess Isis, had smiled on their Queen. Festivals celebrating being alive and their popular Queen occurred from Thebes to Memphis. Senenmut initiated propaganda in carvings and statues, claiming the gods favored the Regent Queen. The feeling of relief could be seen and felt in the palace.

As Moses grew, he assumed the role of big brother to Neferure and the young Prince Tuthmose. An aging Sitre and Neferure's wet nurse Sheriti were given the responsibility of caring for Moses and Neferure. Iset and nurse Ipu, cared for the young Prince, while Senenmut assumed more roles and titles as he aided his Regent Queen. Moses was tall for his age and led the children on many adventures in the palace and gardens. Bae was the constant guardian of Iset and the children, he was with them every day. Iset had always been close to Bae, he had put her at ease when she first arrived in Memphis.

The only conflict the children ever had was when Neferure teased Moses. When he got excited, he often mixed up words in Hebrew and his new Egyptian language. Moses had a very short temper and would become angry when she mocked his stuttering, but the precocious young princess would always hug him and make him laugh.

As often happens when a popular ruler governed, the most popular name for a baby girl in Egypt was Hatshepsut.

Senenmut jokingly stated one evening, "If my Queen does nothing else in her reign, her name will be remembered forever."

Hatshepsut knew it was a fine line for her, she had to be seen as strong and yet she did not want history to remember her stealing the throne. Senenmut wanted to start work on her magnificent mortuary chapel they had dreamed of, he was told to wait, she did not want to be seen eager to build a great monument to herself. Senenmut was allowed to build a canal that one day would bring stone and supplies closer to the construction site from the River. The predictable Nubians stopped sending their tribute of gold the following year, they always challenged a new Pharaoh that came to power. Hatshepsut announced to her Red Court, "An expedition must be sent to Nubia."

"I will inform the Generals to prepare the Southern Army of Ra," Senenmut stated.

"No, I wish to stop these reoccurring battles and loss of life, I want to go to Nubia and establish an alliance with the Nubian King. If possible, I will bring back a young Nubian Prince to Egypt, he will be taught our ways and help our two nations live in peace."

"We can send someone to do as my Queen suggests without her being in danger," Senenmut suggested.

Before she could answer, Ambassador Nehsi spoke up, "I can represent my Queen."

"No, I must demonstrate my ability to rule the army, make the arrangements." Hatshepsut commanded as she stood and left her court.

Two months later, Hatshepsut led an expedition of about

300 soldiers out of Thebes to the distant military docks, with many subjects along the road, wishing her success. More soldiers at the massive Fort Buhen, near the second cataract, would add to her expedition. There the rapids were too strong for the boats to pass, the expedition would continue on foot. She was excited to once again be on an adventure, the recent years in the palace had made her anxious to do something new. She wished for the guidance of her cobra dream, but the last dream she had was just before her encounter with the young prophet, Rachel. No maids were with her, only Menna, Dadu and Bek, she had to command Senenmut to remain in Thebes. He was to raise and educate the children, if anything happened to her.

It was a week of slow travel on the River to the first cataract, the rapids were gentle, now that the river is low. The boats were pulled past the rapids in a canal built long ago by the local people who did this for a living and were experts. Normal boat traffic was only a few freighters but the large army and ships were a welcome boost to the local economy. It was another two weeks farther south at the second cataract when her ships arrived at Fort Buhen. At the fort were hundreds of people around the fortress, traders from Egypt, Nubia, and even Bedouins had come to buy, sell, and trade many goods. The gatherings of the traders occur often throughout the year.

Menna said the Nubian army would soon learn that her army was on a march to Nubia, he was certain that the Nubian traders would send runners warning their King. The fort was the largest that she had ever seen with walls that were 16 feet thick and 33 feet high. Inside were over 1000 soldiers and families of the officers. Hatshepsut, trying to think what Senenmut would do, finally said, "Inform General Hor that I desire his council."

The General had been reluctant for the Queen to be on the campaign, arriving at her quarters, "My Queen wishes my council?"

"Yes," as she continued to remove dust, applying soothing oil and eye makeup. "Be seated," she pointed to a three-legged portable chair. "We have arrived during market it seems, what does my General recommend?"

"We should advance quickly because the Nubian King will be warned."

She offered him some of her wine, which he gladly accepted. "Is it possible that Nubian spies in Thebes have already warned their King, when we first began our march?"

"It is possible but we do not know for sure, my Queen."

"Can we arrive at the capital of Nubia before word gets to the King that we are coming?"

General Hor paused, "Word will reach the King before we do, but if we continue quickly, they will not be fully prepared."

She slowly continued applying oil to her sun-dried skin and waited for him to relax, offering him more of her wine, "You would agree that we have most certainly lost the element of surprise?"

He nodded yes, "That is true, my Queen."

"I suggest that we stay here for several days, we have our soldiers go among the traders and spread the word that the Queen of Egypt wishes to negotiate peace with the Nubian King in person."

General Hor thought about her suggestion for a long time. "My Queen's suggestion has its risks, but the King of Nubia would learn that this is not a typical Egyptian military campaign."

Before he could say anything else, "That is a very good point General, this is not a typical Egyptian army seeking war, we shall wait here for a few days." The General was not sure he had said that they should wait but he could not come up with a good argument. "Thank you for your advice."

The general stood a little unsteadily, saluted, and departed her quarters. She looked at a grinning Menna, "What?"

"The General thinks he has come up with a great plan."

A copper factory was near the fort with its strong sulfur odor, even with the factory downwind, the stench was almost too much to endure at times in her camp. She could not imagine how the workers tolerated the odor and what their families had to endure when they came home at night. Hatshepsut was learning firsthand what life was like in the far outposts of Egypt. This was a life with few comforts, soldiers not on duty, drank a lot of beer and were loud at night until they went to sleep in a drunken stupor. Relieved when it was time to leave, Hatshepsut looked forward to hopefully meeting the King on peaceful terms. The army now almost 1000 men strong, had marched only two days before their scouts contacted the advanced front of a small Nubian army. Menna was sure that a larger force was behind and would arrive soon.

The plan was for General Hor to meet with the Nubia General first, Hatshepsut was hopeful that their much larger force would convince them to negotiate and not fight. She was far behind the front line, out of Nubian archers' range, standing on a slight rise. In the distance she could see General Hor advance toward his counterpart. There was a brief exchange, thankfully he and his soldiers started returning without incident. Hatshepsut smiled at Menna, "Perhaps the General's plan will work," she said sarcastically and with a laugh.

All eyes were watching the General and his party, ready in case the Nubians decided to attack them as they returned, when an eagle flew low over the General and his returning soldiers. All eyes followed the rare majestic bird, a symbol of royalty, the young Prince Tuthmose III was referred to as, "A young eagle still in the nest." The large bird continued to fly low over the soldiers straight toward Hatshepsut, with all the soldiers turning to watch its flight. As it approached her, the midday rays of Ra reflected off the gold that the Queen wore, she was very visible to her army as it passed directly over her and flew toward a rock formation higher up the rise.

Bek was the first to see men hidden in the rock formation, he yelled, "Archers are aiming at the Queen." He forcefully pushed her down to her knees and stood between her and the attackers. Then she heard the sizzling sound of arrows in flight, one landed on the ground close to her. Menna and Dadu immediately joined Bek, they were around her with their shields up. Menna yelled, "Soldiers, archers are shooting at us!" Hatshepsut could not see anything but heard the dull drumming sound of arrows hitting their raised shields. Then she felt a hot stinging sensation in her shoulder, in pain and shock she looked down and saw the arrow, with disbelief she realized that the arrow had gone through Bek's thigh first and then struck her.

Many angry and determined soldiers were now shouting and running toward the archers. The arrows must have stopped because she remembered the severe pain when Bek moved and the arrow was jerked out of her shoulder. She blacked out, when she regained consciousness, she heard Menna yelling, "Are you alright?"

"I am OK," she managed to answer.

Soon order was restored and many soldiers were around them, Dadu was tending to Bek. Menna had applied pressure to her wound with some linen to stop the bleeding, "It is a minor wound, my Noble Lady."

Hatshepsut thought, it does not feel minor, but managed to ask, "How is Bek?"

"Dadu is tending to him."

"How did the Nubian archers get behind us?" she asked.

"I do not know." Menna picked her up and he tried to carry her gently, but with each step he heard her moan softly. Once in her tent, she began to recover from the shock.

Menna stayed with her while Dadu now tended to her wound, he touched her head and smiled, "My Lady has been protected again, the eagle showed us the archers." It was comforting to see his smile as she went to sleep. Voices woke her, it was dark and she could just barely see that someone was with Menna, she moved and groaned.

Hearing her awake, they came to her bed, "My Queen was saved by the gods again, Commander Menna informs me," stated General Hor.

"Did I lead us into a trap, General?"

She was shocked when she heard his reply, "No my Queen, but you did survive an attempt on your life by three of our own soldiers."

"Do you know who paid them?" She thought of her daughter, the young Prince, and Moses in Thebes, "We need to warn Senenmut in Thebes," she said looking at Menna.

"A messenger has already been sent and we do not know who paid the traitors, our loyal soldiers killed the assassins."

Hatshepsut closed her eyes, "The children, it will be too late!"

General Hor watched her as she went back to sleep, "It is true, the gods do protect her."

"It is not the first time the gods have saved our Queen," Menna stated.

"So, all the stories are true," he said as he departed.

It was a restless night and any movement caused her to wake up in pain, when she was awake, her concern was for those in Thebes. The smells of cooking woke her the following morning, when Menna saw that she was awake he asked, "How is My

Lady?"

"I did not sleep well, how is Bek?"

"Dadu is tending to him, he is in good care. Are you hungry?"

"No, but I am thirsty." Menna gave her some water and offered her some warm flat bread, which she took.

After a few bites, Menna said, "General Hor is here, he is very concerned about his Queen."

"Help me sit up and then show him in." Menna went to the tent opening and called for General Hor.

The General was relieved when he saw her, "It is good to see my Queen up!"

"Thank you General, any news about the Nubian army?"

General Hor told her about his first meeting with the Nubian General the day before. The Nubian General had informed him that the King was not with this advance force. When he met again after the attack on Hatshepsut, General Hor had informed the Nubian General that a meeting at a later date will be arranged between the two nation's diplomats. He had also informed the Nubian General that Queen Hatshepsut did not want to destroy the small Nubian force. But if tribute did not continue, she would return with no mercy. A relieved Nubian General said he would inform his King of the Queen of Egypt's demand and mercy.

"My General has represented Pharaoh well, thank you." Hatshepsut hoped that their encounter without any military action had established a dialog with Nubia. Perhaps tribute would be paid without further military action.

"It is an honor to serve my brave Queen and the soldiers have never seen such a display by the gods. All here today know that our Queen is favored by the gods, the stories of how the gods protect our Queen will be told by the soldiers to their families and friends throughout Egypt. Your father, the great General and Pharaoh must have known that the gods had chosen his daughter to be the future ruler of Egypt."

Hatshepsut had never tried to present herself as being chosen by the gods, but it was an interesting concept. Perhaps Senenmut could use this idea to promote her becoming Pharaoh one day. "In time when my people are ready, I will claim the throne the gods have chosen for me."

"My Queen, I look forward to that day."

"General, I will require your advice on all military matters and we will start our return march tomorrow."

"As the Foremost of Noble Ladies commands."

After the General was gone, Menna asked, "Will My Lady be able to continue our march back tomorrow?"

"Yes, I want to get back to the palace as soon as we can."

The following morning Queen Hatshepsut stepped out of her tent and climbed aboard her chariot with a few guards and soldiers cheering around her. Soon her whole army was cheering her name, "Queen Hatshepsut, Queen Hatshepsut, Queen Hatshepsut!" Her spirits were lifted by the cheering from the soldiers, she saluted them. Menna slapped the reins of the horses and started the march back to Thebes. "The support of the army is appreciated," she commented.

"They are proud to serve their victorious Queen," Menna stated.

"But it was not a real victory."

"We met the enemy and our goal was accomplished and no soldiers were lost in battle, it was the best kind of victory. All of Egypt will soon know what happened here."

"We still have to find those who tried to kill me," she was concerned that those behind the assassination attempt may be her own cousins. Egypt did not need to know there was discord among her family.

During the returning march back to Fort Buhen, Hatshepsut had fever and chills the first night. Arriving at the fort, it was suggested by Dadu that they stay so Bek could improve, he also saw that Hatshepsut was feverish. Dadu was doing an excellent job of treating him, "If he can eat, drink, and relieve himself, he will be alright soon," he gruffly commented to Hatshepsut once.

A ship arrived at the fort with a message for the Queen from Senenmut. With dread she broke the seal and unrolled the message, it was written in their secret language. Those around her could see that she was upset and visibly shaken as she read the dispatch, tears made reading the dispatch difficult and she could not finish the dispatch. She went to Bek in his tent crying, "Bae has been killed!" was all she could say as she embraced him for a long time. General Hor, Menna, and Dadu waited anxiously to hear what had happened.

Eventually she was able to tell them, "Iset was attacked and Bae saved her, but he was wounded and died in her arms. His last words were to warn you and me." Bek asked to be alone, she kissed him on his forehead, leaving him alone. Outside his tent, she gave them some confusing information. "Iset and Bae were attacked in the palace by three of the palace guards, the attackers were heard yelling, "Kill her!"

General Hor said, "It makes no sense, I understand why they attacked my Queen, but not her."

"Bae killed two of the guards and the other was wounded and captured by loyal guards. Senenmut said that the Medjay State Police are interrogating the wounded traitor."

"The traitor will wish he had been killed, before the Medjay are finished with him," commented General Hor.

"I hope he is still alive when we return, he will die a slow death on a stake," Hatshepsut stated as she returned to Bek's tent. She could not sleep, going over the recent events kept her awake and she had chills, Bek was sleeping restlessly. Once when Bek was awake, she went to him, "Can I get anything for you?"

"No, My Lady."

"I am so sorry about Bae, he saved Iset and she loved him so."

"Yes, and he loved Iset too. He told me once that he understood how I felt about," he stopped and closed his eyes.

Hatshepsut finished his thought, "How you feel about me?" He did not say anything, laying her head on his chest, "I love you too." She felt his chest rise with his breaths and heard his heart beating. When he was asleep, she went to her bed, many thoughts were going through her mind, one decision she had definitely made, there was to be no future military campaigns for her. When she was away from the safety of the palace, Menna, Dadu and now Bek had risked their lives protecting her. She did not want to risk the lives of those who were willing to die for her.

Royal Palace

Iset and Tyia were watching the children playing after the noon meal, Senenmut was sitting on a lounge near the fountain almost asleep, the children will soon be ready for a nap also. They have stayed in the main forecourt of the Queen's quarters since the attack on Bae and Iset for security. Senenmut is concerned, because they do not know for certain who was responsible. Sitre and Abet were out doing the daily shopping for food and water, no one else had left the secure quarters for two weeks. Senenmut is watchful at night and gets very little sleep, neither does Iset, she still has memories of the attack but mostly she feels guilt.

During the attack she had not helped Bae, she was ter-
rified and concerned for her two-year-old son. After Bae was
wounded, the last attacker had come after her, during the fight
she had heard them shout, "Kill Pharaoh's Wife." Just as one of
the assassins was about to strike her down with his sword, the
Captain of the Guard saved her, by cutting off the attacker's up-
held hand holding the sword. He and several other guards had
heard Bae calling for help and arrived just in time to save her but
not Bae.

Recovering some from her fear, she went to Bae, holding
him in her arms with tears flowing from her eyes. Bae's only
concern was that she was alright and that his brother and the
Queen be warned. When he died, her fear was replaced by anger
and guilt, she wanted revenge. It was learned from the mortally
wounded attacker that they had been paid in gold to kill Iset,
some of the gold had been found. Senenmut recognized the par-
tial stamp on one piece of the gold, it was the missing gold from
the treasurer in Memphis.

Senenmut had sent a message warning Hatshepsut and
then met with the Chief of the Medjay, who was in charge of
the investigation, since the attack was on the royal family. The
port in Thebes was temporarily closed to all out going traffic in
hopes of catching the traitor who had hired the assassins. All
the Medjey stations down river had been notified to search all
boats for someone with a large amount of gold. Iset had not particularly cared for the Captain of the Guards because Menna did
not like him, but he had saved her life. She had thanked him for
saving her life, "I owe my life to you, if I had been armed, perhaps
I could have helped Bae."

"I only wish I had been quicker in aiding the brave Bae
and Pharaoh's Wife, you could not have helped Bae, if anything
you may have been killed also," he stated.

Iset wondered why Senenmut wanted everyone to sleep
in Hatshepsut quarters at night, perhaps she thought, it was so

he could keep everyone close together. Once she had noticed that a lamp in Hatshepsut's bedroom was crooked and appeared broken. Senenmut replied that he would have it fixed later, when it was safe for workmen to enter.

They had many long discussions, trying to determine who had paid to have Pharaoh's Wife killed and not the young future Pharaoh. It did not make any sense, Iset could not have another legitimate heir to the throne, Pharaoh was dead. Senenmut had suggested that she had only heard the assassins call her name, they may have mentioned the prince also, but she did not think so. Iset had asked, if he thought her father hated her enough to risk the wrath of Egypt's army, to kill her? Then there was Ambassador Ipi, he was a hunted man, the person responsible had to be found, so the threat could be eliminated, they hoped the Medjay could find him.

The main forecourt that Senenmut had designed, was the coolest place in the palace during the hottest part of the day. The tall ceiling with windows at the top allowed the hot air to escape and cooler air was drawn in from the room's balconies, the breeze was made more refreshing by the spray of the fountain and plants.

Relaxing, Tyia thought about Moses again, they were still trying to understand his actions on the day of the attack. Iset had planned on taking the children to see a new giraffe that had been recently added to the large palace zoo. Just before they were ready to leave, Moses said that he had a loud ringing in his ears and that he felt odd. When Sitre had questioned him farther, he stated that the light and colors were very bright, he did not want to go outside in the bright light, then four-year-old Princess Neferure decided to stay with him.

Senenmut was sure that if all the children had been with Iset and Bae, the outcome would have been much worse. Everyone quietly agreed that Moses was being protected, too many unexplainable events had occurred.

Iset had returned from putting the children down for their naps and was sitting quietly with Tyia when there was a loud unexpected knock on the door, startling both of them, it was too early for Sitre and Abet to return.

Senenmut jumped up from his nap, he went to the main door and spoke to the Captain of the Guards at length through a small opening, before finally opening the door. The captain entered with the Chief of the Medjay and a woman, she could be best described as an attractive warrior. Dressed in black with a black and white scarf draped over her shoulders, the white side of the scarf could be used for protection from the rays of Ra, the other side would help conceal her at night. She had a wide belt holding a knife and sword, over her shoulder hung a bow and quill of arrows. The Medjay woman's long black hair was pulled back and braded down her back. She was hard to describe, but if anything, her appearance was more shocking and menacing than the Chief of the Medjay.

In a low voice that sounded more like a growl, the man introduced himself to Iset and Tyia, Senenmut already knew him, "I am Penre, Chief of the Medjay in Upper Egypt." He and the woman bowed ever so slightly to Iset, he continued, "This is Captain Anya, she is my officer in Coptos, she captured the man responsible for the attacks." There was absolutely no expression on her face. "Captain, inform Pharaoh's Wife what happened," commanded Chief Penre.

She took one step toward Iset, "I captured a man carrying gold, I wish he had not died before I could obtain more information, My Lady." Her voice was clear, feminine but very controlled and hard, she was not the least intimidated by those around her.

"We are pleased and impressed that you were able to find and capture him, tell us all that you know," said Senenmut.

Captain Anya told how she had searched each ship that came into the port, she had placed other Medjay policeman on boats, commanding that all ships dock and be searched. When she went on board one of the ships and asked the captain if there was anyone on board that had paid in gold for his passage, a man who had heard her, ran ashore. "I chased him through the docks, we passed the fort and he was about to enter a large crowd of people, so I shot him with an arrow." Everyone listened to her matter of fact account told in a calm measured voice with no emotion. "Gold was found on him and I knew that he would die soon from his wounds, his chest was bubbling blood.

He could not answer my questions because he was unconscious, I knew any movement would make him die sooner. I quickly sent a small amount of the gold to the nearby fort blacksmith to be melted. When I dropped a small amount on his hand, he regained consciousness, screaming and looking at his burnt hand."

There was a hushed gasp from Tyia, Captain Anya just looked at her, "I told him to talk or I would give him some of his hot gold to drink." She then displayed the thin round drop of gold that had flattened and cooled after going through his hand.

Iset asked, "Did he say his name was Ipi?" She was guessing that he was behind the attack, part of her hoped it was the Ambassador who had been captured and tortured, another part of her wanted Ipi to be alive so she could watch him die.

"He said the name you mentioned, Ipi paid him to arrange the attack. I asked him where this man Ipi was, and he said in Mitanni."

"So, it was the coward and he is still alive!" Iset stated with contempt in her voice.

"He told me that he had been the Captain of the Guards in Memphis."

"I want that piece of gold," stated Iset as she pointed at it. The Medjay officer looked at Senenmut, who nodded yes. Anya handed the small piece of gold to Iset. "I will wear this until Ipi is dead."

Penre, Chief of the Medjay then displayed a bag that everyone assumed was the remaining gold and handed it to Senenmut, "So, he did die?" asked Senenmut.

"Yes, he died soon after," Captain Anya answered.

"Thank you, I was in Coptos once with Pharaoh's Daughter when the flash flood occured. I am familier with the location of the fort."

"Yes, I saw you and our Queen praying to the god Min and laughing at a baboon."

Senenmut remembered the incident, when the baboon barked that early morning, it had noticed the hidden Medjay Captain. A slight shiver went down his back, he had not seen her. "Thank you for your protection and loyalty, that will be all for now."

After they had departed, Tyia commented, "That woman scares me."

"I admire her," stated Iset, "I will arrange to have the Medjay Captain remain in Thebes."

"Why do you want her to stay here?" asked Senenmut.

"I do not want to ever feel helpless again. I will train with her and when I am ready, I will return to Mitanni and get justice for Bae."

"When Hatshepsut returns, she will make sure the former Ambassador is punished, now that we know where he is," Senenmut stated.

Fort Buhen

Hatshepsut reread the long dispatch from Senenmut, she was sleepy and did not feel well. Their daughter Princess Neferure, Prince Tuthmose, and Moses were safe, no attempt had been made on their lives. The sense of urgency was over, Senenmut was protecting everyone and hopefully the person responsible would eventually be discovered. General Hor had instilled the idea of her being chosen by the gods, she knew that the Hebrew God had chosen her to save Moses and educate him as an Egyptian prince.

It was reassuring to know from the prophecies through Rachel, that Egypt would prosper under her leadership and that she was to be Pharaoh of Upper and Lower Egypt.

As the gentle fog of sleep overtook her, she prayed for a long life, an easy death, to be remembered, and a resting place undisturbed.

She had no dreams as she slept.

POSTSCRIPT

History records that Hatshepsut took over the control of the government on behalf of her young nephew as Regent Queen and within a few years Hatshepsut was crowned Pharaoh. What events caused her to make such a bold move? Tuthmose III, the son of Hatshepsut's half brother and a secondary wife, named Iset was always depicted as co-ruler. On monuments, he was not displaced or disregarded by Hatshepsut and her officials.

Senenmut, the Royal Steward and Royal Architect, completed the Mortuary Temple of Hatshepsut called Djeser-Djeseru meaning, "The Holy of Holies." His memory is preserved in a hidden location in her Mortuary Temple. He acquired over eighty official titles while serving Hatshepsut, the temple he built for her is considered to be the most beautiful temple in Egypt and perhaps in the world.

As Pharaoh, Hatshepsut ruled successfully and peacefully for over twenty years, during her reign Egypt prospered, she was responsible for more public works projects than any pharaoh except perhaps Rameses II. Trade routes that had stopped during the Hyksos rule in Lower Egypt were reestablished, wealth returned to Egypt, making the eighteenth dynasty one of the greatest in Egypt's long history. A successful trade expedition was sent to Punt, a mysterious land near the Red Sea, many items desired by the Egyptians were brought back. On a relief in her temple, the leader of the expedition was a man named Nehsi. Records show that she went on only one military campaign.

She renovated the temple complex in Thebes, called, "The Most Select of Places," it is known today as Karnak.

Hatshepsut erected two large granite obelisks there, historians described them as being 108 cubits tall with the tips covered in gold foil. When the sun hit the obelisks, all of Egypt was filled with the rays of Hatshepsut.

Tuthmose III when older assumed command of Egypt's military, after he gained control of the military, he could have easily taken full control of Egypt if he had desired. One of Hatshepsut's last monuments she started, was an unusual red structure within the temple called Chapelle Rouge or the "Red Chapel." Her nephew, now Pharaoh Tuthmose III, completed the monument after her death.

The chapel is thought to have been in the central court of Maat between her two obelisks. Inside the chapel are many inscriptions depicting events during her reign. One block in the chapel has an oracle speaking for an unnamed god declaring that Hatshepsut will become Pharaoh. For reasons that are uncertain, some twenty years after her death, a nationwide attempt was made to remove her memory and her name from history. What possible series of events could cause this to happen to a once loved and popular Pharaoh?

In 1903 Howard Carter discovered a small tomb with two unidentified female mummies, uninterested, Carter resealed the tomb. In 1906 one female mummy in her coffin was removed. The other mummy on the floor was left in the tomb and resealed again. The Antiquities Museum of Cairo subsequently indentified the mummy as Sitre. Even though she was not of a royal family, she was buried in the royal necropolis.

The other mummy remained largely forgotten in the tomb for over a century. In 2007, the mummy was removed and later identified as Hatshepsut by Egyptian authorities. It is assumed that her priests moved Hatshepsut for security, from her royal tomb, when her monuments were being destroyed after her death. It is appropriate and poignant that Hatshepsut was reburied with her beloved Sitre.

For almost 3000 years Pharaoh Hatshepsut's name was lost to history or was her favorite name, Pharaoh's Daughter, always remembered by the Hebrews and recorded in the Bible?

Moses was educated as an Egyptian prince and remained in the palace until an adult. It was God's plan that he would reject his privileged Egyptian life and chose to live among his people. While defending a Hebrew man, he killed an Egyptian slave master and had to flee Egypt for his life. Moses returned to Egypt when a new Pharaoh came to power, after much suffering inflected on the Egyptians by plagues, Moses was able to gain freedom for his people from Egyptian bondage.

The new reigning Pharaoh had lost his first-born son because of Moses and one of the plagues, did he blame Hatshepsut for all of his and Egypt's suffering? After all, she had saved Moses, adopted him, and educated him. Did he then try to have her name erased from history?

The story of Moses is told in the book of Exodus in the Bible.

Made in the USA
Coppell, TX
11 January 2022

71420056R00166